Soiled Dove

Brenda Adcock

Yellow Rose Books

Port Arthur, Texas

ISBN 978-1-935053-35-4
1-935053-35-3

First printing 2010

9 8 7 6 5 4 3 2 1

Cover design by Donna Pawlowski

Published by:

Regal Crest Enterprises, LLC
4700 Highway 365, Suite A, PMB 210
Port Arthur, Texas 77642

Find us on the World Wide Web at
http://www.regalcrest.biz

Printed in the United States of America

Acknowledgements

There have been too many people over the last six years who have helped me realize my dream to be a writer of reasonably decent stories for the enjoyment of others. Although I though I might die in the process, I will be eternally grateful to Miss Jacqueline Patterson, my high school English teacher who saved my life in college English classes by demanding more than I thought I could do. Through the years since high school, writing has always been a therapeutic solution to most of my problems, real or imagined. My characters have always been much braver than I am and often the person I wish I was. So I wish to thank all of my characters for allowing me to speak through them.

Back in the realm of reality I'd like to thank Gail Robinson, a member of my reading group, my beta reader, and friend. A big thanks to my editor on this project, Patty Schramm, better known to me as "the POV Queen." Too many voices running rampant in my brain to keep track of. My thanks, once again, to Donna for another great cover that conveyed the message I wanted. Of course, I can never fail to thank the woman who gave me a chance, Cathy LeNoir, my publisher and friend. I will always be grateful and hopefully will never let you down. Last, but never least in my heart, are the thanks I owe to my partner of fourteen years, Cheryl. There is no other person on the planet who would put up with my moods and general occasional bitchiness. That really takes a special person and she is. Thanks, baby.

To Cheryl –

Because I never thank you enough.

Chapter One

St. Joseph, Missouri, Early April 1876

LORETTA DIGBY THREW her head back and feigned a groan of pleasure, staring at the hairline crack that began near the top of the window sill and ran halfway across the dingy ceiling of her room. Her first customer of the evening, a well-known member of the St. Joe City Council she wasn't particularly fond of, breathed heavily as his wandering hands slid around her waist and roughly caressed her buttocks. She felt his arousal press against her as he fumbled to untie the lace holding her corset which temporarily denied him access to her breasts.

"Easy, sugar," she said. "We have plenty of time."

She grimaced as the roughness of his beard scraped across her neck. She tried to remember the first client she had serviced to repay her debt to Jack Coulter, the brothel's owner. It had taken almost two years of grabbing, pawing, one-hour customers to work her way up to the higher paying and slightly less repulsive men who frequented Jack's establishment.

As she stood wearing only her corset and light-weight bloomers, she remembered her terror when the man threw her on the bed and mounted her without bothering to remove his boots and pants. The smell of tobacco in his mouth and liquor on his breath sickened her. Her sixteen-year-old mind grew numb and she prayed for it to end. Now, four years later, she was able to ignore the scent of stale tobacco, stale alcohol, and stale sex. No matter how much she disliked what she did to earn a living she knew she was better off than most other prostitutes. Jack liked her, almost as much as he liked the money she brought in each night. She glanced briefly at the regulator clock hanging near her dresser. Forty-five more minutes to endure the councilman before he strutted home to his wife and family.

A scream found its way into her thoughts. "What was that?" she asked, turning her head away from the mouth that sought more of her body.

"Ignore it," the man mumbled against the soft skin along her white shoulders.

Amelia, she thought as she pushed him away and smiled up at him. She placed her hand firmly against his swollen crotch. "Hold that thought, baby," she said softly.

She opened the door and saw a small crowd gathering in front of a room at the far end of the upstairs hallway. She grabbed her robe and tied it around her waist. She pushed her slight frame past half-dressed men and their entertainment for the evening and reached for the doorknob to the room. When the door opened, Loretta stood wide-eyed for a moment, not believing the scene in front of her. A large naked man was on his knees on top of the bed and the newest and youngest girl in the house cowered against the headboard.

"You stupid fuckin' whore!" the man screamed. The back of his hand flew across the frightened girl's face. An ornate gold signet ring on his little finger caught her bottom lip and broke it open as she tried to draw the bed cover up to protect her face from further assault. Loretta saw tears flow down the girl's mottled, freckled cheeks. A violent game of tug-of-war with the bed cover ensued as he continued to hurl curses at her.

Loretta launched herself at the disgusting, naked figure in front of her and threw her arms around his neck. Her hands weren't quite successful in grabbing one another and the man turned quickly to shake her off.

"Get out, bitch! One uncooperative whore is enough," the man yelled as his hand lashed out and caught Loretta, sending her onto her back on the gritty wooden floor. She shook her head slightly while he returned his attention to the teenager cowering under the worn quilt. She grabbed a poker from a set of andirons next to the unused fireplace. Pushing a wavy mass of unruly, honey-colored hair away from her face she saw three faces staring into the room from the open doorway.

"Get Jack," she ordered calmly. "Then get back to work. I'll take care of this fucker."

One of the faces disappeared and Loretta heard the sound of rapidly retreating footsteps on the stairway. The indignant customer had resumed fighting with the buried girl and was leaning over the bed. Loretta shuddered as she caught a glimpse of his ample, snowy white ass. *Jesus*, she thought with a slight smirk, *this guy's got more hair on his ass than his head.* She looked at the poker in her hand and knew she could end the altercation in a few seconds with one good swing. But who would believe a whore had killed him in self-defense? Jack and the other girls didn't need any further attention drawn to them. With a deep breath she dropped the poker, took a step back, lowered her shoulder, and threw her entire one hundred and fifteen pounds into a body tackle. Unprepared for the blow, the man's body flew forward, covering the cowering girl before his head struck the heavy wooden headboard of the ratty, well-used bed. Steeling herself for the man's retaliation, Loretta planted her bare feet solidly on the floor and waited. When nothing happened, she tentatively approached the prone man and poked his corpulent frame.

"Please...help me," a small sobbing voice begged. Remembering what brought her to the room in the first place, Loretta grabbed the man and half rolled him off the trapped girl. A hand finally managed to find its way from under the covers and flailed around. Loretta took the hand and a moment later a disheveled mass of red hair popped from under the covers, gasping for air. Amelia's eyes widened in horror when she saw the unconscious man.

"Did you kill him?" she whispered.

"God, I hope not," Loretta breathed heavily, bending at the waist and resting her hands on her knees to calm down. "Get on out of there, Amelia, and get dressed," she said, straightening up and cautiously touching her bruised cheek. She winced slightly and pushed hair away from her face.

Amelia yelped and grabbed what little of the bed cover she could in a futile attempt to cover her nakedness as the room erupted once again in pandemonium. Loretta whirled around, prepared for another attack, and saw Jack Coulter pushing his way through a gathering crowd of half-dressed customers and girls. Calmly assuring his customers everything was fine while casting threatening glances at each girl, he nodded and closed the door to the room.

"What the hell happened in here?" he seethed, looking from Loretta to Amelia. When neither spoke he stepped next to the unconscious man and felt his fleshy neck for a pulse. Standing up and folding his arms across his neatly dressed chest he looked at the redhead. "He was your customer, Amelia. What happened?"

The teenager looked scared and she stammered to reply as she pointed at her comatose client. "He...he...he..."

"He what? Spit it out for Christ's sake, girl!"

"He wanted me to...to do something...disgusting," Amelia choked out.

Motioning to her for more information, he asked, "Which was what? Did he want to take a piss on you? Tie you up? What?"

Loretta worked hard at keeping a straight face during the interrogation although she could see her employer's patience was wearing dangerously thin. Loretta didn't want to know and had never asked, but suspected Amelia couldn't have been more than fifteen-years-old. Now she was looking at Loretta, her eyes pleading for help. Loretta leaned down and Amelia whispered something to her, new tears making their way down her already tear-stained cheeks. Loretta patted her on the shoulder and whispered back, to which the girl nodded. She was still looking around for something to cover her body until Loretta sighed and took off her robe. She draped it around Amelia's shoulders, leaving her own body wearing only skimpy lace underwear.

Amelia slipped the robe on and, hugging it close to her thin body, carefully made her way past Loretta and Jack into an adjoining room. As soon as the girl left, Loretta said nonchalantly, "He wanted her to suck him off and she bit him. I told you she was too damn young for this shit. What were you thinking when you sent her up here, Jack?"

Loretta watched Jack's eyes skim over her shapely body before he answered. "I was thinking she would have more productive working years by starting young. She's about the same age you were when I found you, Retta."

"Send her downstairs as a bar girl. She's pretty beat up and won't do much good up here anyway," Loretta said as she walked to the bedroom door. She looked at Jack while she turned the doorknob. "She probably wasn't being fucked by her stepfather like I was at her age."

Jack grabbed her lightly by the upper arm, leaned down and smiled. "But look how well you were trained when you arrived here. Remind me to send your stepfather a thank you card." As she yanked the door open, he smacked her firmly on the ass. "Finish up with your customer and get cleaned up. I'll be up later, baby."

Making her way down the aging, thin carpeting of the upstairs hallway, Loretta ignored the questions of the other girls and the leering looks of the men. *Fuckin' perverts.* She had a shapely body and she knew it. She was successful because she had managed to keep her figure over the last four years while avoiding being beaten badly enough to scar her face. She took a deep breath and paused in front of the door to her room to straighten her hair. She pasted a smile on her face before turning the doorknob and strolling back inside. "Sorry about that interruption, sugar. Now where were we?"

IT WAS AFTER midnight when Loretta gently lowered her tired body into a tub of hot water and exhaled a sigh. Her hair was clipped high on her head, but a few long tendrils always managed to slip down her neck and into the water when she leaned her head back. She closed her eyes and reflected over the events of the evening. Amelia had virtually barricaded herself in her room and refused to open the door, even for Loretta. If Jack was smart he would either move the girl back to bar hostess or kick her out completely. If Amelia was smart she would leave. However, if everything the fifteen-year-old had told Loretta was true, she had no family to return to.

A tap on the bathroom door interrupted Loretta's thoughts. "What is it now?" she asked wearily.

"It's Lydia. Ya got a minute?"

No, I don't. "Sure. Come on in. Nobody here but us girls."

Lydia, a twenty-five-year-old woman with mousey brown hair who considered herself the whore in charge of the other girls, stuck her head in the door. It wasn't that she had been rode hard and put up wet, it was more a case of never having been put up, wet or otherwise. Loretta admired her stamina though. It was pretty well known that while Lydia wasn't the best looking of the girls, she would do just about anything a customer requested.

"What are we gonna do about Amelia, Retta?" Lydia asked as she made herself comfortable on the toilet seat across from the tub.

"We?" Loretta asked. "I'd say she was Jack's problem. She sure as hell ain't mine."

"If she keeps actin' the way she is with the gentlemen callers she's gonna give us all a bad name," Lydia huffed. Her hands seemed to flutter around the room as she spoke.

Loretta didn't want to laugh at the woman, but the statement was so ridiculous she couldn't help herself. She unpinned her hair, letting it fall loosely around her shoulders as she submerged herself in the bath water. She stayed there for a few moments before popping back up, using both hands to sweep hair back, away from her face. She laughed bitterly as she blinked away the water. "I can't believe you're worried about our reputations, Lydia. We're *whores*, for God's sake, and it don't get much lower than that."

"This is just a temporary situation. One of my regular, and most faithful, gentlemen has promised to take me away from all this and set me up real respectable like."

Loretta reached over the edge of the tub to pick up a container of shampoo and poured a generous amount into her hand, working it into her hair after she returned the container to the floor. She closed one eye to avoid the sting of the soapy substance and looked at Lydia out of the other. "And would that be before or after he leaves his wife and four kids."

"Why after, of course!" Lydia said indignantly. "Wouldn't be right otherwise."

Loretta re-submerged to get the shampoo out of her hair and smiled as she came back up. "You're living in a dream, Lydia. Ain't no man gonna take any of us out of here. None of us is ever gonna get out. So just accept it for a fact. Men only want one thing from any of us and they'll say whatever it takes to get it."

Lydia leaned her chin on her fist and looked sadly at Loretta. "Don't you ever wish you could start over somewhere though, Retta?"

"Of course I do, honey. But what's done is done. It's a tad too late to be thinking about respectability."

"But if I moved somewhere else, I might could start over. Ain't like I got a big old H stamped on my forehead or somethin'."

Loretta was touched by the sadness in Lydia's voice. She was becoming an old woman before her time and despite her obvious lack of education, she could be pretty smart about some things. "Well, save up what you can. Who knows, maybe I'm just full of shit and we'll all meet the man of our dreams."

"That's the spirit!" Lydia said cheerfully as she stood to leave. "Oh, yeah, I'm supposed to tell you that Jack will be up as soon as he finishes countin' what we made tonight."

"Thanks, Lydia. Get some sleep. The wharf rats get paid tomorrow."

"Oh, shit! Not them again," Lydia moaned as she opened the door and left Loretta blessedly alone...at least for a little while longer.

LORETTA HAD BEEN brushing her hair for nearly three quarters of an hour and it was almost dry. It had a natural wave to it and, as long as she took the time to brush it two or three hundred strokes each night, it remained thick and shiny. She thought her hair was her best asset even though few of her customers ever noticed anything above her neck. Her breasts were well developed and supple. Under the right hands they were more responsive than she believed possible. The flare in her hips added to her delicate feminine figure, making her irresistibly alluring. Four years earlier she had been nothing more than another starving hayseed looking for a better life. Too bad her money ran out by the time she arrived in St. Joseph.

She hadn't been able to stand the drunken pawing of her stepfather another day. She gathered up what she could carry and the few dollars she had hidden away. She chose her sixteenth birthday to escape from her home in Ohio and thought she was fortunate when she met another traveler who got her all the way to St. Joe before attacking her and taking the last of her money. She was scavenging through discarded food bins behind a nice looking restaurant when Jack Coulter found her. She tried to run away from him, but he caught her and seemed nice, offering her a job and a place to stay. It wasn't until she serviced her first paying customer two or three weeks later that she discovered the man Jack really was.

Jack's house was clean and well-appointed. His clientele came from some of the best families in town, along with an assortment of local politicians and police officers willing to exchange one favor for another. He spared no expense to decorate his establishment with the best furnishings and the rooms were all comfortable. Loretta later grew to hate the smell that seemed to permeate the walls of the rooms. She and the other women were well-clothed and healthy for the most part. Although she never used it, she knew Lydia and a few of the other girls smoked opium Jack supplied to them to make them more compliant for his customers. It helped them relax, he said.

Loretta bent over at the waist and tossed her hair over her head, continually stroking the brush through it. There were times she wanted to cut it off so she wouldn't have to spend half the night getting it dry. She was counting the brush strokes to herself when she felt hands sliding into the opening of her robe to enclose her breasts. The scratchy feel of Jack's moustache prickled her neck.

"Sorry, it took me so long, baby. Tonight was a very good night in spite of that little fiasco with Amelia. I put your money on the dresser," he said.

"Thanks, Jack," she said as she sat up and brushed her hair back. She saw Jack's smiling face reflected behind her in the mirror.

"You look beautiful tonight," he said huskily as his eyes met hers in their reflection.

"Thank you again," she smiled, standing to face him. Jack was a charming man, but Loretta was very tired. If what she felt between her legs was any indication, it had been a very good night indeed.

"What did you do with Amelia's client?" she asked as she walked to her dresser and picked up the money laying there and counted it.

"I reimbursed him, of course," Jack shrugged.

Loretta looked at him and held up the bills in her hand. "What the hell is this, Jack?" she demanded. "I know damn well I earned more than this."

"Well," he started smugly as he stripped off his jacket and tie, "since you were part of the reason I had to reimburse that gentleman, I figured it was only fair that I took half from you and half from Amelia. You should have minded your own business, Retta."

"That's horse shit and you know it, Jack Coulter," she said, raising her voice a notch.

"I could have taken the whole thing from your pay. Maybe I should have."

"How much did you have to give that asshole?" she seethed.

"A hundred," he said as he stepped closer. Smiling, he added, "I didn't know he wanted her to suck him off, Retta. If I had..."

"You would have charged him more," she frowned.

"And sent him to a different girl. Our clients don't always tell me what they want up front, you know. Amelia wasn't ready for that. Next time, I'll ask for more specifics about what the client expects. Okay?" He bent his knees slightly to lower his body and looked into Loretta's eyes.

She couldn't help but cast a half smile in his direction. He seemed to believe his explanation solved everything as he pulled her into his arms and drew her into a hungry kiss as his hands began pushing her robe away to allow him access to her body.

"Come on to bed now, darlin'," he breathed huskily into her ear before he turned away.

Chapter Two

"I HAVE A very special customer for you tonight," Jack said, watching Loretta brush her hair and twist it into a neat stack on top of her head, later the following afternoon. She pushed a dark tortoise shell comb that stood out against her light hair into the mass and examined her appearance in the mirror of her dressing table.

"How special?" she asked as she picked up a small brush and began applying dark pink rouge to her cheeks.

"The customer requested you. Wouldn't settle for any of the other girls."

Loretta smiled at her reflection. "That's not new," she said somewhat arrogantly.

"The client will arrive around eight. Just passing through town and will be catching a train early tomorrow morning." Jack squirmed slightly in his chair. "This will be something totally different for you, Retta. You were already booked this evening, but this client was willing to pay nearly five times the rate for your time and tender touches. This will be your only client tonight."

Loretta looked over her shoulder at Jack and cast him a coy smile. "Then I suppose I'll have to be extra nice to him."

LORETTA PACED NERVOUSLY between her bed and the dressing table, stopping periodically to re-check her hair and make-up. She didn't entertain many gentlemen all night, but she was familiar with what her regular customers wanted. With a complete stranger she felt wary and unsure what to expect. She was more accustomed to a few minutes of teasing and flirting before getting down to business. Certainly nothing that had taken more than an hour and usually followed by contented snoring before her client dressed and returned to his family.

She frowned into the mirror and was startled by light tapping at her bedroom door. She glanced at the clock hanging on the wall and took a deep breath. A quarter before the hour. Officially Jack's establishment wouldn't be open for another fifteen minutes. She took a final glance into the mirror and reached for the door knob. A tall, slender body, dressed in a suit, complete with a scarf tied into a large bow around the neck stood in the doorway. A wide-brimmed hat was pulled low, obscuring her client's facial features. One gloved hand held a small bouquet of flowers and a bottle of what Loretta recognized as wine. In the other hand, her customer gripped the handle of a large valise.

"May I come in?" a husky voice asked.

"Certainly," Loretta replied, stepping aside to allow the figure to enter.

"For you," the client said softly, extending the hand holding the bouquet.

Loretta brought the flowers to her nose and breathed in the fragrance. "They're lovely. Thank you."

"Would you care for some wine?" he said, setting the valise next to Loretta's dressing table.

"I don't drink when I'm with a customer," Loretta said.

"Tonight can be an exception." He skillfully removed the cork from the bottle and set it on the dressing table. "Do you have glasses?"

Flowers still in hand, Loretta retrieved two glasses from a small table next to her bed and waited as her mysterious client poured wine into them, filling them halfway.

The stranger handed Loretta her drink and raised his own in a salute. "To an enjoyable evening."

When Loretta finished her wine, the client set his drink down and took Loretta's. She could sense the man looking at her and began to feel slightly uncomfortable under the silent, heated gaze. She watched as he slowly brought a hand up and removed his hat. Loretta stepped back when she saw a thick mass of strawberry blonde hair fall to frame obviously feminine features. The woman smiled benignly at Loretta, seemingly not surprised by her shocked expression.

"Perhaps you should put those flowers in some water," the woman said. She pulled her gloves off one finger at a time and refilled her wine glass. "Would you care for another?"

"Damn right," Loretta said.

"Do you mind if I get comfortable?" the woman asked.

"It's your time."

With nothing more than a smile, the woman set her gloves down, then reached up to untie her scarf. She pulled it off and folded it neatly, placing it next to her gloves. With a flick of her fingers she unbuttoned her jacket and slipped it off, hanging it on the back of the chair in front of the dressing table. She sipped her wine and pushed lush hair over her head.

Loretta set a vase, now filled with the flowers, on the night table beside her bed.

"Come here, please," the woman said softly.

Loretta moved resolutely toward the woman and stopped in front of her. She looked up into hazy blue eyes behind round, gold-tinted eyeglasses.

"Would you do something for me?" the woman asked.

Loretta closed her eyes for a moment and then said, "You've paid for my time. What would you like me to do?"

"Would you wash the rouge and powder from your face for me?

You're very beautiful and don't need anything to enhance your natural beauty."

"Wash my face?"

"Please."

When Loretta returned from the bathroom the woman was seated comfortably on an upholstered chair next to the door. She stood as Loretta came toward her.

"Now you're even more beautiful. Thank you." She reached up and let her fingertips run softly along Loretta's jaw line before removing the comb holding her hair in place. Loretta heard a quick intake of breath when her hair cascaded over her shoulders.

"You have lovely hair. You must brush it every evening," the woman said.

"What should I call you?" Loretta asked.

"I'm sorry. I've been very rude. My name is Josephine, but please feel free to call me Jo," the woman said. She searched Loretta's face. "You've never been intimate with a woman, have you?"

"No, I haven't," Loretta answered, looking steadily into the woman's eyes. She recognized the unmistakable look of desire gazing back at her.

"Does the idea make you uncomfortable?"

"A little. Perhaps you would rather spend the evening and your money with someone more experienced."

"No. I am quite satisfied with our arrangement," Jo answered with a grin. She brought her hands up and touched Loretta's rib cage. "I'm quite certain this corset cannot be comfortable. Please feel free to remove it."

Here it comes, Loretta smirked. *She's no different than my male customers. Ready to get to the goodies.*

"Why don't you remove it for me?" Loretta replied seductively.

Jo laughed. "We have all night, my dear, and I am in no hurry, although it is an extremely provocative offer."

"Then could you at least unbutton my dress?"

"It would be my pleasure," Jo said.

Loretta turned around and lifted her hair away from the neckline of the dress. She wasn't accustomed to such a slow and deliberate pace with her customers. Jo was an unusual woman. Not exactly beautiful, but striking looking. Her facial features were angular, almost severe, but strong and attractive nonetheless. Loretta liked the gentleness and softness in the woman's voice when she spoke. She was obviously accustomed to spending intimate time with other women and that intrigued Loretta. How different could it be? Sex was sex.

Warm fingers caressed Loretta's shoulders as the dress was pushed down over them. Loretta reached up and untied the cord holding her corset tightly against her body. She heard the sharp, quick intake of a breath behind her as the corset loosened.

"Perhaps you should remove the corset privately. I'm not quite ready to see you unclothed...yet," she said as she leaned closer to Loretta's ear. "You're an accomplished temptress for one so young."

"So I've been told," Loretta said. "But apparently not good enough...yet."

"Never underestimate your talents, my dear."

THE CLOCK ON Loretta's bedroom wall chimed ten o'clock. Jo was still lounging comfortably in the upholstered chair and Loretta was curled up on her bed, her feet beneath her as she rested against the headboard.

Jo looked at the clock and smiled. "I didn't realize it was getting so late."

"It's still early yet."

"Would you like more wine? I can order another bottle."

"No. This is more than I usually drink. But it was very good wine."

Jo stood and stretched, then plopped back down in her chair. "You might have to assist me with these boots," she said. "They're a little snug and always create a problem."

Loretta bounced off the bed and turned her back to Jo. "Give me your foot," she ordered. "Then push against me with the other one."

Within a few seconds Jo was contentedly wiggling her toes on the carpet in front of her chair. "God, that feels better than anything I can imagine," she breathed.

"Anything?"

A smirk raised Jo's lips. "So far."

Jo stood again and stared down into Loretta's eyes. "Thank you," she said. Before she realized what she was doing, Loretta began slowly pulling the shirt from Jo's waist, her hands stroking the hot, fevered skin beneath. She watched Jo's face become more relaxed under her touch and spread her fingers across Jo's soft back.

Jo's hand rose to caress Loretta's cheek and she leaned closer, allowing her hands to move into the front opening of Loretta's robe. "You're incredibly beautiful," Jo whispered. She pressed her cheek to Loretta's before bringing her mouth closer to the young woman's. "May I kiss you?" she asked.

Loretta couldn't restrain a laugh. "No one's ever asked my permission before."

"I am."

"I've never kissed a woman."

"A kiss is a kiss," Jo said with a slight shrug.

"And if I say no?"

"Then I would not, much to my regret."

While they were speaking their lips remained centimeters apart.

Loretta felt the hot breath of her customer. "Then who am I to refuse such a request," Loretta said.

A brief smile crossed Jo's lips as they met Loretta's tentatively. As the kiss deepened slightly, Loretta's lips parted, inviting her in. She drew Loretta's tongue into her mouth and traced its edges with her own, her arms lifting the smaller woman closer.

Loretta had been kissed many times, but never had anyone kissed her so gently and with such controlled desire. She wrapped her arms around Jo's neck as she was lifted from the floor and pressed her mouth hard against Jo's.

When the kiss ended and Jo lowered her to the floor, Loretta was light-headed from the contact.

"May I touch you?" Jo breathed heavily.

"Will you please stop asking permission before every movement," Loretta snapped. "It's driving me crazy."

Jo looked down at her and smiled. "That's the idea, my dear. To drive you crazy...with want and desire."

"You've succeeded," Loretta said as she began unbuttoning Jo's shirt. Her efforts were hindered by the feel of Jo's hands lightly caressing her breasts. Fingers rolled her nipples between them, the pressure sending jolts of desire through her abdomen and between her thighs.

"If you don't stop that, I'll never get this damn shirt off of you," Loretta said through clenched teeth as she tried to concentrate on what she was doing rather than what she was feeling.

"You may be disappointed at what you find," Jo said, her lips trailing kisses over Loretta's ear and down her throat, further distracting her.

"I'll be the judge of that," Loretta said, finally giving up on the buttons and ripping the shirt open. She was surprised to find no brassiere beneath, but rather a lovely pair of the smallest breasts she had ever seen. With a smile, Loretta brought her mouth to a breast and sucked it between her lips, running her tongue in circles around the nipple which responded quickly. She felt Jo tremble in her arms.

"I...I must lie down," Jo stammered. "It would be most embarrassing to fall to the floor in a heap during this delightfully intoxicating moment."

A laugh rumbled from deep in Loretta's chest and she turned them halfway, gently pushing Jo backward onto the bed. She slipped her robe from her naked body into a pile at her feet before joining her client.

LORETTA'S EYES FLUTTERED open and she stretched an arm across the jumbled covers on the bed. She felt the coolness of the sheets and sat up. She was preparing to get up when the door to her room opened and a woman with strawberry blonde hair, now covered by a small hat perched toward the front, and wearing a floor-length, deep blue dress with a white lace collar, stepped inside. Round, gold-framed glasses perched on the bridge of Jo's nose, giving her a studious appearance. Her cheeks flushed when she saw the naked young woman sitting up on the bed, staring at her.

"I'm sorry, my dear. I didn't mean to awaken you," Jo said.

"You didn't," Loretta said. "I rolled over and you were gone."

"Yes. My train will be arriving soon and I cannot afford to miss it."

"You look like a different person," Loretta smiled.

"I am a different person." Jo moved to the side of the bed and reached out to stroke a finger over Loretta's cheek. "Thank you for a wonderful night. You are an amazing young woman."

"Thank you. I hope it was everything you anticipated."

"And much more, my dear," Jo said with a slight grin.

"Will you ever come through here again?"

"Possibly, but you and I will likely never see one another again. It's safest for both of us, I believe. I cannot afford to have my personal proclivities known and one day you will find happiness with a good man."

Loretta reached out and grabbed Jo by the forearm when she started to turn away. "No one has ever treated me as well as you, Jo. Or loved me as well."

"Thank you, Loretta. Some day someone will. Someone who doesn't have to hide their desires in the shadows. You are an exquisite young woman. Don't let this life scar you."

Jo pushed her glasses farther up her nose and picked up her valise. "I wish you well, Loretta. Please take care of yourself."

Loretta nodded dumbly, watching Jo leave her room in the pre-dawn hours. She took a deep breath and fell back onto the bed. Truly, she had spent a night like none she could have dreamed of. She hadn't known such pleasure between two people was possible. For the first time in her life she felt cared for rather than used. Even though money had been involved, she hadn't been treated as property. Jo hadn't forced herself upon her, taking her cues from the way Loretta's body reacted to each touch and kiss.

Finally, Loretta scooted to the edge of her bed and stood up. Maybe she could get a relaxing bath before the other girls awakened. As she passed her dressing table and reached for her robe, she noticed an envelope leaning against the mirror. She opened it and withdrew several bills. She counted it and was stunned to find one hundred dollars Jo had left for her. The bills were wrapped in a piece of paper containing a note and a business card. "Thank you for an unforgettable evening. The best of my life. Don't hesitate to contact me if you need assistance. Jo." She flipped the business card over and read the inscription "Josephine Barclay, Esquire. Attorney-at-Law. St. Louis, Missouri."

Loretta was mildly surprised that Jo, who obviously led a secretive life, had entrusted her with her identity. She moved the table next to her bed and pulled up a loose floorboard. She dropped Jo's card and the money into a small box hidden beneath the board. She should receive another fifty as her percentage of the money Jack had charged for her services. She was getting closer to her goal. Perhaps before the first of the year she would be able to leave this life behind.

Chapter Three

HETTIE TOBIAS READJUSTED her small brown valise in her hand while holding her wide-brimmed hat on her head with the other as she peeked down one side of the train platform and then the other. The covered area in front of the busy station in St. Joseph was overflowing with people milling around. Burly men in blue and gold uniforms labored to pull huge rolling carts with metal wheels, loaded with mail, supplies, and baggage down the length of the wooden walkway toward boxcars waiting to head north, south, east and west. St. Joseph was the entry point into the great unknown everyone simply referred to as the West. The accounts she had read in the Indiana newspapers regaled readers with what she suspected were heavily embellished stories of the golden plains of Kansas and the majesty of the mountains in the Colorado Territory and beyond.

Always a bookish young woman, she had been rather thrilled when she received a reply to her query concerning a teaching position in the town of Trinidad in the southeastern corner of the Colorado Territory. Even though she lived a predictable and stable life in Germantown, Indiana, Hettie longed for adventure and the call of the west had been alluring.

She took the hand offered to her by a smiling porter and stepped off the train. No matter how she had planned her trip there would still be a layover in St. Joseph, Missouri and she would have to use part of her savings to find a decent room for the next few nights. She had never traveled by train before and found the continual stopping and starting to load and unload passengers, freight, and mail exhausting. Every time she closed her eyes she was jolted awake by the shudder of the locomotive braking. It hadn't been what she expected in the least and she hoped the remainder of her journey would be more pleasant.

She cast a smile in the porter's direction and walked carefully across the platform to avoid running into small children and harried adults. Despite standing on solid ground her body felt as if it was still in motion. She dusted off her skirt and pushed her spectacles back up onto her nose as she thought about where she should go next. Finally, she approached the ticket window and waited for the man behind the bars to look up. A black visor encircled his head and he finally peered up at her over his round framed glasses.

"Can I help you, miss?" he asked as he set aside the paperwork he had been engrossed in.

Hettie stepped closer with a slight smile. "My train west will not be leaving for a few days. Do you know of a nice but relatively inexpensive place nearby where I might find suitable lodging until then?"

He scanned Hettie's face and body from the waist up and said, "There's a nice rooming house about two blocks from here. Mrs. Covington usually has an extra room and the price ain't bad."

"And which direction might that be?" she asked stiffly. She needed a bath and a change of clothes. She had just spent two long days in a crowded, smelly passenger car, surrounded by any number of unsavory looking characters and crying children.

The man leaned forward and stuck his hand between the bars to point to Hettie's right. "That way two or three blocks. It's a white two-story with a white picket fence. Two large bougainevillea in front. Can't miss it."

Hettie turned to walk away, but paused for a moment. "I'm traveling from here to Trinidad in the Colorado Territory. Can you tell me how long that trip might take?"

"Depends on how many times the train has to stop, but I'd count on at least three days. Maybe four."

"Four days!"

"Could be three," the man shrugged. "Lots of little towns have sprung up along the railroad right of way in the last few years. Course, the train only goes to Pueblo right now. You'll have to take a stagecoach the last sixty miles or so."

"And what about my luggage?"

"We'll keep it locked up in here until your train arrives and then load it."

Hettie began walking toward the rooming house, her mind filled with thoughts. Possibly four more days crammed on a train car. God! What had she been thinking? She knew absolutely nothing about the people or the town she was traveling to. Calvin wanted to marry her. Why hadn't she accepted? Because Calvin was boring. Just another farmer looking for a woman to cook and clean and bear children. She stopped and smiled to herself. She had read that families in the west were large, sometimes more than six children so they could grow up and help work their homesteads. But this would be an adventure. Hettie nodded in an attempt to convince herself. She stopped in front of the large two-story boarding house, took a deep breath, and made her way up the steps.

"RETTA! WAIT UP!" Amelia called out. The puffiness on her bottom lip had gone down considerably, but the remnants of bruises remained around her eyes and there was only so much make-up could do.

Loretta paused and looked in the window of the mercantile store a few blocks from Jack's establishment. Some very nice material was on display in the window. She hadn't seen it the last time she had been to the business district and it would make a beautiful dress.

When Amelia reached Loretta, she was out of breath. Taking her by the arm, Loretta said, "Look, Amelia. Isn't that cloth beautiful?"

"I guess," Amelia shrugged.

"What's wrong?" Loretta said, resting her parasol on her shoulder and twirling it as she smiled at the men passing them on the sidewalk.

"I...I can't do this anymore, Retta," Amelia said.

"Do what?"

"You know what. How can you stand it? All those filthy, panting old men touching you and sweating all over you every night. It's disgusting. I hate it," the young woman frowned.

"Jack has put you back as a bar hostess, Amelia. No one's going to pant or sweat on you there. At least not as much." Loretta looked around absently.

"How can you do it, Retta?"

Her eyes flashing, Loretta looked sharply at the younger woman. "I'm doing what I have to do, Amelia. Jack saved my life. I could have become a crib girl to survive instead. You think you'd like that better? Having men who have never had a bath in their miserable lives and willing to fuck anything half alive climbing into your bed for two bits?"

"Well, I never thought..."

"Don't you ever judge me, girl, you hear. I almost have enough money saved to get out of here and not you or anyone else is going to take that away. If this is what I have to do for now, then I will. Once I leave here no one will ever know what I did in the past."

Amelia laughed. "Jack'll never let you leave. You're his woman and you know it."

"No one owns me, Amelia. Not Jack Coulter. Not anyone. Understand?" Loretta said forcefully.

"But those men...what they want you to do to them...or do to you...," Amelia shivered.

"You have to shut it out of your mind and remember your goal, Amelia," Loretta said gently as she patted the girl's arm. "Now let's go inside and look at that material."

It was true that Jack Coulter wanted his girls to look good both inside and outside his establishment. He considered himself a benevolent brothel owner, providing unreported medical care should any of his girls be beaten up, contract a disease or accidentally become pregnant. Considering that Loretta and the other girls serviced him for no charge in exchange for his medical treatment, she wasn't sure "Doc" Southard was even a real doctor. Jack hired a seamstress to keep them all well clothed and provided more than enough food and drink for their comfort. He knew where his bread was buttered, but he still didn't countenance any back talk from any of them, including Loretta. It was also true she was his favorite and he rarely visited the other girls in his establishment. During the day Jack spent time with his wife and children, returning to his business only in the evenings. He was a handsome man with a smooth way of talking his way out of any situation and into any woman's bed.

Loretta knew she would have to keep Amelia from complaining very much. She had seen what happened when Jack lost his temper. It had been enough to keep Loretta in line more than once, no matter how much Jack enjoyed being in her bed. If Jack actually paid for her services she could have already been gone. Just a few more months, that was all she needed. The boost in her savings, thanks to the generosity of Jo Barclay the week before, brought her even closer to the realization of her plans to leave St Joseph. She didn't trust the other girls enough to let them in on her plans and wished she hadn't said anything to Amelia. The girl was obviously terrified and would do anything to save her own neck.

Amelia and Loretta browsed through the mercantile, talking and giggling as they went. Loretta chose to ignore the glaring looks from the wife of the dry goods owner. Her money was as good as anyone else's and she frankly didn't care what other people in St. Joe said about her behind her back. She tried to resist, but kept returning to the material in the front window.

"May I help you?" a shrill voice behind her asked.

Smiling thinly at the woman's severe face, Loretta said, "Yes, although I'm sure you'd rather not. How much is this material?"

"Two dollars a yard," the woman replied.

"For everyone or just for me?"

"It's imported from Europe."

"For that price someone must have swam it over here on their back," Loretta said, causing a giggle to escape from Amelia.

"Wh...," the woman began.

"But it looks like a fabric befitting a lady," Loretta said quietly. "I'll take two yards. And make sure you measure it accurately, please. I wouldn't want to have to return for more and upset your delicate sensibilities."

Loretta walked away as the woman pulled the bolt of fabric from the window and carried it toward a cutting table. She was muttering to herself as she unrolled the fabric from the bolt.

"Excuse me," a soft voice said, interrupting her mumbling.

"What?" the storekeeper's wife asked curtly.

The tone of the woman's voice startled Hettie and she took a step back.

"I'm sorry, my dear. What can I do for you?" the storekeeper's wife asked more pleasantly when she saw the bookish-looking woman staring at her.

"Do you have any scented soaps here?" Hettie asked quietly.

"Yes. We just received a new shipment a few days ago with some lovely new fragrances. Jasmine is a new one. Let me show you where they are." Abandoning the bolt of material, the older woman led the way to the far end of the store.

The owner of the mercantile stepped from the back storage room carrying a box of goods and set them on the counter. Loretta glanced up from the patterns on a nearby rack and smiled. Rounding the counter he walked up behind the diminutive young woman. "Find anything you like, Miss Loretta?" he asked in a low voice.

"Why yes, I did, Hiram. Thank you." Loretta smiled without looking at the older man. He was a familiar customer and having met his wife on a number of visits to his store she could see why he might look elsewhere for pleasure. "Your wife will be cutting some of that new material for me as soon as she gets around to it."

Hiram O'Toole glanced at the material lying on the cutting table. "That color will look wonderful on you. It matches you complexion," he said. A ruddy blush made its way up his neck as Loretta turned toward him and curled her lips in a smile.

"Why, thank you, Hiram. That was very sweet," she said seductively, looking up at him. "Two dollars a yard is a little more expensive than I had planned for. Once it's sewn, you'll have to tell me how it looks on me."

"Two dollars?" Hiram asked, practically having to wipe drool from his lips.

"Yes, that's what Mrs. O'Toole said it would be," Loretta said innocently.

"Mrs. O'Toole was mistaken, Miss Loretta. It's only one dollar a yard. If you'd like I would be happy to cut the length for you."

"That would be extremely kind of you, Hiram."

Loretta followed Hiram to the cutting table and watched as he measured out the two yards, plus a healthy extra half yard to ensure the cut was straight. As he smoothed the material over the table he glanced up occasionally and admired the soft curves and lines of Loretta's body. He couldn't afford to visit Jack Coulter's establishment often, but when he did he always requested Miss Loretta.

"What are you doing?!" Mrs. O'Toole's shrill voice broke the relative quiet of the store.

"I'm cutting this material for a customer, my dear," Hiram said calmly.

She lowered her voice as she walked up to her husband. "She's a whore, Hiram O'Toole. She could have waited until respectable customers were taken care of."

Loretta bit her tongue and clenched her hand tightly around the handle of her parasol.

"She's a customer," Hiram restated. "As far as I know her money is as good as anyone else's."

Picking up the material, Hiram folded it and when he was sure his wife wasn't looking, he cast a wink in Loretta's direction. Loretta and

Amelia followed him to the cash register, ignoring the daggers Mrs. O'Toole was sending their direction. Loretta took four bills from her purse and slid them across the counter toward Hiram.

"But I said the material was...," he began.

"I don't wish to cause a problem for you with your wife, Mr. O'Toole," Loretta said.

Sliding two dollars back toward her, he said, "The price I told you was the correct one, ma'am. I won't have my wife cheating customers and giving my business a bad name."

"That's very considerate of you, Hiram. You, indeed, are a true gentleman."

As Loretta picked up her package of material and turned to leave she almost ran into a young woman in her mid twenties wearing a conservative green dress and horn-rimmed glasses. "I'm sorry," Loretta said, stepping aside.

"Now where?" Loretta asked as she and Amelia stopped onto the boardwalk in front of O'Toole's Mercantile.

"I don't know," Amelia shrugged. "I don't have any money of my own."

Linking her arm with Amelia's, Loretta said, "How about I buy you a sarsaparilla?"

"I'd like that," Amelia said, smiling brightly.

"Me, too," Loretta said as they made their way through horses and wagon traffic on the dusty street toward a local eating establishment.

Loretta slid into a booth and settled herself before taking a long draw on the straw of her drink. "Damn, this tastes wonderful."

"Better than whiskey," Amelia said.

They chatted for a few minutes, laughing and gossiping about some of their customers. Loretta was looking absently out the front window, when a voice broke into her thoughts. "Excuse me."

Loretta turned and saw the young woman she had seen not long before in the mercantile. "Yes. May I help you?"

"May I join you for a few minutes?" the woman asked. "There don't seem to be any other available seats."

Loretta stood and moved to Amelia's side of the booth. "It's your reputation, honey," she smirked.

The woman set a small package of soap on the seat and cleared her throat. "My name is Hettie Tobias."

"What can we do for you, Hettie Tobias?" Loretta asked, taking another sip of her drink.

"I couldn't help but overhear part of your conversation with that woman at the mercantile."

"Really," Loretta said, glancing at Amelia.

"It wasn't my intention to eavesdrop, but I wanted to tell you I thought her behavior was reprehensible," Hettie said indignantly.

"For her to insinuate you were a...a whore was uncalled for."

"It's the truth," Loretta smiled. The look on Hettie's face made her laugh. "Don't worry, honey. I'm used to it."

"Well, I must say, you're lovely and certainly don't look like I would have imagined."

"What do you think a whore looks like?" Loretta asked, amused.

"Retta!" Amelia hissed.

"Excuse me. Wherever are my manners?" Loretta smiled. "My name is Loretta Digby and this is my friend, Miss Amelia Benson." She paused for a moment before adding, "She's new to the trade."

"Are you a..a...? Oh my. You can't be more than a child," Hettie managed.

"Amelia is a hostess," Loretta said.

"I'm actually just passing through St. Joseph," Hettie said, changing the subject rather abruptly. "I'm on my way west to teach at a small school."

"Congratulations," Amelia said.

"Thank you. I guess," Hettie said. "I'm not sure I'm doing the right thing."

"Where you goin'?" Loretta asked.

"Trinidad in the Colorado Territory."

"Oh, it's real pretty there," Amelia enthused. "At least that's what I heard from a gentleman last month."

"Do you know anything about what it's like in the west?" Hettie asked. "I mean, you must have met men and women from there."

"I have," Loretta nodded with a frown. "The men are a fairly unwashed group. And a little...um...," Loretta searched for the right word.

"A little what?" Hettie asked with concern in her voice.

"Um...eager, I guess. Many of them haven't seen or smelled a woman in quite a while."

"Oh, God!" Hettie breathed, resting her forehead on her hands.

"What made you decide to go west anyway?" Amelia asked.

"The literature I've read makes it sound rather romantic. Running off to a completely different and unknown environment in the wilderness. Seeing things I would never see otherwise."

"Ain't you scared of Indians or train robbers?" Amelia asked. "I heard they even stop the trains and take the women with them for...you know."

"Oh, don't be so damned melodramatic, Amelia," Loretta frowned. "Seems to me the west would be a wonderful place to build a new life." Turning to Hettie she said, "Perhaps you will meet a decent man, get married, and raise a family."

"I have a layover here in St. Joseph," Hettie said. "So I have a few days to decide whether I want to truly go any farther or not."

"I hate to say it, honey, but you should have thought about all of that before you picked up and left home," Loretta said.

"I know," Hettie nodded. "Maybe I'll find someone else at Mrs. Covington's Rooming House who can tell me more."

As Amelia and Loretta slid out of the booth, Loretta rested a hand on Hettie's shoulder. "I'm sure whatever you decide will be the right decision for you. But once you make a decision don't let yourself be turned back by doubts. Your heart will know the right thing to do."

Hettie looked at her with a puzzled look. "My grandmother always told me to follow my heart."

"Well, I hope I look a damn sight better than your grandmother, sweetie," Loretta laughed as she turned and left the eatery.

Chapter Four

AMELIA JUGGLED AN armload of packages into the front entryway of Jack's establishment. Loretta giggled as Amelia struggled to keep the packages containing Loretta's purchases from slipping. The poor girl, who was eager to please, attempted to keep them under control until she reached the table in the middle of the parlor floor.

Camille DeRossi, Jack's favorite prior to Loretta's arrival, stepped out of her room and looked over the banister at the two younger women below. "What's all the noise about?"

"We've been shopping," Amelia said through her giggles. "Loretta found the most elegant fabric." Without thinking, she continued exuberantly. "She can wear it to her first dinner when she starts a new life."

"What new life?" Camille asked Amelia while staring directly at Loretta.

"Why as the Duchess of What-Not or the Countess of Faraway," Loretta said dramatically. "Just as soon as we can convince the Duke or Count to sweep in here and take us all away." She turned her attention to Amelia. "Isn't that right, my dear?" Impulsively Loretta took Amelia in her arms and began dancing around the parlor. "You mustn't talk about leaving," she whispered quickly. Then she released Amelia and they both made a deep curtsey in Camille's direction.

"Where did you get the money to buy all those things?" Camille asked.

"Actually, a number of my customers are respected businessmen who gladly give me a discount," Loretta answered. She knew the answer sounded snobby, but Camille had been watching her every move for the last three years. Since the day Jack abandoned Camille's bed for hers. Personally, Loretta would have preferred he stay where he was.

"You two can stop playing around. Loretta, you're booked for this evening. Amelia, Charlotte is ill and you'll be the only hostess tonight. So get a move on."

"I'm sorry, Camille," Loretta said as she slowly pulled her gloves off. "Did Jack die and leave you in charge?"

"Don't get a smart mouth with me, girl. You're just another whore who can be replaced," Camille snapped. She turned abruptly on her heel and slammed the door to her room.

"She's pissed," Amelia breathed.

"She's jealous," Loretta sniffed. *Not much longer and she can have*

Jack Coulter back. "Let's get this stuff upstairs."

LORETTA THREW HER head back and let a deep husky laugh escape from her throat. "Slow down, Cyrus, honey. We got all evening." Cyrus Langford was a sweet man in his mid-thirties, but had the sexual control of a fifteen-year-old boy. Loretta thought he would make someone a good husband one day, once he learned to control his sexual urges. As minister to his flock, Cyrus always seemed to regret the times he visited Loretta, but it hadn't stopped him from making several visits each year when church business brought him into the city. He always paid for an entire night and was a welcome relief from the usual men who shared her bed.

"God, forgive me," Cyrus mumbled as his mouth and hands wandered over each newly exposed part of Loretta's body. She smiled as she took his face in her hands and kissed him tenderly while he unfastened her brassiere and caressed her full breasts as if they might break.

"You're a good man, Cyrus. God knows that," Loretta said soothingly.

"I'm a sinner, Miss Loretta," he said with a shaky voice as his fingers spread across her smooth back and slid down to her hips.

"We all are, sugar. Otherwise, there'd be nothing for God to forgive."

"You're a smart woman, Loretta. I don't know why you do the devil's work." As Loretta let her hand wander between his thighs, his breath caught. "But you are so very talented at it." Slowly Loretta lowered her body until she was kneeling in front of the man who was beginning to shake slightly in anticipation. Staring into his eyes, she unfastened his trousers and began pulling them down at a tortuously slow rate.

"I've heard other preachers say that as long as a person calls out God's name with their last breath," Loretta said with a smile as her fingernails raked along the backs and sides of Cyrus' legs eliciting a groan, "that He would forgive even your deepest sins. Do you want me to make you call out God's name tonight, Cyrus?"

"Oh, yes," the minister breathed. "Oh, yes."

Loretta felt Cyrus tremble at the feel of her lips moving slowly, tortuously up the outsides of his thin thighs. When he buried his fingers in her hair, she knew it wouldn't be much longer before he lost control of himself. Loretta always began their nights together this way and he never seemed to tire of it. She wondered if he had completely forgotten his sermons against lust and the wages of sin.

Unexpectedly, the door of Loretta's room flew open, startling both of them. Loretta grabbed her discarded blouse as Cyrus' hands attempted futilely to cover his arousal. Loretta couldn't believe her eyes.

"Jack! What the hell are you doing?" she asked angrily. Cyrus not only paid for her services, but was a more than generous tipper in an attempt to assuage his guilt.

"Get out, Reverend!" Jack demanded, barely controlled fury filling his dark eyes as he stood in the doorway. "Pick another girl tonight."

"But I don't wa...," Cyrus began, glancing at Loretta.

"If you don't want another girl, Lydia will refund your money," Jack said as he glared steadily at Loretta. He shifted his eyes to Cyrus and forced a smile. "Something unexpected has come up. Loretta is not available."

Cyrus redressed as quickly as possible and slipped past Jack. He nodded a small, embarrassed smile in Loretta's direction before Jack closed the door.

Still holding her blouse across her chest as Jack approached, Loretta said, "What was that about, Jack? Cyrus is one of my best customers."

The reply came as a vicious backhand across her mouth. Her blouse fell to the floor as she brought her hand to her mouth and felt the warm blood that had begun to run down her chin. Before she could react, a second blow slammed into her face and knocked her to the floor. Angry tears formed in her eyes from the pain and she tried to blink them away. Jack grabbed a hand full of thick, light amber hair and jerked her bleeding face back so she could look at him.

"You a lying, filthy, fucking whore," he spat. "You think you can just pack up and leave."

Her mind was fuzzy and she shook her head. "Wha...what are...you talkin' about...Jack?"

"I saved your ass four years ago!" he screamed. "You would have starved or frozen to death in a back alley if I hadn't taken you in! And this is how you repay me?"

Loretta was confused and couldn't think. "I...I don't...know...," she tried to say through her rapidly swelling lip.

Jack dragged her to her feet and shoved her roughly across the room and onto her bed. As she watched through widened eyes, Jack began stripping his trousers off.

"Jack, tell me...what...I did," she pleaded.

"Amelia tells me you're planning to leave," he said calmly. His sudden change from anger to calm sent a terrified shiver through Loretta's body. "But you're never going to leave here, Retta. Understand?"

She nodded. "I'm not...going anywhere."

"You're goddamn right, you're not," he said through clenched teeth. "No one leaves Jack Coulter."

"Jack, please," she said as she reached toward her nightstand.

"No!" he said firmly as he slapped her again. "No protection this time."

She tried to bring her knee up between them to push him away, but was dizzy from the blows to her head. "Jack, please don't," she begged as he grabbed her wrists and forced them over her head. Getting a knee between her thighs, he brought it up forcefully into her crotch. She cried out at the pain and tears rolled down the sides of her face and onto the bed. She had been with many men in the past four years, but had never been seriously hurt. There was nothing gentle as Jack forced her legs apart and drove into her painfully. Blood from her face, mingled with her tears, began covering his shirt collar as he pounded against her relentlessly. He was hurting her and she could feel the tender skin of her crotch tearing and burning as Jack's sweaty body battered against hers.

It seemed like an eternity before Jack released her hands and withdrew from her exhausted and ravaged body. She couldn't look at him as she pulled her legs up to her chest and curled into a ball, sobbing from pain and anger. Jack was standing at the end of the bed, panting.

"Nobody leaves me," he stated again. "No one! I own you!"

She ground her teeth together as she turned to face him. "Nobody rapes me and no one owns me."

"A whore can't be raped, you stupid bitch," he seethed as he reached out and grabbed her legs. Loretta kicked with whatever strength she could muster, managing to land one well-placed kick that doubled Jack over. When he straightened up once more, he jerked her off the bed, her body landing on the floor with a thud. She groaned as she tried to catch her breath and push herself up. She wasn't expecting the bone-crushing pain in her side as Jack lashed out and kicked her across the ribs and abdomen, sending her collapsing to the floor. Was this what happened when you die, she thought as Jack continued to kick her body. Please, God, she prayed, hoping what she told Cyrus earlier was true. Everything around her sparkled briefly before it turned black as she felt the force of Jack's foot for the last time.

"RETTA. PLEASE WAKE up, Retta. Please," a shaky voice whispered. Even the gentle movement against her shoulder sent waves of pain and nausea through Loretta's beaten body and she moaned at the movement.

"Shhh," the voice said. "You have to be quiet, Retta. Otherwise, Jack...," the voice said. At the mention of the man who had raped and beaten her, Loretta's eyes managed to open into swollen slits and she tried to curl into a protective ball once again. But her arms and legs weren't working the way they were supposed to. Unbidden, tears rolled across her face.

"My God," a man's voice said softly. "We have to get her to a doctor."

"No...no doctor," Loretta wheezed.

She felt a cool cloth against her face, which felt stiff, especially around her mouth. "Let me get some of this blood off your face, Retta. You can't leave here lookin' like this."

"Amelia?" she managed. "What..."

"Be quiet, Retta. I got Cyrus with me. We'll get you out of here," Amelia whispered.

"No," Loretta said. "Jack will hurt you, too."

"We're both gettin' out of here," Amelia said resolutely. "Where's your stash?"

"Loose board. Under nightstand."

"Cyrus, can you pick her up while I get her money?" Amelia asked as she stood.

"Yes," the preacher said as he knelt next to Loretta. "I'll be as careful as I can, Miss Loretta, but I'm positive it will hurt," he said gently as he stroked blood-matted hair away from her swollen face.

Loretta found the damp cloth Amelia had been using and stuffed it into her mouth. She could barely see the concern and compassion filled eyes of her customer. Cyrus slid an arm around her shoulders, the other under her knees and brought her carefully against his chest. The cloth in her mouth muffled the scream that washed over her from the excruciating pain ripping through her ribs and abdomen as he lifted her from the floor. She managed to bring an arm up and squeezed Cyrus' upper arm with the strength she had left. A moment later, Amelia was next to them.

"Got it," Amelia whispered.

Loretta was beginning to shiver in Cyrus' arms. "Get a quilt or something to cover her with," he whispered. "She can't be out half-naked."

Loretta felt warmth spread through her body as a quilt was gently tucked around her body. "Wait here, Reverend, while I check the hallway," Amelia said. She cracked open the door to Loretta's room slightly and peeked out. She breathed a sigh of relief when she saw no one. She led them silently down the stairs and toward the back entrance. Amelia held her breath as the back screen squeaked open, but heard nothing from inside the building. They stayed in the alleyways near the brothel as much as possible and didn't stop again until they were several blocks away. By then Loretta had begun trembling and moaning loudly enough to be heard through the cloth in her mouth.

"Now where, Amelia?" Cyrus asked as he leaned against the side of a building and shifted Loretta's weight slightly in his arms, causing another moan.

"I don't know, Reverend. It ain't like I've ever had to do this before, ya know?"

"Do you have any friends who can take you in, at least for tonight?"

Amelia laughed derisively. "Oh, yeah. Us whores are just eat up with friends."

"There must be some place," he sighed. "We have to go somewhere before it gets light out."

"Just give me a minute," Amelia said as she took a deep breath. "I could use some of Loretta's money and find a hotel room, I suppose. Where are you stayin', Cyrus?"

"The Clarendon, but you can't stay there," he said shaking his head.

"Why not?"

"It's full already," he said. With a laugh, he continued, "Mostly with other ministers."

"Wait!" Amelia said. "I might know a place, but I need to go there alone first. No sense in you carryin' Loretta all that way if it don't work out. Can you stay here with her for about an hour? I shouldn't be gone longer than that."

"Of course, my dear. I'll take good care of her until you return," Cyrus said softly as he gazed down at the small battered body in his arms.

"I know you will, Reverend," Amelia said as she touched his arm lightly. "Loretta always said you were a good man even though you had been sorely tempted."

"Loretta is a good woman even though she's had a hard life. Now hurry, Amelia. I don't like the way her breathing sounds."

LORETTA'S HEAD LOLLED on Cyrus' shoulder as he carefully slid down the wall of the building, still cradling Loretta. The movement startled her and she tried to speak, but only mumbled incoherently.

"Shhh, Retta," a familiar soft voice whispered. "You've been hurt. Don't try to move. Amelia's gone for help."

Cyrus! she thought through the fog that had enveloped her mind. The steady, rhythmic rise and fall of his chest made her feel safe as she floated into a pain-wracked sleep. Later, when his body jerked, fear ran through her again.

"How is she?" she heard Amelia ask, her voice filled with concern.

"Sleeping. At least I think she is," Cyrus answered quietly.

"I found a place we can take her," Amelia said. "This is Hettie. Retta and I met her yesterday. Can you get up?"

"I don't think so."

"Hettie, if you grab Cyrus under one arm and I grab under his other one, we might be able to get him up," Amelia instructed.

"My God!" a strange voice breathed. "Who would do such a thing?"

"One fuckin' mad pimp," Amelia said harshly.

"Language, Miss Amelia," Cyrus cautioned with a grunt as the two women prepared to help him stand.

"Sorry, Reverend," Amelia said. "But it's the truth."

"And the truth shall set you free," the unknown woman said as Loretta felt Cyrus grip her securely and begin to move.

"Indeed," he said. "Indeed."

"On three," Amelia said as she took a deep breath.

AMELIA SILENTLY LED the little group through alleyways toward Hettie's rooming house. Hettie walked next to Cyrus, occasionally glancing up at his kind face and the bundle held securely in his arms. What had she been thinking when she agreed to help these total strangers? She had barely remembered the young girl who appeared at her door an hour or so earlier. Now she was letting two prostitutes hide in her room for God knew how long. And there was a man involved. She simply could not permit him to stay in her room as well. It wouldn't be the proper thing to do under any circumstance. She had been alone with a man before, but that was of her own choosing. The tall, rather handsome man carrying the injured woman was apparently a man of the cloth and while Hettie was sure he could be trusted, beginning her new life with such an impropriety was unthinkable. Or would have been in Indiana. She left home to seek adventure, but this wasn't exactly what she'd had in mind. And consorting with prostitutes? What would her parents and Calvin think? She smiled to herself as the thought of the scandal sent a pleasant shiver through her body. She hadn't reached the Colorado Territory yet and her adventure had already begun.

Cyrus and Amelia waited near the back door of Mrs. Covington's Rooming House while Hettie entered through the front door and made her way to the back. It was the middle of the night and the house was quiet as she unlocked and held open the back door. Cyrus had to turn sideways to make his way past Hettie. They waited as she relocked the back door and led them to her room on the second floor. She unlocked the door to her room and struck a match for the light next to the bed. Amelia took the quilt from around Loretta's body and spread it over Hettie's bed, careful to avoid getting blood on the bedcovers. When Hettie had made the room as bright as possible, she turned toward the bed.

"Dear God!" she said. "She's...she's naked."

Cyrus removed his coat and rolled up his shirtsleeves. "If you could bring us some warm water and clean cloths it would be very helpful," he said looking at Hettie.

"Are you a doctor?" she asked, unable to tear her eyes away from Loretta's naked body.

"No, but I studied to be one before I became a man of the cloth," he said. "Amelia, as soon as we have her cleaned up, you and Miss Hettie should leave." His face reddened slightly.

"Why?" Amelia asked.

"She may have been...be injured in her...um...private area. I will need to check," he said quietly.

Amelia snorted. "Like I ain't seen that before, Reverend."

Hettie stood at the foot of the bed, her mouth agape, looking between Cyrus and Amelia. She finally cleared her throat and said, "I helped my sister deliver her baby last year. I can assist as well."

"First, get the water and cloths," Cyrus said gently. He hesitated a moment before reaching down and stroking Loretta's hair. "And a funnel of some kind if you can find one."

Within a few minutes, the small room was a flurry of semi-quiet activity. Hettie and Amelia carefully washed dried blood from Loretta's face and from cuts on her side and abdomen. When they finished, Cyrus carefully opened Loretta's mouth and peered inside, manipulating her jaw. He took each arm and felt along its length, bending her elbows. Hettie handed him a funnel she found in the kitchen. He pressed the wide end against Loretta's chest and placed the smaller end in his ear and closed his eyes in concentration.

He instructed the two women to help him turn Loretta onto her side as gently as possible and knelt next to the bed, placing the funnel on her back. When he stood a few minutes later, he was smiling. "Her heartbeat is strong and although I'm certain she has several broken ribs, her breathing sounds fine, so I don't believe her lung has been punctured."

"I'll see what I can find to wrap her ribs with," Hettie said.

"Good," Cyrus said. "Umm...Amelia?"

"What?" the girl asked as she looked up at him.

"I know you girls use something for...to...you know...prevent diseases and...well...pregnancy," he said uncomfortably.

"I think Loretta rinses herself out, but she makes her customers use a cover. You know that, Cyrus," Amelia said nonchalantly.

He cleared his throat and glanced at Hettie. "Yes, I know, but I don't think Jack used a cover when he did this. The skin is badly torn."

"Oh," Amelia said. "I didn't bring anything for that, Cyrus."

"I saw a hot water bottle in the bathroom earlier this evening," Hettie volunteered.

"That would work, but it might already be too late," Cyrus nodded. "We can try though. Amelia, you and Hettie see what you can find that we can mix with the water. Something acidic."

"For what?" Amelia asked.

Hettie reached over and took Amelia by the arm. "Come with me. I know what to look for."

Cyrus raised a questioning eyebrow as he looked at Hettie. "And we'll need something to catch the fluid as it passes out of her body,"

Cyrus said quickly.

While he waited for the women to return, Cyrus sat on the edge of the bed and used his fingers to brush Loretta's hair back, looking at her once beautiful face. "I'm so sorry this has happened to you, Retta," he said softly. "I'll do what I can and hope it's enough." Without another thought, he slid off the bed and knelt beside it, interlacing his fingers as he said a silent prayer. Unexpectedly, a hand found its way to his hair and stroked it. When he looked up in surprise, Loretta's swollen lips were trying to move.

He grabbed her hand and brought it to his lips. "Don't try to talk, Miss Loretta. You've been badly injured." She nodded slightly, taking a ragged breath. "Amelia and Hettie will be back in a minute," he said. "I'll try not to hurt you any more than necessary."

When Hettie and Amelia returned, Hettie assisted Cyrus while Amelia held Loretta's hand. By the time they were finished, Amelia's hand was white from being squeezed hard and she had to shake it to return circulation to her fingers. Hettie handed Cyrus two small white tablets and helped prop Loretta up far enough to swallow them. Whether from pain, the pills, or exhaustion, Loretta fell into a deep sleep as they cleaned up the room.

"You did a wonderful job, Reverend," Hettie said as they carried the basin to the bathroom and emptied it. "Perhaps you should have become a doctor after all."

"Where did you get the laudanum tablets I gave Loretta?"

"From my doctor before I left Indiana. I don't need them and thought they would help."

"They will give her time to rest. I decided not to complete my studies because I couldn't tolerate seeing all those people suffering in pain everyday," he smiled. "I decided to save their souls instead."

"And what about your own soul?" she asked.

"I'm still working on that, Miss Hettie, I'm sad to say," he frowned.

"Loretta is a prostitute, is she not?"

"Yes, she is," Cyrus acknowledged. He turned to face the young woman and lifted his chin a little. "And I have been her customer on several occasions. As a matter of fact..."

Hettie held her hand up to stop him. "It would not be my place to judge you, Reverend. I am a sinner, as well."

"I highly doubt that, Miss Hettie," he smiled gently.

"I have been with a man out of wedlock," she said as she looked away. "That is why I am willing to travel west to leave my sinful past behind and start anew."

"We all make mistakes, my dear. That is why we can be comforted by our faith in God. He forgives our mistakes and makes us whole again."

"Do you really believe that?"

"Considering my profession and my own sins, I suppose I have to," Cyrus smiled.

"Your flock is extremely fortunate to have a man who understands what sin is."

"Somehow I don't think they would agree with you," Cyrus frowned. "I am somewhat in the same situation you are. I have accepted a new position in Colorado where I can rebuild my life and renew my faith. This was my last trip into St. Joseph."

A WEEK LATER, Loretta was able to push herself up on a stack of pillows. Her injured ribs made it difficult to take a deep breath and the bruises on her body and face were beginning to fade although they were still clearly visible. Amelia sat beside the bed, scooping up another spoonful of oatmeal and bringing it to Loretta's mouth. It tasted good, even though Amelia had gotten a little carried away with the sugar. Loretta winced slightly as she took the oatmeal into her mouth.

"Too hot?" Amelia asked.

"No, it's fine, sweetie. I'll be glad when my lip heals though."

"Cyrus says it will in another week or so. Same with the other cuts, but you might have a couple of little scars. Gonna take longer for your ribs though."

"Yeah. I'd kill to take a deep breath," Loretta said with a small smile.

A light tap at the door startled Amelia. She stood quickly and set the bowl on the nightstand. She walked to the door, leaned closer to it, and whispered, "Who is it?"

"Cyrus and Hettie," a soft female voice said.

Amelia looked back at Loretta and smiled, then opened the door. Loretta noticed Cyrus was holding the hand of the familiar looking woman beside him.

"You're looking much better today, Miss Loretta," Cyrus said as he crossed the room to stand next to the bed.

Loretta reached out and stroked his arm, attempting a crooked smile to protect her lip. "Thanks to you, Cyrus. You saved my life. I'll never be able to repay you," she said quietly as a tear escaped from her eye and rolled down her cheek. Her hand quickly brushed it away. "I'm sorry."

"You should contact the police," the woman next to Cyrus said tersely.

Loretta looked at her curiously, trying to remember where she had seen her before. "I'm a whore," Loretta snapped. "The police are frequent customers to my employer's establishment. It's not likely they would do anything." Loretta looked at the woman through bruised and swollen eyes. "Do I know you?"

"I'm sorry. My name is Hettie Tobias. I spoke to you and Amelia for a few minutes the day before you were...assaulted. In that little café."

Loretta looked at Amelia in disbelief. "You went to a total stranger for help?"

"There wasn't no one else, Retta. You know the other girls wouldn't have done a damn thing," Amelia said defensively.

"Language, Miss Amelia," Cyrus reminded her softly.

"Sorry, Reverend. If it hadn't been for Cyrus I couldn't have gotten you out of there. Jack would have come back and finished you off for sure."

"It's all right, Amelia" Loretta looked at Hettie. "I thought you were leaving for someplace out west," she said.

"I've postponed my journey," Hettie said, glancing up at Cyrus, a light blush coloring her cheeks.

Cyrus cleared his throat, a smile teasing at his lips. "As it happens, Miss Hettie and I are both traveling to the same town in the Colorado Territory."

Loretta lifted an eyebrow, looking at Cyrus and then back toward Hettie. "Reverend Langford is a fine Christian man." She was unsure what Hettie actually knew about her relationship with Cyrus or what he might have told her.

"Hettie knows," Cyrus said softly. "I've told her everything."

"Then she's a fine Christian woman," Loretta smiled.

Cyrus sat on the edge of the bed and took Loretta's hand. "Um...we were thinking, Miss Loretta," he began, looking at Hettie. "Jack is looking everywhere for you and Amelia. Miss Hettie and I thought perhaps the two of you might consider traveling with us to Colorado."

"I'm not afraid of Jack Coulter," Loretta said defiantly. "But I sure as hell ain't workin' for him again."

"Perhaps all you need is a fresh start," Hettie said, touching Loretta's arm. "Once you get there you can do what you advised me to do and follow your heart."

Loretta thought for a few minutes. "I will give you the money to purchase tickets for us, but all my belongings are at Jack's."

"You can take some of my clothes. I think we're about the same size."

Loretta shook her head slightly. "Thanks, but I can afford to clothe myself. Take part of my stash and purchase two or three dresses for me. I might as well start a new life with everything fresh."

"I checked at the depot and the next train to Pueblo leaves in three days," Cyrus said. "It will take three or four days to get most of the way to our destination by train. I know you'll be in a great deal of pain because of your ribs. Do you think you can stand the jostling around?"

"Reckon I'll have to."

Chapter Five

"I DON'T SEE anyone familiar," Cyrus said softly as he knelt in front of the wooden wheelchair holding a woman who wore a heavy black mourning dress and adjusted her lap quilt. A black veil attached to a wide-brimmed black hat covered her face.

"How much longer before the train arrives?" she asked.

Cyrus withdrew a silver pocket watch from his vest pocket and flipped it open. "Half an hour. If it's on time. Are you doing all right?"

"I'm smothering in this damned dress," she said.

"Language, Miss Loretta. And patience," he whispered as he stood and patted her lightly on the shoulder.

"As I recall, Reverend, patience was never one of your virtues either." Loretta chuckled as she remembered Cyrus' inability to contain himself when he spent an evening with her. The chuckle was followed by a fit of coughing which caused her to wrap her arms around her ribcage to lessen the pain from her damaged ribs.

"Leaving town, Reverend Langford?" a familiar voice asked as Cyrus leaned over Loretta.

"There, there, Mrs. Tobias. It won't be much longer now," Cyrus soothed. He smiled as he watched Jack Coulter approach. Dressed impeccably as usual, Jack puffed on a cigar as he glanced around the depot platform at the passengers waiting for the westbound train.

"How are you, Jack?" Cyrus asked, resting a hand on Loretta's shoulder and squeezing lightly. "What brings you down here today?"

His eyes scanning the platform, Jack shrugged. "I'm just keeping an eye out for a couple of friends I'm expecting to be here."

"Are they coming in on this train?"

"No. Probably departing and I wanted to wish them well."

"Really?"

"Have you see Retta or Amelia while you've been here?"

"No, I haven't. I had planned to say goodbye and wish them both well before I left, but I was asked to assist a friend in getting her mother on board the next train and didn't get the chance. I hope you will give them my kindest regards."

Jack laughed and leaned closer. "I'm sure you'll miss them, especially Retta."

Loretta sat quietly in the wheelchair, barely daring to breathe as Jack continued his conversation with Cyrus.

"Oh, Cyrus. There you are!" Hettie said as she walked quickly across the platform. "Are you feeling all right, Mother?" she asked as she knelt beside the wheelchair.

Loretta nodded slightly and brought a glove-covered hand under her veil as if to wipe her nose.

"We should get mother into the shade, Cyrus. It's getting terribly warm out here," Hettie said.

Jack removed the bowler from his head and bowed in Hettie's direction. "I don't believe I've had the pleasure, ma'am. I'm Jack Coulter. The Reverend and I have known one another for quite a while. I'm sure I would remember such a lovely woman as yourself."

"Hettie Tobias," she answered as she shook Jack's hand. "Reverend Langford and I only met a few days ago. My mother's health has not been good lately and this trip has taken a toll on her, I'm afraid."

"And what might your destination be?"

"Colorado. I've accepted a teaching position there and my mother, a widow, is making the journey with me. I feel much better knowing I will still be able to care for her."

"How long ago did your father pass away?"

Hettie's eyes shifted quickly to Cyrus. "Last month. It was quite unexpected and our travel arrangements had to be hastily made. That's why it was such a blessing when I met Reverend Langford during our layover here in St. Joseph."

A whistle sounding in the distance snapped everyone to attention. Small black puffs of smoke from the approaching train's stack created a buzz among the waiting passengers. Some began rounding up small children and hoisting luggage from the platform, anxious to begin their journeys.

"Have you made arrangements with the station master to take Mrs. Tobias aboard?" Cyrus asked.

"Yes, he said it might be best to wait until everyone else boarded to avoid delay," Hettie said. "If you'll excuse me, I should check Mother's trunk. I had a difficult time with the latch this morning and wouldn't want it to come open unexpectedly."

"It was a pleasure to meet you, Miss Tobias," Jack said with a charming smile as he tipped his hat. "I hope you have a pleasant and uneventful journey."

"Thank you," Hettie replied. She turned and quickly made her way to the far end of the loading platform toward the luggage dolly.

Jack extended a hand to Cyrus. "The girls and I will certainly miss you, Reverend," he said with a wink. "If you decide to make a visit this way again I hope you'll stop by. You'll always be welcome."

Just as long as I pay up front, Cyrus thought as he took Jack's hand. He watched Jack leave and stroll down the platform. He leaned over Loretta's shoulder and mumbled, "That was a close one."

"How is Amelia?" Loretta whispered.

"Hettie's gone to check on her. It won't be much longer."

HETTIE MOVED QUICKLY down the steps at the far end of the platform, stopping halfway down to see where Jack Coulter was. Sure the coast was clear, she made her way to the large cart filled with trunks and valises. Pretending to examine the locks on a large black trunk she said, "Are you all right in there, Amelia?"

"It's hotter than the devil's own hell in here. How much longer?" a muffled voice asked.

"The train is nearly here. Once the train departs I will go to the baggage car and let you out. Jack Coulter is here."

"Oh, no!"

"Sh-h-h. It's all right. He stood less than two feet from the wheelchair and didn't have any idea who was in it. Be patient and you and Loretta will both be safely away from here."

Cyrus and Hettie waited until the final passenger boarded before rolling the wheelchair to the steps onto the passenger cars. Hettie smiled as she glanced down the empty platform and saw the trunk being loaded into the baggage car which was five cars from theirs. She looked over her shoulder and saw Jack Coulter leaning against the wall of the depot watching as she and Cyrus prepared to help her 'mother' onto the train.

"He's still here," she said under her breath as she pulled the lap blanket away.

"I know. Don't pay any attention to him." Cyrus bent over the wheelchair and saw Loretta's hazel eyes staring back at him. "Just put your arm around my neck, Miss Retta, and I'll carry you on board. I'll try not to hurt you."

Loretta did as she was told and felt Cyrus' arms slip under her knees and around her back. Looking at Hettie, he said, "When I lift her, stand between me and Jack as you fold the chair so he won't be able to see anything."

Hettie nodded and stood behind the chair. Loretta was a small woman, no more than five-foot-three inches and barely weighed over a hundred pounds. He lifted her easily from the chair, waiting as Hettie folded and lifted the chair behind him. Cyrus took the three steps onto the train, turning quickly into the passenger car while the conductor took the folded wheelchair from Hettie and stored it in a passageway compartment.

Halfway down the car, Hettie stepped into a seat next to a window and Cyrus placed the woman in black on the seat next to her before taking his own seat across from them. While they waited for the train to pull away from the station, Hettie shook out the lap cover and placed it over the woman's legs as the train finally began to move.

They sat quietly until Cyrus let out a sigh of relief and smiled broadly. "I can't see the depot any longer. We did it!"

With a sweep of her hand Loretta pulled the veiled hat from her head and let her long dark blonde hair fall over her shoulders. Jerking the cover from her lap, she pushed her body up. Reflexively her arm went around her damaged ribs and she bit back the pain. "We have to get Amelia out of that trunk before she dies from the heat. And I have to get out of these God-awful clothes before I faint."

Cyrus stepped into the aisle and escorted Hettie and Loretta toward the baggage car. As they walked between cars, Loretta took as deep a breath of fresh air as her ribs would allow. She hadn't breathed air as fresh since she'd fled Ohio home nearly five years earlier. She was free of Jack Coulter at last, and so was Amelia. She smiled, enjoying the scent of freedom.

The baggage compartment attendant tried to explain to Cyrus that the baggage compartment was off limits to passengers. Aside from the passengers' baggage, the compartment also held mail being transported west. The clerk stared suspiciously at the women standing impatiently beside Cyrus. His eyes were drawn to the diminutive blonde in particular. She was a pretty young thing, but looked tired.

"Let me out of here!" a girl's muffled voice yelled. "Goddammit!"

His eyes wide, the clerk slowly approached the trunk at the back of the car. He glanced over his shoulder at Cyrus' concerned face. Finally, he leaned down to the trunk and pressed his ear against it. Amelia chose that moment to kick the top of the trunk with as much strength as she could muster. When Cyrus saw the clerk's reaction he pounded on the door into the car. The clerk stumbled back to the door and opened it, allowing Hettie and Loretta to rush past him, leaving Cyrus to explain.

Hettie unlocked the clasp on the trunk and flipped the top open. "Are you all right, Amelia?"

"Yes, but I gotta pee somethin' fierce!" the teenager exclaimed as she clamored from the cramped space.

"Hey! You can't bring a person on board in a trunk," the clerk said forcefully. "I'll have to get the conductor."

"Wait!" Hettie said, digging in her purse. "I have a ticket for her."

"If you got a ticket, then why the devil is she in there?"

"She's trying to get away from a jealous boyfriend," Loretta said calmly, smiling flirtatiously at the middle-aged clerk. "I'm sure you can understand something like that, being such a fine upstanding gentleman yourself."

Although it took her a few minutes, Hettie triumphantly pulled four tickets from her purse. "There," she said, thrusting the tickets at the clerk. "Here are our tickets."

"Still seems like a mighty strange way to travel," the clerk said as he examined the tickets closely.

Cyrus cleared his throat and said, "I'm sure you can understand, sir. It was either this sort of subterfuge or force this young woman to continue to fight off the unwanted advances of a man who simply refuses to take no as an answer. What would you do if she were your daughter?"

"I'd shoot the sonuvabitch."

"Language, sir. Amelia is a young girl and still a virgin. She was in fear of losing her innocence to the unwanted advances of an impetuous and inpatient young man."

Loretta stifled a laugh, while Amelia simply stood wide-eyed, staring at Cyrus. "I have got to get out of these widow's clothes," Loretta said.

"I still got to pee," Amelia said, clamping one leg in front of the other.

"Loretta, take a dress from the other trunk and I will go with you and Amelia so you can change and...relieve yourselves," Hettie directed. "Cyrus, is this gentleman satisfied with our tickets? We're all tired and should return to our seats before the conductor comes by to collect them."

Cyrus cocked a questioning eye at the clerk as Hettie closed and relocked the trunk. The confused clerk stared at the three women and shrugged as he handed the tickets to Cyrus.

"Thank you, sir. You are indeed a fine Christian gentleman. You will be remembered in our prayers for your assistance with this delicate matter," Cyrus intoned.

"I don't recommend it for your future travels."

"I assure you it shall never happen again," Cyrus said as he backed out of the baggage car behind the women.

As the door of the car closed, Amelia whispered, "You told that man a lie, Reverend. You know I'm not a..."

"I'm sure God will forgive me, Amelia. It seemed the only prudent thing to do at the moment."

While Cyrus returned to their seats, Hettie accompanied Amelia and Loretta to a restroom. Loretta couldn't wait to strip out of the heavy black clothing and into something lighter. Hettie carefully helped her lift the dress over her head and checked the wrappings around her ribs.

"Are they too tight and uncomfortable?" Hettie asked.

"They'll be all right in a few days. I just need to rest and let them heal. Believe it or not, I have been hurt worse," Loretta replied.

"God, I feel five pounds lighter!" Amelia said as she rejoined them. "I shouldn't have drank all that water I had in the trunk, but it was damned hot in there!"

"Amelia!" Hettie said. "That's no way for a young lady to speak."

"Sorry, Miss Hettie. I used to have better manners."

"And you will again now that you and Loretta are starting a new life and can forget the awful things that happened in St. Joe."

Loretta washed her face and managed to make her hair more presentable as she listened to Hettie talk with Amelia. A new life, she thought, wondering if she would ever be able to forget her past or out-run it. She couldn't remember the last time she had been happy and looked forward to the next day. She couldn't begin to imagine what a new life might bring. Whatever it was would have to be better than what she had left behind. But she had been disappointed before. She thought she would find a better life when she escaped from her lecherous stepfather only to find Jack Coulter. Now that she had escaped from Jack, was the train taking her to something better, or something worse?

Chapter Six

Outside Trinidad, Colorado Territory, Early May 1876

CLARE MCILHENNEY REINED her horse to a stop behind half a dozen steers she was herding toward a mountain pasture higher in the foothills of the Sangre de Cristo Mountains near the Spanish Peaks. The sound of gunfire drew her attention toward the north. She turned quickly away from the cattle she was trailing and urged her horse in the direction of the sound.

She topped a hill half a mile away and spotted three of her hands caught in a crossfire by two small groups of riders. She pulled her rifle from its case behind her saddle and chambered a round as she dug her boot heels firmly into her horse's sides. She raced toward the rear of one of the groups pinning her men down and began firing when she was barely within range, drawing the men's attention to the new threat.

Clare was pissed off. This was the fourth time in as many weeks her men had been attacked as the dispute over the property boundary between her ranch and that of her neighbor, Thaddeus Garner, continued to escalate. A few feet of dirt hardly seemed like something worth dying over, but if she allowed Garner to continue encroaching onto land that was clearly hers she could eventually lose the whole thing. Tired of the fighting, she disregarded her own safety and plowed straight ahead into the faces of the men ahead of her, firing rapidly. Instead of stopping to join her men she galloped toward the second line of attackers. Two of the men ahead of her fell, wounded, as she flew through their line.

Out of the line of fire, she stopped, breathing heavily and reloading her Henry repeating rifle. It was old, but had served her father well, until that tragic day nearly twenty years before. The sight of her father and mother lying on the ground, dying, filled Clare with rage again and she spurred her horse forward. As a single unmarried woman, the law did not support her claim to her father's land, but she would never give it up without a fight. By the time she approached the group attacking her men from the west again, she could see they were beginning to retreat. She kept up a withering fire in their direction, barely allowing them to mount their horses unscathed and ride away.

Clare watched the dust rise beneath the horses' hooves and stared after them while her own horse pranced and circled around beneath her.

"Are you trying to get yourself killed?" a Spanish-accented voiced yelled.

Clare turned her head to see her friend and ranch foreman Ino

Valdez hurrying toward her. He ran up to her and began checking her horse.

"He's fine," Clare said, still looking in the direction the men had fled. "Garner's men, right?"

"Who else? We caught them driving a few head over the boundary and they disagreed where the line was," Ino shrugged. He pointed toward the property line where a fire smoldered.

Clare pulled her horse's reins to the side and rode him across the cut barrier between her property and Garner's. She stopped next to the remnants of the small fire, leaned off her saddle, and wrapped her gloved hand around a branding iron. It sizzled slightly when she spit on the metal. "Still hot," she muttered.

She returned to her side of the fence line, the Garner brand in her hand. "It's about time Thad Garner and I had another chat," Clare said. "Then we need to go into town. I ordered enough barbed wire to fence this whole damn place if necessary."

Ino looked worried. "That's not going to make you a popular woman around here. Never been any barbed wire out here. Once an animal gets tangled up it's nasty."

"It's Garner's fault," Clare snapped. "Ever since he moved in here he hasn't been satisfied with his own damn spread and thinks he can steal mine! It...will....never...happen," she said with emphasis on each word. She turned to the other hands. "I left a few head halfway to the upper meadow. Get them up there. Ino come with me. You might need to stop me from killing someone."

CLARE REINED HER horse to a halt in front of the main entrance to Thaddeus Garner's house and swung off the saddle. She took the steps onto the front porch two at a time and pounded on the heavy wooden door. A petite, fragile-looking woman in her forties opened the front door. Virginia Garner reminded Clare of an out-of-place southern belle.

"Thaddeus home?" Clare blurted, gripping her rifle tightly in one hand.

"Why, no. He and a few of the men went into town. I don't expect him home for a day or two. Is there something I can help you with?"

"No, ma'am. I'll find him. We need to talk," Clare said. She nodded at the woman and turned to rejoin Ino.

She bounced up into the saddle and squirmed a little to sit comfortably. "Son of a bitch is in Trinidad. Probably setting up an alibi," she mumbled.

"If he was here, he'd of already shot you off that horse," Ino said.

"First thing tomorrow morning we'll take the last of the stragglers to the upper meadow. I want the Burress boys to spend the rest of the day riding the boundary between our place and Garner's while we go into town to pick up the wire. After the herd is settled in I want everyone to make that fence their *numero uno* job."

"Garner's just gonna tear it down," Ino said, shaking his shaggy head.

"Then I want anyone who touches it shot! We've worked too goddamn hard to get this ranch to the brink of paying for itself without having some Johnny-come-lately think he can take it away without a fight. I won't let an asshole like Garner stop us now." Her eyes hardened with determination. She was no longer the woman she had been when she first came to the Colorado Territory twenty years earlier.

EARLY THE FOLLOWING morning Clare waited patiently astride her horse as Ino gripped his saddle horn and swung his thin, but well-muscled body easily onto his horse's broad back. Nearly fifty, Ino Valdez was a Mexican vaquero who had accidentally wandered into Clare's life. Then, like a stray cat, he simply decided to stay. He worked hard and rarely complained. She glanced over her shoulder at Caleb and Zeke Ramsey. They were young, but had stayed through the last winter and proved they, too, were willing to work hard, and endure her cooking. She had already sent the Burress cousins, Hall and Dewey, to ride the fence line between her property and the Garner spread, looking for breaks. Seldom did a day pass without at least two or three breaks in her fence line. She was certain the Garners were responsible, but had never actually caught them cutting the wire. Clare moved the reins on her horse to lead the small group away from the compacted dirt that served as the ranch house front yard.

Every spring a few head of cattle had to be driven into the upper meadow to join the main herd. Clare and her hands spent most of the winter riding to the meadows in the higher elevations to bring strays back down the mountain to the lower meadows. Not being the brightest animals on God's green earth, they would die if caught in a sudden snowfall. They would stand in a field of snow covered grass and never use their heads to uncover the grass beneath the way buffalo did and had no clue the snow itself could save them from dying of dehydration. In the spring, when calving began in earnest, the higher elevations would come alive with wildlife. Rising temperatures and the appearance of still wobbly calves usually meant Clare would lose a few of her herd to wolves or mountain lions looking for an easy kill. The busiest months were just beginning.

In the hazy gray-blue early dawn, the four riders slowly made their way into the foothills of the Sangre de Cristos in search of wayward animals. The cowboys settled into a familiar and easy conversation as they rode toward the meadows overlooking the ranch. Clare rode silently, as she always did. There was work to be done and it never seemed to lessen. Even though her men worked hard for their meager pay, she knew it was nothing more than a paycheck to most of them. The ranch was her life and she protected it as fiercely as a parent would a child.

Clare spotted two small clusters of cattle. She stood up in her stirrups and looked over her shoulder. She noticed Ino slumping forward slightly in his saddle.

"Ino! Quit day dreamin'! You and Zeke get that steer over there!" she ordered. "Caleb, with me."

Ino and Zeke reined their horses to the right and trotted toward the wayward animal while grabbing the ropes from their saddles. The steer was a big animal and ignored the two men as they approached. Ino slapped his rope against his leg and leaned down near the steer, making a clicking sound with his tongue to get him moving. The steer wasn't impressed and resumed its slow grazing. Zeke laughed as he let a portion of his lariat out and swung it around, striking the steer's hind quarters with a snap.

Clare and Caleb encircled three heifers they'd located on the far side of the hill and encouraged them back on course by slapping their ropes against the chaps covering their legs. Clare smiled and pointed toward Ino and Zeke. "Looks like they have a problem," she said.

Clare heard Ino's voice as he prodded the stubborn animal to finally move. She watched the steer turn away again as the heifers approached. "You want me to get him for you?" Clare called out with a laugh.

Ino waved his hand at her dismissively as he opened the loop at one end of his rope. Clare watched as the vaquero swung his rope and released it, letting it fall over the steer's head. Zeke draped a second rope around its neck. They pulled the slack from the ropes and began up the hill, dragging the reluctant steer behind them. Clare turned in her saddle in time to see the steer jerk against the ropes attempting to escape, nearly pulling Ino from his saddle in the process.

"Ino! Let's go!" Clare yelled back at him. She was about a hundred yards ahead of him and his stubborn friend.

"Yeah, yeah!" he called back with a smile.

"Ino!" Zeke yelled suddenly as he began backing his horse up.

Clare's eyes widened as she saw the rope in Ino's gloved hand go slack. Before he was able to react, the animal lowered its head and charged into the side of his mount. The horse managed to stay on its feet, but reared, tossing Ino from the saddle. He hit the ground hard, momentarily stunned. Zeke tried valiantly to keep the steer under control and avoid another charge as Ino scrambled to get to his feet. In a limping run, Ino reached his horse, but couldn't bring his leg up far enough to remount or release the rope. It was all he could do to avoid being trampled by his own horse's hooves or hit by the angry steer. He managed to pull his rifle from its case near the saddle and chambered a round.

"Ino! No!" Clare hollered as she raced back toward him. Her rope was already in motion and Ino lowered his rifle. The steer pawed the ground and lowered its head once again. As the big steer leaped toward Ino, Zeke was nearly jerked from his saddle. Ino grabbed the saddle horn with both hands and leapt onto his horse's back as Clare launched her rope and caught one of the steer's hind legs, stopping quickly and jerking the animal's feet out from under him. Once the animal was on the ground, Ino collapsed over his horse's shoulder for a moment to catch his breath. As soon as Caleb joined them, Clare transferred her rope to him and moved her horse alongside Ino and touched his shoulder.

"What the hell happened, Ino?"

"Dunno. Maybe he got hold of some loco weed or something, but he sure as hell wasn't ready to go anywhere," he answered, shaking his head.

"You all right?"

"Landed on a rock when I fell. Hurts like a son-of-a-bitch."

"Turn around and let me look."

Ino turned slightly in the saddle and bit his lower lip as he unbuttoned his coat. Clare lifted it and sucked in a breath. Blood soaked the back of the vaquero's shirt. Carefully she pulled the shirt out and looked under it. There was a two inch tear below his right shoulder blade.

"Might need a few stitches," she said. "Other than this cut are you hurt anywhere else?"

"No, just knocked the wind out of me, I reckon. I'm sorry, Clare."

"Not your fault," she said.

She dismounted and checked the condition of Ino's horse. She patted the animal's neck when she finished her inspection. "Might have a bruise or two, but otherwise he looks okay," she reported.

Ino smiled as he stroked his horse's mane. "Sorry, fella."

"He'll have a couple of days to rest until we get back from town," Clare said. "Think you can manage those heifers while we take care of this bad boy?"

"Yeah. No problem," Ino nodded.

Zeke and Caleb both had ropes around the steer's head and forced him up the mountain between them even though he managed to fight them most of the way. He was fast becoming one of Clare's most disagreeable animals and would find himself curing in the smokehouse by the next winter if they couldn't keep him calmed down. Even though he was one of her best breeders, he could be replaced.

By the time they released their strays to mingle with the rest of the herd it was well after midday. When the riders returned to the ranch, Ino stretched out on his bunk and buried his head in a pillow as

Clare cleaned his wound and stitched it up.

"You're gonna have a pretty good bruise," she said quietly. "Probably be a little sore too."

"It shouldn't have happened. I was careless."

"You're never careless. That steer was just meaner than you today," she said with a smile. She patted his bare back and stood up. "Get rested up today. We'll wait and go to town tomorrow morning. A few drinks will make your back feel better. That and maybe a few tender ministrations from Miss Mavis." Clare knew the vaquero had taken a fancy to one of Willis Manning's saloon girls and couldn't blame him. With a full head of dark, copper-colored hair and twinkling green eyes, Mavis Calendar was the object of many a man's fancy and she had taken a fancy to the vaquero. Clare smiled as she left the bunkhouse. She figured Mavis was a couple of years younger than her own forty, but she was certain Mavis' interest in Ino was far from daughterly.

Chapter Seven

THE TRIP FROM St. Joseph, Missouri to Pueblo, Colorado was a long one, especially for Loretta. Without the benefit of a sleeping car, she was forced to sleep upright in her seat next to Amelia. The swaying movement of the train cars over the tracks lulled her off to sleep many times during the four day trip. But every time she drifted into a few moments of rest, the train lurched to a stop in yet another town. It seemed as if there were hundreds of stops to take on passengers or mail. The jostling of the train didn't help the pain she still felt along her ribcage and abdomen. Occasionally, Hettie found a secluded place where she could check Loretta's bandages and attempt to readjust them into a more comfortable position. Cyrus apologized daily for having nothing to give her for the pain. On the second day, she asked him to leave the train during a layover to purchase a bottle of whiskey. If nothing else, she would drink enough to help her fall asleep and not care about the pain. The lack of sleep, combined with the whiskey, made her nauseous, but she managed to keep enough food on her stomach to survive the journey.

She spent most of her time staring at the wheat growing in huge, seemingly endless fields across the flat prairies of Kansas, the stalks radiating sparkles of gold from the warming sun. She often thought about what she would do once they arrived in Colorado. She would certainly have to find a job to support herself. If nothing panned out for her, she could always return to the one thing she knew how to do well. She folded the lap blanket into a pillow of sorts and rested her head against the metal frame of the passenger car window, watching the changing landscape as the train lumbered along. For three days and nights, the train made its way across flat golden prairies. On the fourth day, Loretta noticed the pale outline of mountains in the distance, as yet too indistinct to see in much detail. She watched all day as the mountains grew larger before her and she eventually saw snow-capped peaks.

"What mountains are those?" she asked when she saw Cyrus watching her.

He leaned closer to the window for a better look. "The ones closest to us are called the Sangre de Cristo Mountains. In Spanish it means the blood of Christ. Beyond those are the tallest mountains in the west, the Rocky Mountains."

"They're beautiful," she said softly. "When will we arrive?"

"We should be in Pueblo tomorrow about midday. I spoke to the conductor earlier and he assured me we were making excellent time. I'm sure you'll be glad to be able to walk around again. How are you feeling?"

"Better," she said with a wisp of a smile. "The bruises on my face are much lighter now. The others will take longer, but no one will see them."

"You're still a beautiful young woman, Retta," Cyrus said sheepishly. "You and Amelia have a lot to look forward to."

"Thanks to you and Hettie. Someday I'll repay you for everything you've done."

"No need, my dear. I'm beginning a new life myself and, whether or not you intended it, you're helping me do that."

"Like I've always said, you're a good man, Reverend. Not perfect, but still a decent man."

"DID YOU SEE the mountains?" Amelia asked excitedly as she leaned across Loretta to peer out the passenger car window.

"Pretty hard to miss them," Loretta answered. She pushed her hands through her thick hair and tried to tame the stray tendrils that had fallen over her face. She would have killed for a tub of warm water to wash away the coal grit from the engine that had drifted through the cracked windows of the car. It seemed to coat everything with a fine film of black powder. As the train slowed on its approach into the Pueblo station a little before noon, Cyrus and Hettie began gathering their belongings. They were all eager to finally be able to stand and walk outside the confines of the train car.

Although they all would have liked an overnight layover in Pueblo, the stagecoach to Trinidad would depart a scant two hours after the train pulled in. It was a rush to locate a wagon to haul their luggage, everything they each owned in the world, from the train depot to the Wells Fargo office and then locate a nearby place to eat.

It was a little after two in the afternoon when Cyrus helped Hettie onto the Wells Fargo stagecoach that would take them the final sixty miles to their new life. The driver and station manager hoisted the travelers' luggage into the baggage section at the rear of the coach and tied them down. Cyrus took Amelia's hand to assist her aboard while Loretta stood back, seemingly mesmerized by the mountains to the west of the town. The driver and his shotgun rider climbed onto the seat over the coach. The driver picked up the reins for his team of six horses while his companion brought a rifle across his lap and adjusted himself on the seat.

The bearded driver looked over the side of the coach and pulled his hat down firmly. "We're ready to head out as soon as you're on board."

Cyrus nodded and took Loretta's elbow and guided her toward the door of the coach. "This might be rougher than the train, Loretta. Can you make it a little farther?"

"I'm fine, Cyrus," Loretta nodded.

She placed a foot on the lowest step. Cyrus gently lifted her up while Amelia took her hands and pulled her inside. Cyrus stepped up into the coach and pulled the steps inside before closing and securing the door.

"If you want to sleep I can lower the window shade," he said.

"How long will it take to get to Trinidad?" Hettie asked.

"A few hours, hopefully before dark falls," Cyrus said, patting her hand.

Loretta remained quiet most of the afternoon as she watched the mountains draw closer and loom larger. Lush green carpeted the hillsides and bright white and yellow wildflowers sprang up and seemed to flow from the tree line in wind-blown waves. The coach eventually made its way across a bridge over a rock-strewn river and she watched as blue and white water tumbled over boulders and along the stretches of rapids farther downstream.

"What is that river?" she asked.

"Must be the Purgatoire River," Cyrus said. "The gentleman at the stagecoach office in Pueblo said it ran through Trinidad, so we must be getting close. Got its name from the French trappers who used to roam this area. Most folks can't pronounce it and call it the Picket Wire."

"*Purgatoire* is French for purgatory, isn't it?" Hettie asked.

"I guess things weren't always hospitable around here."

Hettie looked at Cyrus and smiled. "It seems as if you've come to a place in need of your services, if the river's name is any indication."

Loretta kept her eyes closed, but listened to the chit-chat between Cyrus and Hettie. She had first noticed the way they interacted before they left St. Joe. Cyrus had held Hettie's hand many times during the two weeks before Loretta was sufficiently recovered to travel. She had seen the way Hettie looked at Cyrus when she thought no one else was watching. A touch here or there, something humorous whispered between them. Loretta smiled to herself. Hettie claimed to be a sinner, as Cyrus certainly was, and perhaps that was exactly what he needed. Another sinner who could understand his spiritual anguish and try to heal it while healing her own.

Chapter Eight

DESPITE LORETTA'S INSISTENCE that she was feeling much better, Cyrus helped her from the coach before making his way to the rear of the conveyance to claim their belongings. While they waited, Hettie made inquiries about hotel accommodations for a night or two.

"Are you feeling all right, Retta?" Amelia asked as the two young women sat down on a bench outside the station to wait for Cyrus and Hettie.

"Just tired," Loretta said. "I hope I can sleep without the constant click-clack of the train wheels on the rails."

"I don't think anything could keep me from sleeping tonight as long as I'm horizontal."

Cyrus joined them shortly afterward and wiped his brow with a handkerchief. "I've arranged to have our luggage delivered as soon as Miss Hettie tells me where to have it taken. Then I have to find the deacon from my new congregation. Hopefully, we won't be more than a day or two at a hotel."

"Then where will we go?" Amelia asked.

"My new church provides a home for its minister and his family."

"How are you going to explain all of us, Cyrus? We're not your family," Loretta asked.

"When we stopped a couple of days ago I wired the church and explained that due to unexpected circumstances, I was bringing my sister and sister-in-law with me. If anyone asks, Amelia is my sister and you, Miss Loretta, are my sister-in-law."

"Considering how close we've been in the past, I suppose we are almost like family," Loretta teased.

Crimson crept up Cyrus' face as the two women laughed. "What's so funny?" Hettie asked as she joined them on the platform.

"We were just discussing our new little family," Loretta said. "Where will you be staying?"

"Oh, the head of the local school board has promised me a place to live. It will take them a day or two to make the final arrangements. In the meantime, the clerk told me we should be able to find suitable rooms at the Columbian Hotel. He said it wasn't far from here."

"I'll find a carriage," Cyrus said.

Loretta took a deep breath. "I think I'd rather walk, if no one minds. My limbs are stiff from sitting so long."

Amelia entwined her arm with Loretta's and said, "That sounds wonderful to me as well."

Cyrus got directions to the hotel from the station master and arranged to have their luggage delivered before they set off on a leisurely stroll to explore their new surroundings. The small group of travelers wandered slowly along the streets of Trinidad. Loretta was amazed at how modern parts of the growing city seemed. Perhaps it wouldn't be the dusty, wild place she had imagined. The group checked into the Columbian Hotel and settled quickly into their rooms. Cyrus would have a separate room while Amelia, Hettie, and Loretta would share a room with two beds. As soon as their luggage was delivered they unpacked enough clothing for a couple of days. Hettie freshened up and re-twisted her hair into a bun set close against the back of her scalp.

"You girls rest. I am going to arrange an appointment with the head of the local school board and perhaps take a peek at the school. Reverend Langford will be meeting with the deacons from his church, but should be back before dark. Then perhaps we can all sit down to a good meal for a change."

Hettie pinned her hat in place and picked up her satchel. "Do I look presentable?" Hettie had changed into an ankle-length blue gingham dress, trimmed with white scalloped fringe accenting the collar and sleeves. A belt surrounded her waist and showed off a surprisingly trim figure.

"You look like a school marm," Loretta said with a grin.

"Then I have achieved the proper appearance." Hettie smiled as she readjusted her glasses and left the room.

Amelia stretched out on the bed closest to the window. "God! This feels so good after sleeping sitting up for days."

Loretta lay down next to her young friend. "Do you think it's more comfortable than the beds at Jack's?"

"I don't give a damn, Retta. At least I'm not going to have worry about some fat, panting old fart pawing me and trying to ride me like I was wearing a saddle," Amelia snorted.

"You know, you're going to have to be mindful of your language now. It wouldn't be seemly for one of Miss Hettie's students or a preacher's sister."

"I know, but I don't have to pretend when I'm with you."

"I've been meaning to thank you for over a week, Amelia. I would probably be dead now if you hadn't come back for me."

Amelia couldn't meet Loretta's eyes. "What happened to you was my fault," she said quietly. "Camille told Jack about what we said that morning. When he called me into his office, he hit me. I...I was scared."

Loretta smiled at her. She knew her beating by Jack had been partially Amelia's fault, but she knew Amelia wasn't much more than a child. It would have been easy for a man like Jack to frighten her into talking.

"You did the Christian thing in the end," Loretta said to soothe Amelia's guilt.

"Yeah, that's us," Amelia laughed. "A couple of real Christian whores. Now we're livin' with our very own minister."

They burst into giggles until tears ran down their cheeks. Finally Amelia sat up slightly and propped her head on her hand. "Were you...I mean had you ever...you know, been with a man before you were at Jack's?" she asked shyly.

Loretta stared at the ceiling and blinked hard. "Yeah, sort of. My father died when I was ten. My mother remarried about a year later. It was hard for her to keep us going taking in sewing from time to time. When Horace offered to marry her, she accepted to give us a better life. But I was never comfortable with the way he stared at me. My body filled out a little earlier than some of the other girls and I felt awkward. A few months after they married, my mother's sister fell ill and she went to help her out for a few weeks. A day or two after Mother left Horace began brushing up against me and stuff like that. Then one night he came into my room and climbed into my bed. He'd been drinking and passed out before anything happened. There were nights when I wasn't as lucky." Loretta swallowed hard at the memory. "The day I turned sixteen I packed what I could carry and left home."

"Oh, I'm sorry, Retta. Did you tell your mama?"

"She didn't believe me even though it was going on practically under her nose. She couldn't afford to lose her meal ticket. I guess she thought it was a small enough price to pay." Loretta snorted. "At least he wasn't pawing her."

Loretta flashed a grin at Amelia and continued. "Then I met Jack and he saved me from living on the streets and begging for food. Whoring was a way to pay him back. What about you?"

"I never been with a man before I went to St. Joe. My folks died in a flood and no one else in our family wanted to take me in. They were all mostly dirt-scratch farmers and had their own families to worry about. So I left and Jack saved me, too. I thought I could just cook or clean or something domestic like that to repay him. I didn't know what he did until I was already beholden to him. I tried. Honest, Retta, I did. But I couldn't do those things you and the others did."

"Don't judge me, Amelia."

"I'm not! You were always kinder to me than the others."

"You're a kid."

"I always thought I'd like to have kids of my own one day, but now...I don't know."

"You're still young, honey. You have a chance to start over. So don't worry, some day you'll find a fine young man who'll treat you like you should be treated."

"As long as I don't tell him I was a prostitute," Amelia muttered with a frown.

'Except for that one unfortunate night you were never more than a bar girl. Don't forget that. It's your choice to tell or not, but if a man really loves you he won't care."

"Do you believe that?"

"For you, I do."

"You're still young too, Retta."

"Yeah, but I've been around the block so many times I lost count. I'll never be able to tell anyone about my past and hope to hell I never run into an old customer."

They lay on the bed, each absorbed in their own thoughts until they drifted off to sleep. An hour later Loretta blinked her eyes open and rubbed her face, wincing at the soreness in her jaw. She slid off the bed and crossed to look at her face in the mirror hanging over the small dresser. Her bruises had faded to a pale yellowing around her eyes and along her jaw line. She poured water from a pitcher into a large bowl alongside the dresser and scrubbed her face and arms. She dug make-up from one of the valises and applied it to the bruised areas until she was satisfied they wouldn't be noticed. She ran a brush through her long wavy hair. She pulled her hair over her shoulder and fashioned it into a long braid that hung down the middle of her back.

During their walk to the hotel Loretta noticed a sign in the window of a hole-in-the-wall café advertising for a waitress and she planned to ask about the job. She could live with Cyrus, but would eventually have to find a way to support herself. She looked through her clothes until she found a plain light green dress. It was one of the new dresses Hettie had purchased for her and the garment fit almost perfectly. Without her corset she was amazed at how comfortable the dress was. It was a plain dress, but at least it didn't look like it belonged in a whorehouse. She appraised her looks in the mirror and reached for a cloth next to the water pitcher. She dampened the cloth slightly and scrubbed most of the make-up from her face, leaving only a light dusting of powder to obscure the yellowing bruises. She looked into the mirror once again and the sight of herself almost took her breath away. With her hair tamed and her face showing the innocent look of a young woman of twenty, she felt like a new person, unspoiled and innocent. Was this how she looked to Jo Barclay that one night? She blinked back tears at the sight of the woman she should have been for the last four years. She took a final glance at Amelia and slipped out of their room.

LORETTA STOPPED AND gazed at the sign in the window again. She took a deep breath, straightened the front of her dress, and grabbed the door handle. The establishment was locked and she looked around, placing her hands on her hips. The café was next door to the Cattleman's Saloon. Although it might look unseemly for a young woman to do so, she walked to the saloon entrance and pushed the doors open. Memories of her days with Jack flooded back when she saw the long bar, two or three women lounging near the bar or on the laps of dusty-looking cowboys. All heads turned toward her and she almost left. Steeling herself, she marched up to the bar and waited for a middle-aged man with a handlebar moustache to saunter toward her.

"What can I do for you, miss?" he asked as he dried his hands on a towel.

"What time does the café next door open?"

"In about an hour."

"Do you happen to know who I would need to speak to about the waitressing position?"

"You're lookin' at him." He extended a hand over the bar. "Willis Manning."

"Loretta Dig...Langford," she returned as she shook his hand.

"New in town?"

"Just arrived today. My...um...brother-in-law is the new pastor at the Presbyterian church here."

"And your husband?" Willis asked with a glance at her hands.

"My husband was killed in an accident last year. His brother, Reverend Cyrus Langford, invited me to join him here."

"Ah, I see. Do you have any experience?"

More than you'll ever know. "Some, but I'm a quick learner."

"Don't pay much," Willis said, twisting the tip of his moustache.

"I don't require much."

"Can you cook?"

"I've been known to," Loretta answered with a smile.

"My wife is the cook, but sometimes she gets sick or one of our kids does and she has to stay at home with 'em. I usually close the café then."

"I'm confident I could handle the job, Mr. Manning. Have others applied?"

Willis laughed. "Nope. I'm a barkeep and my wife is a Mexican. Not exactly in the upper crust, if you know what I mean. If you want to give it a try, I'm willing to give you a shot. But I should warn you, Rosario is pretty picky about how things are done. The café is hers. I opened the damn thing to shut up her naggin'. I can hire you, but if she ain't happy with your work, she can fire you just as quick."

"When can I start?"

"Is an hour too soon?"

"I'll be here," Loretta said, extending her hand again to seal the deal.

"Got a new girl for us to break in, Willis?" a woman's voice asked.

Loretta recognized the smell of the perfume the woman was wearing. She had used it herself. She turned and saw the face of someone who looked to be in her mid- to late thirties, but it was hard to tell through the make-up. She didn't look cheap, but had definitely been around more than one corral. The woman looked Loretta up and down, giving her a smile through ruby red lips. Finally extending an extremely white hand, she said in a confident voice, "Mavis Calendar." Loretta understood the inflection in Mavis' voice. She was a prostitute and made no excuses for it. For an instant something in Mavis Calendar's eyes told Loretta the woman knew who she had been. Loretta smiled back and took her hand. "Loretta Langford."

"I hired her to help out Rosario," Willis interjected.

"Too bad," Mavis said as she released Loretta's hand and perused the young woman closely. "We could use some younger blood around here."

Loretta opened her mouth to say something then thought better of it. Instead she turned back to Willis. "I'll be back in under an hour, Mr. Manning. Thank you so much."

"I'll let Rosario know to expect you."

In her excitement Loretta couldn't wait to get back to the hotel to tell Cyrus and Hettie about her new job. She turned and ran into the firm body of a tall cowboy who had just entered the saloon, followed by three other men who stepped around them and made their way to the bar. The cowboy's hat was pushed back on his head, revealing a boyish face. His mouth leered down at Loretta as he grabbed her by the shoulders to steady her. Loretta inhaled the scent of dust and leather that wafted off the stranger.

"I...I'm sorry," she mumbled.

"Join me for a drink," he said. "Then maybe you and me can get together upstairs for a little poke. 'Bout time old Willis got some new girls in here." He held onto her upper arm tightly and started toward the bar. "Lookie what I found, Pa."

"She don't work here, Clement," Mavis said. She approached them and winked at Loretta. "Clement here don't mean no harm," she explained. "He don't meet many proper women so his social skills leave a little to be desired."

"Always been good enough for you, Mavis," Clement sneered.

"Your *money's* always been good enough for me, sugar. Don't confuse that with affection."

Clement's eyes blazed and his hand flashed out, catching Mavis with a glancing blow across the face. When his grip loosened, Loretta seized the opportunity to jerk her arm away. Clement reached for her again. She side-stepped away and grabbed the front of his shirt, pulling him closer. The smile on his face vanished when she brought her knee up quickly into his groin. His hands flew to his crotch and he fell to his knees in front of the now heavily breathing Loretta. The snickers of the men at the bar came to an end when a gunshot rang out. All eyes turned toward the saloon entrance.

Loretta saw the silhouettes of three people standing in the

entrance to the saloon and backed away quickly. The figure in the center held a still-smoking rifle pointed toward the ceiling. Loretta could smell the scent of burned gunpowder and watched as the rifle was lowered until it was parallel with the floor. When the men standing at the bar made a belated attempt to reach for their pistols the sound of a round being chambered was enough to stop their movements. Loretta doubted they would have had a chance against the weapon leveled at them.

"Stay off my property, Garner," a deep husky voice said. Light from a front window fell across the stranger as she took a step closer to the bar, revealing a strong, handsome face with well-defined angular features and a square jaw. Loretta felt her heartbeat quicken as she realized the stranger holding the rifle was female. The woman's hat was pushed back off her head and rested against her upper shoulders.

"We weren't on your property, Clare," an older man with graying hair and moustache growled. "Everyone around here knows you don't own that land you're squatting on. It's free range. You're breaking the law by fencing it."

"The cattle on it are mine." The woman held a leather-gloved hand out toward a Hispanic man to her left. He placed a branding iron in her hand. She tossed it onto the barroom floor and it slid to the toe of Garner's boot. "I think that belongs to you," the woman snarled. "Took it out of a fire where some of *your* men were preparing to brand *my* cattle on *my* property."

"Let's go talk to the sheriff about that, Clare" Garner said with a shrug. "I'm sure it was an honest mistake."

"Everyone knows Beutler works for you," the woman Garner called Clare said with a laugh. She gripped her rifle tightly and moved closer to the bar. "Consider this your final warning, Garner. You won't get another one."

Loretta saw movement out of the corner of her eye as Clement reached for the branding iron on the floor. "Watch out," she said.

Clare turned her head in time to see Clement Garner close his fist around the iron. She swung the butt of her rifle back forcefully and caught him square in the face. Blood spurted from his broken nose and he howled in pain as she turned and shoved him onto his back with her boot. She brought the rifle around and pressed it against the young man's forehead. His watering eyes widened in fear.

"Tell your boy not to do anything stupid, Thad," she snarled. "I'd hate to tell his mama he died because he's a jackass."

"Back off, Clement," Garner ordered.

Clare pulled the rifle barrel back, leaving a deep, round imprint in the middle of Clement's forehead.

"Let's get on back to the ranch, boys," Garner said. He took a step forward and stopped next to Clare. "We'll finish this later, McIlhenney."

"I'll look forward to it," she said softly.

Clare laid her rifle on the counter with a nod toward Willis Manning. As her two companions joined her, she pulled her hat off and ran a hand through shaggy brown hair that fell an inch or so above her shoulders.

"Ino, when we settle up here, check at the dry goods store to see if that wire I ordered has come in so we can get the hell out of here," she said.

Loretta exhaled the breath she had been holding and glanced at the clock behind the bar. She would have to hurry to tell Cyrus about her new job and then get back for her first day of honest work. Before she turned to leave she leaned toward Mavis. "Who is that?' she asked, motioning toward the woman at the bar.

"Clare McIlhenney. Owns a ranch over near Spanish Peaks."

"I've never seen a woman dress or act like that," Loretta said as her eyes scanned the rancher from head to toe. Clare wore chaps over her denim pants and scuffed boots. The long sleeves of her light blue shirt were rolled up to her elbows showing off well-muscled forearms.

"Them's chaps," Mavis said. "They protect a cowboy's legs when he's riding through heavy brush. Some of it's pretty thorny."

"She seems a little thorny herself," Loretta observed.

Mavis laughed. "When Clare first got here, she was soft as a down pillow. She had to toughen up or die. Now, if you'll excuse me."

Loretta watched as Mavis stepped next to the Hispanic cowboy with Clare McIlhenney as he picked up a shot glass and threw the contents into his mouth. He grinned broadly when Mavis linked her arm in his and drew him into a full, hungry kiss.

"How long you in town for?" Loretta overheard Mavis ask.

"Overnight. Clare needs to pick up a few supplies."

"Will I be seeing you later, sugar?"

"If you can make time for a lonely old vaquero," the man said with a laugh.

"I'll always have time for you," Mavis said seductively as she leaned closer to him.

Loretta watched Clare drain the contents of her shot glass in a single gulp. Her hair fell down into her eyes and she brushed it over her head with her hand again.

Another saloon hostess, wearing a low-cut, red and black gown that displayed ample cleavage and was split open from the floor to nearly her crotch, strolled down the stairs and looked around the room. Her eyes stopped and a broad smile lit up her face. "Clare!"

Clare barely had time to steel herself before the woman with dark chestnut hair flew into her arms. Clare lifted her off the floor and spun her around in a tight circle before setting her down again.

"Good to see you again, Peg," Clare said, leaning down to kiss the woman on a heavily rouged cheek.

Loretta backed toward the swinging door to the saloon, prepared to leave. She stopped in her tracks when Clare McIlhenney's walnut-colored eyes met hers. Clare nodded at her before turning her attention back to the others standing near her and picked up a second shot glass.

LORETTA STOOD ON the boardwalk near the saloon for a few minutes. She had to return to the hotel and let Cyrus know she had found a job and would be starting immediately, but she needed a few minutes to gather her thoughts. She had never seen or met a woman like the rancher called Clare McIlhenney.

She was a woman who apparently thought nothing of walking into a bar or mingling with the saloon girls who were so obviously there to entertain men. Flashes of the night she spent with Josephine Barclay swept through her mind. Their arrangements were made secretly and Jo had entered through a back door before the male patrons arrived. Seeing a woman act so openly like a man was unusual, to say the least. Perhaps everything was different in the west.

Finally setting her feet in motion, Loretta virtually ran back to the hotel and burst into the room she shared with Amelia and Hettie.

"Where have you been?" Amelia asked. "When I woke up you were gone without a note or anything."

"Where's Hettie?" Loretta asked, breathing heavily.

"She went to Cyrus' room. They're worried and gettin' ready to search for you. Wait!" Amelia called out as Loretta left the room and walked toward Cyrus' room. When her knock on the door was answered, she saw Cyrus' scowling face.

"Where the devil were you? Hettie and Amelia have been sick with worry."

"I'm sorry, Cyrus, but I've found a job. And I start in less than an hour. I came back to tell you I won't be here until later tonight."

"What kind of job?" Hettie asked suspiciously.

"Waitressing at the café next to the saloon. The owner of the saloon owns it. His wife runs it and needs help," Loretta explained.

"I don't like it, Retta. Being next door to a saloon, you don't know what kind of trash may go there," Cyrus objected.

"It can't be any worse than the trash I dealt with in St. Joe," Loretta snapped. The hurt look on Cyrus' face made her wish she could take the words back.

"I'm sorry, Cyrus," Loretta said, placing her hand on his arm. "You have always been extremely kind to me. I..."

"No, no. You are right, Miss Loretta. I should be the last person to judge you. You are more than capable of caring for yourself." He stepped toward her and pulled her into a warm, friendly embrace. When they broke apart, he continued to hold her by the shoulders.

"But promise me you will be careful. In fact, I will drop by later and escort you home. A young lady shouldn't be walking alone after dark in a strange town. We know very little about Trinidad yet."

"What did you and Hettie find out about the homes you were promised?"

"I've seen mine," Cyrus answered. "It will require some work to make it feel like a home, but there's ample room for the three of us."

"The school board keeps a room at a local boarding house for their teacher," Hettie said with a smile. "I visited there today after our meeting. It's small, but well kept. It will be an adjustment since I've never lived alone before, but I'm hoping you will all take the time to visit from time to time."

"You'll see me every day," Amelia said from the doorway.

"I have to get back to the café," Loretta said. "Perhaps you could all come by for a meal this evening."

"We will," Cyrus said. "Be careful."

Chapter Nine

THE MINUTE LORETTA walked into the small café, Rosario Manning, began a non-stop tour, explaining what she expected from her new waitress. She tossed Loretta an apron and continued chattering on rapidly, speaking a strange and confusing combination of English and Spanish. Loretta only caught about a third of what she was being told. When she looked confused, Rosario grabbed her by the hand and dragged her, pointing to an object she only knew the Spanish word for.

Rosario was a short, rotund woman, her eyes squeezing shut when she smiled broadly. A long black braid, similar to Loretta's, trailed down her back. Loretta had to walk a few steps behind the woman to avoid being whipped in the face by the braid when she turned around quickly, which happened more often than Loretta would have liked. Rosario smelled of cooking spices and something else Loretta couldn't place, but seemed friendly enough.

After a fast introduction to the restaurant business, Rosario picked up a pad and pencil and thrust them toward Loretta. "Now we wait. Not long," Rosario said. The sound of arguing drifted from the kitchen area and Rosario harrumphed. She strode purposefully into the kitchen and flung the swinging doors open. "Hector! Carlos! What you do?" she exclaimed. A fine cloud of white filtered through the room. Loretta stifled a giggle as she watched two young boys with full heads of black hair and deeply tanned skin involved in hurling handfuls of flour at one another. They stopped instantly at the sound of Rosario's voice and stood sheepishly looking at her with dark brown eyes that stood out against their now white faces.

Rosario shook her head and spat out a string of Spanish. She was obviously chastising the boys, but there was no doubt in Loretta's mind that Rosario loved the rambunctious children. Rosario glanced over her shoulder apologetically. "My *niños*," she said with a shrug. Returning her attention to her children she said, "Clean up *muy pronto* and go to *su padre*." The boys began scurrying around the kitchen casting shy smiles at Loretta.

WITHIN THE NEXT week, Loretta quickly settled into a comfortable rhythm at Rosario's. Rosario was happy because with the additional help she was able to open earlier and stay open later. Willis was happy to finally see the little café beginning to turn a respectable profit. Customers flowed easily between the saloon and the café and some of the local business people began having their families join them for an occasional evening meal.

Mavis stood near the end of the bar and glanced through the archway leading into the café, watching Loretta move easily between tables with her arms laden down with steaming platters. She noticed the congenial way Loretta interacted with regular customers at Rosario's, especially the male customers. She was quick with a laugh or a smile and the men seemed to be enchanted by whatever she said to them. However, Mavis noticed their wives didn't seem quite as smitten. Loretta had a way of leaning closer to the men and touching their shoulder or arm lightly when she refilled their coffee cups or set a hot plate in front of them. She seemed equally friendly with the women, but there was just something unusually flirtatious about her behavior toward the men.

Mavis picked up a glass of water and sipped it. To her it seemed obvious that the preacher's sister-in-law was familiar with ways to please men. She had spoken to the waitress on a few occasions and found her to be friendly and charming. The men certainly found her attractive, which was always good for business.

A young cowboy sauntered up to the bar next to Mavis and tipped his hat back. "Buy you a drink, Miss Mavis?" he asked.

"You legal yet, Farley?"

"Yes, ma'am. Today's my birthday."

Mavis tapped a finger on the bar and called out to Willis, "Give this *man* a drink, Willis, and a shot for me!" She gave the cowboy a sultry glance. "Your folks know where you are?"

"My pa does," Farley said with a sheepish grin.

"I'll just bet he does," Mavis said.

The door to the saloon swung open hard enough to hit the wall as four men strode in and went directly to the bar. Thaddeus Garner slapped coins on the bar. "Whiskey, Manning. And leave the bottle," he ordered. Clement Garner threw his shot down and wiped his mouth with the back of his hand before he moved closer to Mavis and stepped in front of Farley. He wrapped an arm around Mavis' waist and jerked her back against him suggestively. Obviously, he had overcome the humiliation of his previous visit.

"Let's go upstairs, Mavis," he said.

Mavis took his hand and removed it from around her. "I've already got a customer, Clement."

Clement Garner glanced over his shoulder and laughed. "He's a pup, not even weaned off his mama's tit yet."

"He's a man today and we've already made an arrangement." Mavis looked around Clement's shoulder and winked at Farley. "Isn't that right, Farley?"

Clement Garner was no more than a couple of years older than Farley. Mavis was certain the boy was a virgin, but his innocence was sweet. She smiled and hoped he didn't think people and cows fucked the same way.

A smile lit up Farley's face. "Yes, ma'am, it surely is."

Clement sneered as his eyes swept the younger man from head to toe. "He won't last ten minutes."

Mavis moved away and took Farley's arm. "That'll be five minutes longer than you did."

Anger filled Clement's face as the other men at the bar laughed. He took a step to grab Mavis, but was stopped by his father's hand on his arm. "You walked into that one, boy," Thaddeus said. "Try Monique or one of the other girls if you can't keep it in your pants. We got all night."

Clement shrugged off his father's hand and poured another shot. His eyes followed Mavis and Farley up the stairs to the second floor.

THE SETTING SUN barely shone over the top of the Spanish Peaks when Clare, Ino, and, Frank Carson, rode into town to pick up the barbed wire she had ordered over a month before. She was still angry the order hadn't arrived on their last visit. She took two rooms at the Columbian Hotel while Ino and Frank took their buckboard and horses to the livery stable before meeting again at the saloon for a drink and something to eat. Clare frowned when she saw her neighbor, Thaddeus Garner, standing at the bar. She nodded at Willis and waited silently for him to pour three shots.

"I see you're still insisting on running barbed wire on that property you're squatting on," Thaddeus said as Clare downed her drink.

"Yeah. I've been having a problem with disappearing cattle," she said.

"It's a hard life," he said with a smirk.

Clare motioned to Willis to pour a second shot. "You know, Thaddeus, I don't know what your problem is with me, but I've never done anything to you. You've been a pain in my ass since you moved here and I'd like to know why. It can't be just because I'm a woman."

"You'll figure it out one day," Garner said as he reached for his drink.

"Let's eat," Clare said, grabbing her rifle and leading her hands into the café.

Ino and Frank sat down while Clare took off her hat and hung it on the spindle of her chair. She rested her rifle against the edge of an extra chair. "Take your hats off," she ordered. "This ain't a barn."

Both men removed their hats and attempted to smooth their hair down with their hands.

"What can I get you to drink?" a voice asked as menus appeared in front of each of them.

"Coffee," Clare answered flatly, picking up her menu and looking at the choices for the day.

"Think we're gonna have enough wire to finish fencing the property that butts up against Garner's?" Ino asked as a cup of coffee was set in front of him.

"If it ever comes in," she grumbled.

"Maybe Garner will give up for a while when they start their own branding," Ino said.

"I doubt it. We might have to put some extra night riders out on the fence line. At least until calving season is over. Otherwise Garner will rob me blind."

"The Army's still wantin' to buy our stock to feed the soldiers over at Fort Kearney," Ino said.

"I can get a better price by driving the herd to Pueblo," Clare said. "But while we're gone, the house and barn would be undefended."

"We can hire some extra hands to make the drive and leave four or five behind to guard the ranch," Ino said.

"There's always herds comin' up the Goodnight-Loving to Pueblo. Maybe you can combine your herd with one of those," Frank suggested.

"Maybe," Clare said with a shrug. "I figure we'll have a couple hundred head to take to Pueblo once we get through calving and branding. We could make the trip faster with only our herd. Maybe get them there before the bigger herds come north from Texas." She sipped her coffee and watched the waitress chatting with a man, woman, and teenage girl across the room. The waitress was the same dark blonde Clare had seen in the saloon two weeks earlier. "Frank, once the branding is done, take a trip up to Pueblo and see who you can set up as a buyer. See if it would be worth it."

CLARE WATCHED THE attractive, young woman gather up empty plates from a table and carry them into the kitchen, bumping the swinging doors open with her hip. She re-entered the café, wiped her hands on her apron and returned to Clare's table. "Sorry about the wait," she apologized. "It's busy this evening. My name is Loretta. What can I get for you this evening?"

Clare saw Frank look at Loretta appreciatively as she and Ino placed their orders. She felt an unexpected twinge of jealousy when Loretta smiled and turned her attention to Frank. She couldn't help but notice the blonde's dazzling smile. Loud voices behind her caused Clare to look away. She frowned as Thaddeus Garner and his men noisily entered the café. They found a table facing Clare's and continued carrying on raucously while Loretta took the orders to Rosario.

"What you lookin' at?" Clement sneered at the family seated at a nearby table. He was obviously intoxicated.

The man at the table stood and quickly assisted his wife and children up and escorted them away from the table and toward the front counter. Clare frowned as the husband handed Loretta a few bills before shepherding his family outside.

"Hey! How about some service over here?" Clement said loudly, banging on the table. He was laughing at the reactions of the other patrons until his eyes met Clare's. She was facing him and shook her head slightly, continuing to drink her coffee. Her glare temporarily stopped his laughter.

Loretta approached the Garner's table to hand them menus and take their orders. Clare saw the leer in Clement's eyes when he saw Loretta.

"Well, if it ain't the little ball buster," Clement said as his hand rubbed against the crotch of his pants.

There was going to be trouble. Clare could feel it and moved her rifle closer. Some people never learned, she thought. When Loretta left to get their drinks, Clement leaned forward and said something to the men at the table with him, which brought another round of laughter. The table Clare shared with her hands was close enough to Garner's to overhear some of what was being said.

Clare thought the waitress seemed uncomfortable as she returned to take the cowboys' order. She set drinks in front of the men and asked, "What can I get for you gentlemen?"

Clement stared at his menu. "You smell good enough to eat," he said, smiling up at Loretta. "How about a double order of that?"

"If you're looking for a cheap lay go next door," she said crisply. "If you want dinner I'll be glad to take your order."

"That's two rejections in one evening, Clement. Give it up," one of the men said with a grin.

"You think you're too good for me?" Clement snapped.

"I know I am," Loretta retorted while maintaining her smile. "You're drunk and need food in your belly. I suggest you start with a strong cup of coffee." Clare admired the waitress's feistiness as well as the calm way Loretta ignored Clement Garner while she wrote down the orders from the men with him.

"Food up," Rosario called out as she slid three steaming plates into the service window.

Loretta walked purposefully back to the front counter and slid the Garners' order across it to Rosario. Clare watched Clement follow her with his eyes. Loretta used a small towel to pick up the plates, balancing them carefully to avoid being burned, and carried them to Clare's table. "Be careful of the plates," she warned as she set them down carefully. "They're very hot."

"Hey, McIlhenney!," Clement said in a loud voice. "You still cozying up with that wetback? If you was a real woman, maybe you could find a real man."

Ino started to stand, but Clare grabbed his forearm and stopped him. "Not worth it," she murmured.

When Loretta re-approached the Garners' table with drinks Clement leaned back in his chair and dropped a hand to his side. As he brought it up again, he ran it over Loretta's ass and gave it a firm squeeze.

Clare flinched when Loretta's hand flew out and slapped his face. Laughter erupted from the men at his table and his eyes turned dark with fury. "Shut up!" he yelled as he stood and grabbed Loretta by the wrist. "Who the fuck do you think you are?" he growled, jerking her closer.

"Let her go, Clement," Clare's dusky voice ordered.

He threw Loretta's arm away and glared at Clare while Loretta moved out of reach.

"This is none of your damn business, so butt out, squatter," Clement snarled.

Clare's eyes shifted around the room and saw everyone watching to see what would happen. Her eyes turned darker as she brought them back to stare at the cowboy.

"You don't belong in here with decent people, you pervert!" Clement spat.

Anger suddenly flashed in Clare's eyes and the men accompanying her winced slightly. "Now it's worth it," she muttered. She wiped her mouth with a napkin before slowly standing and walking around the table toward the drunken cowboy. "You should teach your boy better manners, Thaddeus," she said, never taking her eyes off Clement.

"He's a grown man, McIlhenney," Thaddeus grinned.

Emboldened by his father's response, Clement clenched his fist and spun toward Clare to strike her. But too much whiskey made it easy for her to side-step him. As he tried to swing a second time she grabbed his arm and slammed him into the table, face first.

"No, no, no!" Rosario hollered as she sailed through the swinging door from the kitchen, rolling pin in hand. "Willis!"

Within a matter of seconds the small eatery became a flurry of activity as Clare glared down at the bleeding man. Willis pumped the action of his shotgun and brought it to his shoulder. The doorway between the café and the saloon rapidly filled with curious on-lookers, some sipping from mugs of beer and hanging onto one of the bar girls.

"Do somethin', ya pussy!" a cowboy from the saloon called out with a laugh.

"I'll shoot the first one that makes a move," Willis said as he took two steps into the café. "Get out while you still can, Clement," Willis warned.

"That bitch hit me for no good reason, Manning. Why don't you throw her out?" Blood dribbled down Clement's chin and small spatters flew from his lips as he spoke.

"'Cause I reckon she ain't the one actin' like a damn jackass," Willis stated, tossing Clement a napkin to staunch his bleeding. Clement wiped angrily at his face and threw the napkin down on the table.

Willis escorted the Garners and their hands from the café and Rosario poked Loretta in the ribs, causing her to wince. "New customers," she said, nodding at another table.

Loretta stepped over to Clare's table. "Thank you," she said.

Clare brought a forkful of enchilada to her mouth. "I could use a refill on the coffee."

Loretta nodded and left to serve her new customers.

"You plan on seeing Mavis tonight?" Clare asked Ino as Loretta refilled their coffee cups. She watched a flush appear on her foreman's ruddy cheeks and grinned. "Just get up in time to load that wire." Frank laughed as they all relaxed again.

Ino and Frank finally pushed their platters away and leaned back in their chairs.

"Damn! That was good," Frank sighed as he rolled a cigarette.

Ino and Frank shared a match to ignite their cigarettes while Clare moved her eyes from table to table. She knew one or two of Rosario's customers, but not the family she watched stand and walk toward the counter to pay their bill.

Clare picked up the check for the meal and walked to the front counter. She nodded at the woman and young girl who stood to the side, waiting for the tall, gangly man Clare had seen Loretta speaking to earlier in the evening.

"You should have tried the cobbler," she overheard Loretta say.

"This isn't a safe place for you to work, Retta," the man stated in a low voice, leaning closer in an attempt to not be overheard.

Clare glanced over the baked goods on display in a glass case near the counter.

"He was drunk, Cyrus. No one was hurt," Loretta said calmly.

"I can't believe they allow customers to carry loaded weapons in here," he continued.

"Not exactly St. Joe, is it? Don't worry. I've seen worse than this. Now take Miss Hettie and Amelia home and calm down."

"I'll come back and escort you home when the café closes."

"That's not necessary. That cowboy won't even remember what happened when he sobers up."

Clare watched Loretta during her huddled discussion with the man. Their conversation seemed friendly enough, but she could see the worried look on man's face. The waitress was a beautiful young woman, certainly beautiful enough for any man to want. Clare frowned as she waited to pay for her meal, certain that neither she nor the young waitress had seen the last of Clement Garner.

WHEN CLARE AND her men returned to the saloon, bellies full, business had picked up. Clare spotted a poker game near the back of the saloon and excused herself to join it. Ino and Frank returned to the bar and ordered another drink. Ino had no sooner thrown the drink back than two arms slid around his chest and he caught the scent of flowery perfume.

"You didn't let me know you were comin' into town," a woman's voice purred.

Turning in the woman's arms, Ino smiled when he saw her face framed by a full head of red hair. "Clare's order at the mercantile is supposed to be here, Miss Mavis."

"Then I'm glad you got here early tonight, sugar. You eat already?"

"Yeah. Just finished."

"Lookin' for a little dessert to top off your meal?" she whispered.

"Don't see how I could pass that up," he said with a grin.

"Where's Clare?"

"Playin' poker."

Mavis looked over her shoulder and spotted Clare holding five cards in her hand, slouched down in a chair with her hat pushed to the back of her head. She was a study in concentration. "Hey, Peg!" Mavis called to a woman who was draped over another customer at the bar.

"Yeah," Peg said.

"How's about takin' a drink over to Clare? Tell her it's on me. And keep an eye on her. You know how she can get."

The woman nodded and motioned toward Willis for the drink.

"That's mighty nice of you, Miss Mavis," Ino smiled.

"Well," Mavis began as she played with the buttons on his shirt and looked slyly up at him. "If I'm gonna be entertainin' her best hand all night, it seems the least I can do."

"All night, huh?"

"Unless, of course, you're not up to it," Mavis teased.

"Just make sure I'm up in time to load our buckboard with a few supplies."

"You got nothin' to worry about, sugar," Mavis said as she poked him playfully in the chest. She slid her fingers between the buttons and pulled him away from the bar and toward the stairs to her room. "If anybody asks, Willis, tell 'em I'm indisposed tonight," she said as they passed the bartender who only nodded and continued wiping down the bar.

Clare was engrossed in her game, but noticed Ino and Mavis out of the corner of her eye. She liked Mavis Calendar. Amazin' Mavis. That was what some of the men in town called her and Ino certainly enjoyed spending time with her. She was startled by a slender hand sliding over her shoulders as a drink was set in front of her. "From Miss Mavis," Peg whispered, sending a chill down Clare's spine. "If you get tired later, you can bed down with me, sugar."

"Thanks, Peg. I have a room at the hotel." Clare said as she upped her bet. She watched the brunette stroll back across the bar. There was something about the way Peg moved that intrigued her. The woman had a thin waist with hips that flared out slightly from the tight corset she wore and Clare wondered what would happen if the string holding her bodice together popped loose.

"Your bet," a man across from Clare said, bringing her thoughts back to the game.

Clare picked up her third shot and held it as she scanned the three men at the table. She leaned back in the hard wooden chair, trying to relax. So far the whiskey wasn't helping. She lost the first three hands as she struggled to get a fix on how the men at the table played. Her fourth hand was a much better one and she tried not to let it show on her face. She played with the small stack of chips in front of her and wagered a small amount. Ino taught her to lure the other players in with small bets that indicated a weak hand. She wasn't convinced it was the right thing to do, but decided to take his advice. By the time the round ended, she had taken a sizeable pot and was feeling confident. Perhaps too confident.

As the shots continued to be set in front of her, she began losing. She couldn't think, but couldn't force herself away from the table. By the time her chips were down to the break-even point, she felt warm breath next to her ear and inhaled the scent of sweet floral perfume. "You should call it a night and get some rest, sweetie," a familiar soft voice said.

Clare turned her head toward the voice and saw Peg, leaning next to her. "I'm fine," Clare muttered. "Just a bad streak."

"Just too much liquor. Quit while you're even, honey."

When Clare ignored her advice, Peg reached in front of her and took the cards from her hand and tossed them in. "What the hell are you doing?" Clare demanded. She stood up quickly and spun around to face the shorter woman with chestnut hair. Before she could say anything else, she noticed the room hadn't stopped spinning when her body did. She push her hat back on her head and gave Peg a crooked grin. "I reckon you're right, Peg."

"You know I am, sugar. Now go on upstairs and go to sleep."

"I got a room at the hotel," Clare mumbled.

"Well, I ain't lugging your sorry ass all the way to the hotel."

"Just need some fresh air." She leaned over and picked up her old Henry rifle. "Tell Ino not to be late in the morning. We got work to do at the ranch."

"Stubborn woman," Peg said as Clare moved toward the door.

Clare rested for a moment against the post in front of the saloon before she began the walk to the Columbian Hotel. She was tired and teetering on the edge of drunkenness, but was looking forward to a hot bath at the hotel. She walked slowly down the deserted street.

Halfway to the hotel she heard footsteps behind her and clenched her hand around her rifle. She waited until the footsteps were closer, then stopped and brought the rifle up to hip level, pointing it at whoever was following her. She blinked to clear her vision and lowered the rifle once again. "Sorry," she mumbled.

"Are you all right?" Loretta asked. "I was on my way home and noticed you seemed to be having a little trouble walking."

"Too much liquor can do that." Clare reached up and dragged her hat off, letting her hair fall unevenly in her face. "I didn't mean to scare you."

"Are you staying at the hotel?"

"Eventually," Clare answered.

"Why don't I make sure you get there before I head home?"

"I'm fine, but you shouldn't be out alone this late at night."

Loretta laughed. "You sound like my brother-in-law. I can take care of myself."

"And I obviously need to sober up some. A walk would do me good. Where do you live?"

"At the parsonage of the Presbyterian Church near the edge of town."

The women walked silently for a while. Then Loretta said, "We've never been properly introduced. I'm Loretta Langford."

"Clare McIlhenney."

"Rosario tells me you're a rancher."

"Of sorts."

"And I gather you're not particularly fond of the Garners."

"Not particularly."

"And apparently you're not much of a talker either."

Clare stopped and looked down at Loretta. "Not unless I have something to say that anyone gives a damn about."

"Is that your subtle way of telling me I talk too much?" Loretta blinked up innocently.

"No, ma'am."

Loretta glanced at Clare as they continued toward the parsonage. Despite her slightly inebriated condition and somewhat grim exterior, Clare McIlhenney was a striking woman. She had angular facial features and, when she allowed anyone to see what was in them, seductive brown eyes under heavy eyelids.

Periodically, they would hear a noise and Clare would raise her rifle slightly and look around. Loretta noticed how quickly her eyes turned from hazy to alert. "Are you expecting trouble?" she asked.

"Trouble always happens when you least expect it. I've found it's best to keep an eye out for it."

They were less than a block away from the parsonage when Loretta saw a figure walking briskly toward them. Clare began to bring her rifle up once again, but Loretta stopped her. "It's Cyrus. My brother-in-law," she said quietly.

Cyrus closed the distance between them in a near trot and placed his hand protectively on Loretta's elbow. "Are you all right, Retta?"

"I'm fine, Cyrus. Miss McIlhenney was kind enough to walk me home."

"I meant to leave sooner, but Elder Jessup stopped by to discuss a church matter," he explained. He turned to Clare. "Thank you for escorting Loretta safely home, Miss McIlhenney. If I'm not mistaken, this is the second time tonight you've come to her assistance." Cyrus extended his hand. "Cyrus Langford."

Clare shifted her rifle to her left hand and took his hand awkwardly. "Reverend. Welcome to Trinidad." Clare looked at Loretta, her eyes unfathomable, and nodded slightly. "Good evening, ma'am."

Clare turned around and began the five block walk back toward the Columbian Hotel.

When he was certain they were out of earshot Cyrus said, "I'm glad someone escorted you, Retta, but Miss McIlhenney wouldn't have been my choice."

"She is a little tipsy, but..."

"That's not what I'm talking about. I was telling Elder Jessup about the events at the café tonight. He is very familiar with Miss McIlhenney and the man she lives with." He leaned in closer and whispered, "There's talk that she's murdered some men, but the Sheriff could never prove it."

"Possibly because it wasn't true."

"Well, regardless, her reputation isn't exactly stellar. She lives alone on her ranch with six men. I shudder to think what might be going on out there."

Loretta laughed. "Are you suggesting Miss McIlhenney might be fornicating with six men? Then I can understand why the ladies in town might be jealous."

"She's hardly a lady and has quite a violent temper. I think we all saw a demonstration of that this evening."

"She was defending me, for Christ's sake," Lorettta fumed, "while everyone else in the café, including you, cowered at their tables. I, for one, appreciated it very much. She and her men will be gone tomorrow and that will be the end of it."

Loretta picked up her pace toward Cyrus' house. She knew that although Cyrus was a good man, he wasn't a particularly brave one. It hadn't been Cyrus who stepped forward when Clement Garner acted inappropriately. In fact, not a single man came to her rescue. Only

Clare McIlhenney, an intriguingly intense woman, had.

BY THE TIME Clare opened the door to her room at the hotel she had sobered up considerably. She propped her rifle next to the bed and began stripping her clothes off. She would have to wear the same clothes the next day, but prepared a hot bath anyway.

Despite the spring weather, the nights were still cool. The window was slightly ajar to allow a cool breeze into the stuffy room. Goose bumps appeared on her skin, hardening the dark nipples of her breasts as she stepped into the tub and sank into the warm embrace of the water. She stared into the water as it gently lapped against her body, her fingertips idly tracing the outline of the scar on her shoulder.

IT WAS A beautiful day. The sky the bluest blue eighteen-year-old Clare McIlhenney had ever seen, stretching overhead like a clear ocean of air, unmarred by even a wisp of a cloud as far as her eyes could see. She couldn't recall ever seeing a sky so clear. Terrance McIlhenney found a shaded grove of trees to stop for the day. Clare's eight-year-old brother, Stillman, was absorbed in a game of pitching stones into a small circle drawn on the ground with a stick. While her father fed and watered their horses, her mother kept watch over their dinner cooking over an open campfire.

Clare promised to return within the hour and set off to explore the area near their camp. Her father said they were within a day or two of their destination. It had been a long and tedious journey. They were forced to leave most of their personal belongings behind when they left Pennsylvania. It seemed they left behind more of the life Clare had known at each river crossing and before each steep canyon descent. She glanced over her shoulder at the horses her father purchased in Pueblo to replace their exhausted oxen. They left the wagon train they had traveled with for the past four months and turned south, leaving behind new friends along with the memories of the trials along the road west.

Clare plucked a tender shoot of prairie grass, put it in her mouth and sucked the sweet taste of it. Every step brought back another memory of their long journey. It had been an unnecessary ordeal, she thought. She had done nothing to be ashamed of, or at least nothing shameful enough to warrant her parents' sudden move across the continent in search of a new beginning. They never spoke of their hasty decision to leave their home, but Clare knew she was the reason. Sometimes, when she was alone, she could still smell a hint of lavender similar to the scent of Annalee's favorite toilet water.

A smile tugged at her lips whenever she thought of Annalee Sullivan. Clare couldn't blame Annalee for her misfortune. The young woman had been desperate to defend herself and her honor. It was nothing more than a single, chaste brushing of their lips, much as sisters might do. Except they weren't sisters. Annalee's mother nearly fainted at what she imagined would have happened if she hadn't abruptly entered the room in time to prevent her daughter from being defiled by a pervert such as Clare McIlhenney. The venomous disgust in Mrs. Sullivan's voice when she spat out the word made Clare cringe. Pervert!

A small break in the rocks ahead drew Clare's attention away from the past and she climbed up the rise to reach it. It was too dark to venture far into the cave and she stood a few feet inside the entrance to allow her eyes to adjust from the bright sunlight outside. She had only taken two or three tentative steps inside when she heard the loud report of gunfire. She whirled around and ran from the cave toward their camp as fast as her legs would carry her, hiking her long skirt up to prevent it from becoming snagged on low brush. It didn't seem as if she'd walked so far. She stopped to catch her breath and get her bearings, making certain she wasn't running in the wrong direction. She topped a small rise and looked down to see her father firing his Henry repeating rifle while sheltering Stillman and her mother. Four men fired over the top of a ravine a few dozen yards from the McIlhenney camp, their horses milling behind them.

Clare raced down the low lying hill toward their wagon, but before she reached it she saw her father fall. Her mother picked up the rifle and continued to fire toward the men without much accuracy. She skidded to a stop next to her mother, took the rifle from her shaking hands, and pushed her back to protect Stillman.

"Tend to father," she said as she took aim around the front of the wagon and squeezed off another shot. It hit the dirt at the lip of the ravine, causing the men to duck. She used the seconds until the attackers recovered to reach under the seat of their wagon and grab the box of ammunition her father kept there. As she reloaded the rifle chamber she heard Stillman sobbing behind her. A quick glance over her shoulder told her Terrance McIlhenney was dead. She didn't have time to grieve even though tears forming in her eyes blurred her vision. She never saw the man coming around the side of their wagon until a bullet ripped through her shoulder and spun her toward him. She saw her mother grasp Stillman and shield him with her body seconds before she saw the life disappear from her mother's eyes.

She tried to bring the rifle up to defend her brother, but a blinding pain shot through her scalp. She heard Stillman call out her name, seemingly from far away, as darkness fell over her.

Clare didn't know how much time had passed when she regained consciousness. She squeezed her eyes shut again attempting to block out the throbbing pain in her shoulder and along her forehead. The sky above was the same brilliant, cloudless blue it had been earlier. The sound of feet shuffling in the dirt startled her and she turned her head toward the sound. She saw the blurry image of a man leaning over her mother's body and her hand reflexively tightened around her rifle. She grabbed a spoke on the nearby wagon wheel, biting her bottom lip as pain stabbed at her arm. She managed to sit up and lean against the wheel, propping the rifle on her knees.

"Get away from them," Clare ordered in a raspy voice. Despite her bravado, her hand trembled as she leaned against the wagon wheel, barely able to hold the heavy rifle.

The man's eyes widened when he turned and saw the rifle pointed at him. "You're alive!" the stranger said as his hand moved quickly over his chest to make the sign of the cross.

"No thanks to you. You murdered my family," Clare spat.

"Let me help you, senorita. You're hurt. I didn't shoot anyone except those two," he said, pointing to two bodies sprawled on the ground nearby. "The others, they run away like the cowards they are."

Clare stared up at the strangely dressed man. He was shorter than her father. Hell, he was shorter than she was. Not more than five-and-a-half feet tall. He wore blue and red striped pants, partially covered with leather over his thighs and shins. Despite the summer heat, he wore a blousy, pale yellow long-sleeve shirt and a leather vest. A pair of revolvers hung from his waist and the largest hat Clare had ever seen hung down his back revealing shaggy, black hair. The skin of his face was dark and a black mustache that needed trimming draped across his upper lip. He stood over Clare and smiled in an attempt to win her trust, and avoid being shot himself. She noticed his teeth were amazingly white against his skin and dark hair.

"I am Ino Valdez," he offered.

Clare rested the rifle on her knees and squinted up at him, trying to decide whether she could trust this stranger who had appeared out of nowhere. She was scared and wanted to trust him. "Clare McIlhenney," she managed while finally trying to stand upright.

Ino rushed to her side and grasped her arm to help her stand. Blood trailed down Clare's cheeks from the grazing wound along the right side of her forehead and her left arm was virtually useless. Ino propped her against the water barrel on the wagon and went quickly to the tailgate. He returned a few minutes later with a quilt and an armful of supplies. "Let me see your shoulder, senorita. The graze to your head can be cleaned fine, but I am sure the shoulder is much worse."

Clare nodded and used the rifle to steady herself as she lay down on the quilt. Ino started to reach toward the neckline of her dress. He drew his hands back when Clare brought the rifle up again. "I won't hurt you, senorita. I have to see if the bullet is still inside," he said.

She nodded and swallowed hard. He unbuttoned the neckline and bodice of Clare's simple dress and pulled the material away as gently as he could. He rolled her onto her right side and checked for an exit wound. "It's still inside," he muttered.

He rolled her onto her back again and covered her body except for the wound site. Clare blinked rapidly and looked up at him, her dark brown eyes determined. "Have you ever removed a bullet before?" she asked.

"Si." He reached down and picked up a bottle of whiskey he'd found in the wagon. He twisted the bottle open and lifted her head slightly. "Drink this. It will still hurt, but you won't care as much," he said as he lowered the bottle to her parched lips.

The taste of the liquor burned her mouth and she coughed, causing pain to shoot through her shoulder. Ino continued to encourage her to drink until her saw her eyes beginning to become unfocused. "I am sorry, senorita," Ino muttered. He downed a healthy swallow of the whiskey before pouring the remaining alcohol over her wound. As the whiskey burned into her shoulder, her scream died on her lips as she passed out.

Clare groaned as she began to awaken once again. She felt a cool, rough hand press against her forehead. Her eyes snapped open and she tried to bring the rifle up to fire.

"It's okay," he said softly, his hand pressing against the barrel of the rifle.

"You're still here?" she asked.

"Si. I couldn't leave you here alone for the coyotes," he said with a shrug. "Wouldn't be right."

"Thanks."

"And your honor is still intact," he added with a smile. "You thirsty or hungry?"

"Just thirsty."

Ino lifted Clare's shoulders slightly and pressed a canteen to her mouth. "Where were you and your family headed?"

"Trinidad," Clare answered as she lay back down carefully. "My father bought some land about twenty miles outside of town from a land agent in Pennsylvaia so he could start a ranch."

"Now what you gonna do?"

"Start a ranch," Clare said. "And catch the bastards who killed my parents and brother."

"They long gone," Ino said. "Where is this land your papa got?"

"It's on the deed, I guess."

"You rest the next day or two. Then I take you to Trinidad. Let the doc check my sewing. You can find out where the land is there. Someone will buy it from you."

"It's not for sale," Clare snapped. "It's all I have now."

Ino scratched the stubble along his jawline. "A woman can't own land unless she's got a man."

"My father is dead, I inherit it."

"Then I wouldn't tell no one your papa is dead. Homestead it maybe and live there a long time. Like a squatter, you know. Then maybe you can keep it."

Clare chewed her lower lip. "When we get to Trinidad, you can check at the land office and find out where the boundaries are for me. Tell them whatever you have to."

"I'm heading home to Texas," Ino protested.

"What you got there?"

"Well, nothing, but I wasn't planning to settle down."

"I ain't asking you to marry me! Just to tell a little lie. Then you can be on your merry way back to Texas."

"You know anything about ranching?"

"No, but I can learn. I'm a hard worker. You can teach me."

And Ino had been teaching her for the last twenty years. He was her friend, the person she trusted more than anyone else in the world, and the only one who knew all her secrets, good and bad.

Clare slid beneath the water to wash away her unbidden tears. She hated the times she was alone with her thoughts. She had done everything she could to carry on her father's dream and at every turn there was someone or something there to try to stop her. She survived the attack on her family. She'd survived attempts to run her off her land. She survived being alone. Survival was her penance and she would always do what she had to in order to earn forgiveness. Her failure to control her emotions and desires had led to the death of everyone precious to her. Surviving was hard, sometimes harder than dying.

Clare rested her head on the back of the tub and stayed there until the water began to cool. Relaxing made her tired and she closed her eyes. The smiling faces of her mother, father, brother, and Annalee were joined by a new face. She rolled her head from side-to-side as Loretta Langford's face joined the faces of those she had lost. Loretta was a beautiful young woman with wavy hair that reminded Clare of honey still on the comb. A deep rich amber.

She opened her eyes and stood up quickly, grabbing a towel and drying her body. There was no reason to be thinking about a woman as young as Loretta Langford. At forty, Clare could easily be her mother. The woman was in her thoughts only because of what happened that evening. Nothing more. She and Ino would leave Trinidad early in the morning and she would never have to pay penance for the death of another person.

Chapter Ten

RESTED AFTER A good night's sleep, Clare was up and dressed early the following morning. When she returned to the saloon at daylight, she found Ino, Frank, and Mavis sitting at a table in the saloon enjoying a cup of coffee.

"I'm sure that's better than mine," she said as she joined them.

"I'll get you a cup," Mavis said. "How about a plate of scrambled eggs to go with it?"

"I wouldn't turn it down. Thanks, Mavis." Clare followed Ino's eyes as he watched Mavis walk away. Without makeup and fancy clothes to enhance her looks or figure, Mavis was still a beautiful woman. "Did you have a good night's sleep?" she asked Ino.

"Off and on," he answered with a silly grin on his face.

"When are you gonna make an honest woman out of Mavis? She's gettin' too old for workin' in this saloon."

Ino picked up his coffee cup and took a drink. "You're a good boss, Clare, but I ain't got nothin' to offer a woman like Miss Mavis. She deserves more than a life scratchin' a livin' out of a piece of dirt. Hell, I ain't even got a piece of dirt."

"Half the ranch belongs to you."

Ino shrugged her off. A few minutes later Mavis set a plate in front of Clare. She finished off her breakfast and took a deep breath. "That was delicious, Mavis." She leaned back and drank her coffee, giving her food a minute to begin digesting. Finally she said, "Guess I'd better get over to the dry goods store and try to keep from smacking Horace in the face again."

On Clare's previous trip to Trinidad she had gotten into an argument with Horace Barlow, the dry goods owner, over her order for more barbed wire. She was sure he was reporting her orders to Thaddeus Garner.

"Try to control your temper and your mouth this time," Ino said with a snicker.

"I'll get the wagon and horses and meet you there," Frank said.

"I'll get them, Frank," Clare said. "I want you to go to Pueblo before the branding starts. Maybe we'll get a jump on the other ranchers. Get back as soon as you can."

"Okay, boss lady," Frank said before downing the remainder of his coffee.

The corners of Clare's mouth twitched into the semblance of a smile. She pushed her hat down on her head and left the saloon. The dry goods store was a block south of the saloon and she could see its disagreeable owner setting his wares outside on the walkway. She slipped her fingers into the pocket of her jacket and pulled out a receipt to confirm her order.

"ARE YOU READY?" Hettie asked as she carefully placed her small hat on her head and pinned it down.

"Where are we going?" Loretta asked.

"The dry goods store. I promised Cyrus I'd get some material for curtains in the parsonage. Something to match the furniture already there and make it look more inviting and pleasant."

The parsonage was located at the edge of town and the two women walked leisurely down the main street, looking more carefully into store windows along the way.

"So what's going on with you and Cyrus?" Loretta asked as she examined items in a store window.

Hettie looked shocked. "What do you mean?"

"I've seen the way he looks at you, Hettie. Cyrus is a good man. Surely you've noticed."

"I like Reverend Langford very much. But we haven't been here long enough to meet very many people. I'm busy getting the school set up and learning about my new students. It doesn't leave much time for anything else."

"I know Amelia doesn't cook worth a damn and I'm at work most every day. Are you still cooking for them?"

"I like to cook and can't at the boarding house," Hettie answered with a blush.

"And now you're making curtains."

Hettie looked self-conscious as she continued down the boardwalk. "I came here to start a new life, Loretta."

"So did Cyrus." Loretta hesitated before continuing. "If you're concerned about my former relationship with Cyrus..."

"No. Well, yes. I mean we have discussed that and he's been very open about his past."

"But it still bothers you," Loretta said.

"Perhaps a little."

"Cyrus has left that all behind him, Hettie. Is it because we live in the same house? I can assure you nothing has happened between us and it won't."

"I trust Cyrus, but he is a man and a man has...well...needs. I succumbed to those needs once and I won't again until I am married."

"If he cares for you, he'll wait."

Anxious to change the topic, Hettie asked, "How are you doing after that unpleasant altercation at the café?"

"I'm fine. He was drunk," Loretta said. "He offered me money to bed him."

Hettie stopped, her hand flying to her mouth. "You shouldn't be working in such an establishment, my dear. Does Cyrus…"

"Nothing happened and I was well protected. It's nothing I haven't seen or dealt with before. I'm not some wilting blossom in need of shade, Hettie."

"It's disgusting."

"It's how I made my living before I left St. Joe, but I won't return to it." Loretta put her hand on Hettie's forearm. "This is a new life, remember."

"I know. I suppose I never imagined something like that would happen so quickly."

They continued chatting until they stepped onto the wooden walkway in front of the dry goods store. "If I see material I like," Loretta said, "I may purchase enough to make a new dress I can wear to work. Something simple."

Hettie stopped inside the store and looked around.

"We should each find something obscenely sinful to make us feel better," Loretta said. "Cyrus doesn't need to know we think it sinful," she added with a giggle.

"Just help yourselves, ladies, while I put these goods outside," a thin man wearing an apron called out to them as he bustled by.

While working for Jack Coulter, Loretta had developed something of an appreciation for certain bath oils and scented waters. Unsure where such items might be located, she strolled up and down the aisles looking at everything. She picked up several items and read the unfamiliar labels on the bottles and boxes. Perhaps women in the west didn't use scented bath oils, she thought. But she had noticed the perfume Mavis Calendar wore and liked it. Used much less liberally, it would be a pleasant scent.

While she browsed through items near the rear of the store Loretta heard the shopkeeper's raised voice. "All that was delivered was half the wire you ordered. The rest will be shipped as soon as it's received in Denver,"

"How long?" a low voice asked.

"Probably the end of the month. It's becoming a high demand item all of a sudden."

"That's not good enough, Horace. I've already been waiting a month. I noticed Thad Garner doesn't seem to be havin' a problem getting his wire. Why is that?"

There was a vaguely familiar sound to the second voice. Loretta peeked around a display at the end of an aisle. She recognized Clare McIlhenney's profile.

"I don't work miracles, Clare. I just place orders. Do you want me to place another order or not? I have customers I need to help."

"Just place the damn order. I'll make do with what I have until it arrives. Will you send the order out today?"

Loretta saw Hettie approach the front counter carrying two bolts of fabric, waiting patiently for the storekeeper to complete his business with his customer.

"What can I do for you, ma'am?" the storekeeper asked.

"When you have a moment, I'd like four yards from each of these bolts," Hettie said softly.

"If you want what came in, it's on the rear loading dock," Horace said dismissively to Clare as he turned his attention to Hettie.

"Did you find suitable fabric, Hettie?" Loretta asked as she strolled down the aisle toward them.

Clare seemed surprised to see Loretta again. When Hettie turned her attention back to placing her order for fabric with the storekeeper, Loretta asked, "Are you feeling better today, Miss McIlhenney?"

"Yes, ma'am. I have goods to load, if you'll excuse me."

Clare nodded and turned quickly to leave the store. Once she disappeared, Loretta joined Hettie at the counter. "That's lovely fabric," she said, fingering the deep burgundy fabric.

"I think it will make very elegant, but conservative curtains for Reverend Langford's home."

Loretta leaned against the counter and looked up at Horace with a smile that never failed to get the attention of most men.

"Did Miss McIlhenney have a problem with her order?" she asked.

"Loretta! That's none of our business," Hettie admonished.

Horace harrumphed. "She always does. She's a squatter on some land in the foothills."

"A squatter?" Loretta asked. Clement Garner had called Clare McIlhenney the same thing the night before, but Loretta still wasn't sure what that was.

"The land she says is hers isn't registered in her name. A couple of ranchers have tried to run her off, but something bad always happens to them. Rumor is she's killed some men, but I don't know if it's true. She's been living out there with that Mexican fella, Valdez, for years." He looked around to see if anyone was close enough to overhear their conversation. "I heard tell they're married, but she don't use his name. Her only friends are saloon girls and prostitutes. That's mighty strange behavior for a married woman, if you ask me."

Loretta felt the hair on the back of her neck begin to rise. She pushed away from the counter. "I'll wait for you outside, Hettie," she said curtly. She didn't know anything about Clare McIlhenney, but for some reason the denigrating way the store owner talked about her bothered Loretta. "I suddenly have a need for some fresh air."

Chapter Eleven

"INO! GET THOSE new ponies ready. We need to get them broke before branding starts," Clare called as she saw her foreman walking out of the stable. Clare was already bone-tired, but there was barely a moment to rest no matter what time of year it was. In the month since her last trip to Trinidad, she and her hands had been working long hours tending to the herd and stringing barbed wire along the property that abutted Thaddeus Garner's. Small puffs of dust rose from beneath her feet as she approached the corral. She squinted up at the sun that was beginning to rise over the mountains, sending red and orange streaks knifing across the blue sky. This was a good time of year. She pulled herself up onto the corral rails and waited. She'd purchased four new ponies the month before even though they hadn't been broken to saddle yet. She'd given them time to get acquainted with their new surroundings and feed and used to having the weight of a saddle on their backs. Today would be the first time any of them had felt the weight of a rider as well. She wasn't looking forward to being tossed around on the back of a horse until it calmed down and could be ridden. It was just another chore guaranteed to leave her backside sore and her bones rattled. Saddle breaking the new horses was a chore she had been putting off too long already. If she was going to drive the herd to Pueblo in the fall she would need extra horses in the remuda.

Ino stepped out of the side gate of the stable leading a tall sorrel that wasn't looking too pleased about being disturbed. Clare dropped down fom the fence and grabbed a blanket and saddle from the nearby railing. Ino spoke to the sorrel in Spanish with a low, soothing voice while stroking the horse's head.

"Speak to him in English, dammit," Clare growled.

"What's the difference?" Ino said with a shrug. "'Whoa' is 'whoa' in any language."

Clare carefully placed the blanket over the animal's back as he began dancing around a little. "Hold him steady," she said. "You're probably right anyway. This way when I call him a goddamn jackass he won't know what the hell I'm saying." She shushed the horse and stroked his sides until he calmed down once again.

"This is a smart one, Clare," Ino commented when she lifted the saddle and swung it over the animal's broad back, wiggling it a little to adjust its position.

"He takes the saddle pretty good though," she said as she bent over and pulled the cinch under the horse's belly and drew it tight. She chuckled to herself. "Yeah, he thinks he's a real smart guy," she said. She lifted her knee forcefully and drove it into the horse's belly, causing him to expel the breath being held to prevent the cinch from tightening. With a quick jerk she snugged up the cinch and grabbed the saddle horn to test its stability. "Okay. Let him walk around a few minutes before one of us gets on," Clare said.

"Want me to take this one?" Ino asked.

"Don't matter," Clare said as they climbed onto the corral railing. "I figure you and me can do two of them and leave the other two for whichever hand loses the draw after they get in from watching the herd. That way we all get an equal butt-bustin'."

"You and me gettin' too old for breakin' horses, Clare. Leave it to the hands."

"Speak for yourself, old man." Clare turned her head and winked at him. "Besides, if you're still man enough to handle a frisky young filly like Mavis, I reckon you can handle one of these ponies."

"But Miss Mavis is a much smoother ride," Ino said with a grin.

"Well, talkin' ain't gettin' it done," Clare said with a sigh and slid off the fence. She strolled casually toward the sorrel, speaking softly as she approached. Ino held the bridle while Clare took the reins in her hand and moved to the horse's left side. She placed her left hand on the saddle horn and tested the cinch on the saddle before placing her left foot in the stirrup. She pulled her body up and held her weight in the stirrup for a moment before swinging her right leg over the horse's back and settling in the saddle. "Let him go," she said in an even voice and prepared for the horse's reaction. Initially nothing happened, but then she moved the reins and gripped them tightly, pulling back slightly and clamping her thighs firmly against the saddle. Ino backed away, anticipating the horse's response. Within seconds the horse launched itself into a twisting, bucking attempt to dislodge the rider on his back. When the action began, Ino scurried back to the fence and jumped on it to watch. Clare was a good rider, but he knew eventually she would wind up on her back in the dirt. She hung on and stayed in the saddle until the animal bucked close to the corral fence, jamming her right leg and side into a cross beam and post. Stunned, she hit the ground, landing on her face. She caught her breath and shook her head as she started to stand.

"Look out!" Ino hollered.

Before she could make another move, the sorrel was rearing up over her. It brought its front hooves down, striking her with a glancing yet powerful blow as she tried to roll away. Ino raced across the corral and waved the animal off. Once the horse moved away Ino knelt down beside Clare.

"Clare! Clare!"

The only response he received was a sharp grunt. He tried to pull her up, but she fell back to the ground with a loud groan.

"You okay?" he asked, already knowing the answer.

Clare's eyes finally blinked open and she squinted up at her foreman. "Help me up," she rasped.

She gritted her teeth as Ino helped her to a sitting position. She pressed her hand against her abdomen just below her right breast. She tried to take a deeper breath, but couldn't. She saw blood on her hand as she pulled it away. "Broke ribs, I think," she managed between shallow breaths.

"I'll get the buckboard ready and take you to the doc." Ino placed his hands under Clare's arms and lifted her to her feet. "You're bleedin'. Let's get you out of the corral."

Clare struggled to drape her left arm over Ino's shoulder as he half-dragged, half-carried her toward the gate.

LORETTA WAS SETTING a plate in front of a lunch customer near the front window of Rosario's café when she noticed a buckboard being drawn to a fast halt in front of the doctor's office a block down on the main road of Trinidad, kicking up a cloud of dust in the process. Loretta made sure her customer had everything he needed before she moved closer to the window and watched a cowboy jump from the buckboard seat and run into the doctor's office. Moments later Ino and the doctor dashed from the office toward the back of the buckboard and began helping someone out. A breeze had carried away the dust cloud temporarily and Loretta recognized the grimacing face of Clare McIlhenney. She moved with difficulty and had to be lifted onto the walkway by the two men.

Nearly an hour later business at the café dwindled down to only one customer. Rosario handed Loretta a covered tray to take to Willis and the girls in the saloon. When Loretta appeared at the bar of the saloon she was descended upon by people who acted as if they hadn't eaten in a week. They began devouring Rosario's cooking, which Loretta had to admit was wonderful, emitting sounds of pleasure as they chewed.

The doors to the saloon swung open and Ino strode into the bar. He slapped his hand on the polished wood and held up two fingers. Willis wiped his mouth and poured the drink, setting it in front of the vaquero.

"Didn't expect to see you in town again so soon," Willis said.

"Didn't expect to be," Ino answered before he threw the drink back and swallowed. "Clare's hurt," he added.

Immediately Mavis and Peg joined Ino, carrying their plates with them. "What happened, sugar?" Mavis said as she shoved the plate in front of him.

Ino shoveled a spoonful of rice into his mouth. "We was breakin' some horses and one of 'em got her pretty good." He chewed and washed his food down with a mug of beer Willis set in front of him.

"Got a deep cut on her stomach and doc said she's got some broke ribs. He wants to keep her in town until tomorrow."

"I'll bet she ain't takin' that gracefully," Peg said with a laugh.

"Did he have to tie her down?" Mavis asked.

"Damn near. She's too bruised up to put up much of a fight right now though. He gave her something for the pain and it knocked her right out...for now."

"You staying in town until you can get her home?" Mavis continued.

"Doc says maybe she can go back to the ranch tomorrow, but can't do nothing for a while."

"Better you than me, *amigo*. You know she'll ignore what the doc says unless she's half-dead," Willis said. He turned around and saw Loretta waiting to take their plates back to Rosario. "Tell Rosario she'll need to fix up a plate to take to the doc's this evening, will ya?"

THE SUN FELL behind the roofs of the taller buildings in town, leaving a reddish-orange haze still filtering through the dust along Main Street. Loretta stepped out of the café and pulled the door closed behind her. A white cloth covered the tray in her hands and she placed a hand over it to prevent it from being blown by a light breeze. She crossed the street quickly toward the doctor's office. The hand-painted sign hanging next to the front door read: Samuel Wayne, M.D.

Loretta stepped inside and closed the door quietly. A low desk sat inside the door and four high-backed chairs lined the walls. Other than that meager furniture, the room was Spartan, but appeared clean.

"Hello?" she called. "Is anyone here?"

A moment later a tall man with a beard cut close to his face entered from a back room, drying his hands on a white towel. He smiled when he saw Loretta and the look on his face was friendly. He wore brown pants with a faint stripe running the length of his legs and a brocade vest over a cream shirt, tied at the neck with a loose, loopy bow.

"Can I help you, miss?"

"I've brought food from the café for your patient and a bowl for you as well," she answered. When he looked at her curiously, she added, "It's stew. Rosario said it would cure anyone."

"I've had it before and she's right. It's very nourishing as well as tasty." He reached to take the tray, but Loretta continued to hold it.

"Why don't you enjoy your meal while it's still hot? I can assist your patient," Loretta said.

"That's very kind of you. However, I can assure you my patient may be a little disagreeable."

"Pain can cause one to be that way," Loretta said as she set a bowl, bread, utensils, and a napkin on the desk.

Wayne shook his head and smiled. "Disagreeable is more of a natural condition for Clare."

While the doctor sat to eat, Loretta carried the remaining meal into the back room. The room was semi-dark with only a small lamp burning next to a bed in the far corner. The curtains were pulled shut. Loretta walked quietly toward the bed and set the tray on a small table next to it. The woman lying under the cover looked pale and fragile, nothing like the woman Loretta had last seen nearly a month before. A sheet was tucked neatly under her arms. Her hair was brushed away from her face and rested on the pillow beneath her head. She appeared to be resting and Loretta was torn as to whether to awaken her.

"What do you want?" a voice asked as Loretta prepared to leave.

Dark eyes met hers when she turned around. "I've brought you something to eat. Rosario sent some stew," Loretta whispered in the semi-darkness.

"I'm not hungry. Take it away," Clare said, turning her head to face the wall. "And there ain't no need to whisper."

"If you don't eat and rebuild your strength the doctor may not let you return home tomorrow," Loretta said. "I can't imagine you'd enjoy staying here longer. I can feed you if you'd like."

"I don't need anyone's help. I can take care of myself. Just leave it if you insist."

"Let me at least help you sit up a little so you don't drown from the broth."

Clare glared at Loretta as if the look would frighten the younger woman away.

Loretta lowered her voice and leaned down. "No one will ever know you needed help. It will be our secret. I will simply hold the spoon and let you do the hard work, like chewing and swallowing. Or I can go get your man and let him feed you."

Clare fought to stop the smile which threatened her lips. "My man? I ain't got, or need, no man." She cleared her throat. Before she could speak again Loretta slid an arm under her shoulders and pulled Clare's upper body up. She grabbed a pillow and slid it behind Clare's back before lowering her carefully onto it, leaving her propped up enough to eat. She tucked a napkin under Clare's chin and held the bowl close to the patient's mouth, dipping a spoon into the broth of the stew. Clare opened her mouth and felt the hot liquid flow into her mouth.

After several spoonfuls of broth, Loretta asked, "Would you like something more solid now?" Too curious to keep her mouth shut, Loretta said, "The storekeeper at the dry goods store seems to think you're married to Mr. Valdez."

Loretta captured a chunk of potato in the spoon and offered it to Clare. Halfway through the bowl Loretta held Clare's head up a little farther and gave her a drink of water before continuing. The two women sat quietly through the remainder of the meal.

"Ino Valdez is my foreman, not my husband," Clare mumbled. "He saved my life a long time ago."

Loretta wasn't sure why, but was happy to learn Clare wasn't married. "Perhaps you should straighten the storekeeper out."

"I don't give a good goddamn what that jackass or anyone else says or thinks about me."

"Is there anything else I can do for you before I go?" Loretta asked as she gathered up the bowl and utensils.

"No," Clare said softly. "Thank you."

"You're welcome. I've always thought hunger was stronger than stubborn," Loretta said with a smile. "Rosario said she would send breakfast over early."

"Could you...help me up?" Clare asked. Her face flushed slightly and she looked down at her hands. "I...uh...I need..."

Realization rushed through Loretta and she set the tray back down. "Of course. I should have thought about that. Where..."

"That door," Clare said with a nod of her head.

Loretta opened the door across the room before returning to ease Clare from the bed. Clare gripped Loretta's shoulders until she steadied her legs beneath her. Slowly the women shuffled across the small room. When Clare was settled Loretta closed the door and waited to assist her back to the bed. Loretta's own ribs were mostly mended and she knew movement was probably excruciating for Clare.

By the time Clare was settled once again she looked exhausted. "Would you like me to come back later and help you get ready to sleep?" Loretta asked.

"No, thank you. I'll be fine until morning."

"Sleep well then."

THE SUN PEEKED over the tops of the buildings on Main Street as Loretta once again carried a covered tray toward the doctor's office. She had volunteered to come in early any time the doctor had a patient who had to stay. She rather enjoyed helping someone who couldn't help themselves. Or at least she had enjoyed spending time with Clare the evening before, even though conversation had been somewhat lacking.

"I've brought breakfast for your patient," she announced to a woman sitting at the front desk.

"She'll be leaving soon," the woman replied. "Good luck."

Loretta smiled and nodded, then walked to the door of the room used to house patients. She tapped lightly at the door and walked in. Glaring dark eyes met her as she entered. "How are you feeling this morning?" she asked cheerfully.

"Like shit," Clare growled. "How soon can I get out of here?"

"I don't know. I'm not your doctor." Loretta set the tray on the table and began tucking a napkin under Clare's chin.

Clare shoved Loretta's hand away. "And I'm not a fuckin' cripple. Set the tray on my lap and get out."

Taken aback, Loretta said, "I'll wait for the tray. You obviously don't require my assistance."

"I don't *require* anyone's assistance!"

"Everyone needs help from time to time, Miss McIlhenney. It's not a personal failing. But I'm glad you're feeling better. I'll come back for the tray."

Loretta's hazel eyes turned darker as she spoke. When she was gone Clare tried to identify what she had seen. Anger? Hurt? Disappointment? The waitress from the café was a pretty young woman, but she didn't know anything about Clare and Clare wasn't about to invite anyone into her personal life. She had survived all these years without friends and didn't need one now. Slowly she brought a mug full of coffee to her lips and tasted it. Then she dug into the plate full of eggs and ham and downed a glass of orange juice and the rest of her coffee. After some painful movement she managed to get the tray back on the table before throwing the covers off and standing while holding on to the edge of the bed. It took her nearly an hour to dress herself. When Ino showed up with the buckboard she would be ready to return to the ranch.

TWO WEEKS LATER Ino arrived in town with the buckboard. Horace Barlow had finally sent word the remainder of Clare's wire had arrived. As usual his first stop was at the Cattleman's Saloon. After several drinks he invited Mavis to join him for dinner at the café next door. When they were seated at a table, he took a deep breath and sighed, mumbling under his breath.

"What's wrong, sugar?" Mavis asked, Brushing hair away from his forehead. "You look exhausted."

"I ain't no nursemaid, Mavis," he said. "It's hard takin' care of the stock, the hands, and Clare. She's meaner than the worst steer we got."

"How's Miss McIlhenney feeling these days?" Loretta asked as she set menus on the table.

"She's drivin' me loco," Ino answered. "She's usin' a cane to walk now, but won't stop helpin' long enough to let her ribs heal. I been with that woman almost twenty years now and she still don't trust me. We had a fight today and she told me to get out. Can you believe that? That damn ranch is half mine...sort of."

"She's just frustrated because she can't do much," Loretta said, then walked away to help another customer.

Ino looked at Mavis and sighed. "I know she's frustrated, but so are me and the boys. She never could cook worth a damn and we're gettin' pretty damn tired of jerky and beans. I don't know about her, but I need help."

"Why don't you hire someone to go out there to cook and clean? At least until she can get back on her feet."

"That's what we argued about! But she don't want no stranger poking around in her business," he said with a fake laugh. "She needs someone to take care of the house so even when she gets back to ranching she won't have to do it. Spread's gettin' too big."

Ino watched as Loretta scurried around the restaurant taking orders, delivering plates, and refilling drinks. "How much you think that girl makes workin' here?"

"I don't know," Mavis answered with a shrug. "I wouldn't think it was much. Maybe ten a month, but she gets some extra from tips, I guess."

"Is that good?"

"It's not terrible. What're you thinking?"

"Clare needs a housekeeper. When it was just me and her mostly we were okay. Now we got five more hands that gotta be fed and the house is much bigger than the original cabin. If she's serious about makin' a drive to Pueblo, we'll have even more hands to feed."

"Where you gonna find a woman who'll put up with living at the ass-end of nowhere and be willing to cook for your hands *and* put up with Clare's bad temper? That's a tall order, baby."

"How much you reckon we'd have to pay for that?"

"At least twenty a month. Maybe more."

"How about twenty-five and a place to live?"

"You thinking about stealing Rosario's help away?"

"Maybe."

"Then you'd better talk to her brother-in-law, the preacher. He's responsible for her."

THE NEXT MORNING, after loading the barbed wire, Ino trudged up the steps to the home of Reverend Cyrus Langford and knocked on the door. When the door opened, a fresh-faced young girl smiled up at him. He pulled his hat off and nodded. "*Senorita.* Is Reverend Langford at home?"

"Yes, he is." Stepping back, she invited Ino inside. "Please have a seat in the parlor and I'll tell Cyrus he has a visitor."

"*Gracias.*"

Ino looked around the modest home, finally looking at the pictures hanging on the walls. Obviously relatives, none of them were smiling. They all looked angry about something. The men wore black suits and white shirts and most were seated. A dour-looking woman wearing a dark floor-length dress stood stiffly beside each man with her hand resting on his shoulder.

"How may I help you, sir?" a deep voice asked.

Ino whirled around and saw a man who looked very similar to the men in the photographs standing in the doorway to the parlor.

"Sir, my name is Inuncio Valdez. I am here on behalf of my employer, Clare McIlhenney. Miss McIlhenney is the owner of a ranch near the Spanish Peaks, outside of Trinidad. She was recently injured in an accident and would like to offer the position of cook and housekeeper to your sister-in-law, Senora Langford."

"Mrs. Langford is already employed in town."

"Miss McIlhenney is prepared to offer Senora Langford not only the generous monthly wage of twenty dollars, but a place of her own to live in at the ranch, away from the main house."

"Your employer wishes to hire my sister-in-law as a servant, sir."

Ino wasn't sure what to say to that. In actuality, Clare didn't wish to hire anyone and it had taken him most of the morning to memorize what Mavis told him to say when making the offer.

"Miss McIlhenney has six other employees who work her herd and needs someone to cook for them. Her home has many rooms and since her accident she has been unable to clean as well as she would like."

"So you are talking about a temporary position?"

"I'm sure it would become permanent if Miss McIlhenney was satisfied with the work."

"You expect my sister-in-law to give up a permanent position in town near her family in favor of a temporary one in the middle of nowhere that *might* become permanent?"

"*Si, senor,*" Ino answered, twisting his hat in his hands.

"That's ridiculous, Mr. Valdez," Cyrus said with a chuckle.

"But *senor*..." Ino began.

"Amelia said we had company, Cyrus," Loretta said as she entered the room and saw Ino. "Mr. Valdez," she continued with a smile. "How nice to see you again. How is Miss McIlhenney?"

"Apparently that's why Mr. Valdez is here, my dear. It seems Miss McIlhenney wishes to hire you as her housekeeper. I've told him it's out of the question."

"Why?"

"It's barely more than you earn now and it's so far away from town."

"Miss McIlhenney also offers you a home to use as your own," Ino interjected quickly.

"Oh, Cyrus! That would be wonderful. To have my own home."

Cyrus turned to Ino and said, "I need to speak to my sister-in-law privately for a moment. Will you please excuse us, sir?"

Cyrus took Loretta by the elbow and escorted her from the room and into his study. When he closed the door he said, "You cannot take this position, Loretta. It's out of the question."

"Why? I came here to start over, just as you and Hettie did. This is my chance to do that. I could save the money and..."

"I've spoken to many people in town and, from everything I've gathered, Clare McIlhenney is not the kind of person I would feel safe having you live around."

"Is she a whore or a gambler? Those are the kinds of people I am used to living around or have you forgotten so soon," Loretta snapped.

"She lives alone far from town. She and Mr. Valdez have lived together for many years and no one is certain what their relationship is. There are rumors she has encouraged the Indians in the area to attack her neighbors and has murdered or assaulted a number of people."

"Those are rumors, Cyrus. Since when do you listen to such things? Even if she has done any one of those things I'm certain she had a valid reason. She told me herself that she and Mr. Valdez are nothing more than friends."

"There is no good reason to live in sin, Loretta," Cyrus hissed.

She took a step closer and said firmly, "You did, *Reverend*. How dare you forbid me to live my life as I see fit! I owe you a great deal for saving my life, but I don't owe you my life. What would your precious, pious congregation think if they knew you were living under the same roof with two former prostitutes who are not related to you? Save Amelia, please, but I will make my own decisions."

Cyrus looked stricken by the angry tone of Loretta's voice. "I'm sorry, Loretta. Perhaps I have taken my promise to protect you too seriously. However, regardless of the consequences, I will not agree to let you take this position without at least one stipulation. You must be allowed to come into town one weekend a month so that we might see you."

"I can live with that, Cyrus," Loretta said with a smile. "And I must give Rosario a chance to find another waitress before I leave and I already know just the right person for the job."

A WEEK AND a half later Ino took the buckboard into Trinidad to pick up Loretta and her belongings. His ears were still stinging from the tongue-lashing he had received from Clare over the hiring of a housekeeper and cook for the ranch. Clare was furious and threatened to fire him over the matter more than once. In return, he threatened to leave and take all the other hands with him. He couldn't understand why Clare was being so damn stubborn about one small woman who would be relieving her of the cooking and household chores she hated so much.

"You need help, Clare, and your goddamn pride is ruining your good judgment!"

"You don't know anything about this woman, yet you propose that I pay her and turn her loose in my home!"

"What you got she might take off with? Look at this place! It's filthy and you can't take care of it by yourself right now. All I'm trying to do is make things easier for you."

"And make me pay for that privilege! I ought to take it out of your pay and then we'd see how long you'd be willing to put up with that. And you agreed to take her to town every month. I won't pay you for those days so you can lollygag around in town for a weekend with Mavis. Or do you have your eyes on someone younger now!"

It had been all Ino could do not to raise his hand against Clare. Instead he stomped out of the house and hitched the horses to the buckboard, leaving in the early evening. Despite all the arguing they had done, Ino never found a good time to tell Clare he had promised her old original cabin to Loretta, in addition to her pay each month.

Before he made it into town a thunderstorm rolled over the mountains filling the sky with lightning and dumping a downpour. The storm lasted all night and part of the next morning, but when he drew the horses to a stop in front of Reverend Langford's house, Loretta was ready to leave. She seemed much more excited about the new adventure than the reverend or the schoolmarm who showed up to say goodbye. The only other person who seemed thrilled for Loretta was her younger sister-in-law, Miss Amelia.

The air was damp and chilly, but Loretta's face was flushed was excitement. With a smile she faced forward in the seat of the buckboard and took a deep breath. As the road took her farther away from Trinidad, Loretta swiveled on her seat to look back at the small but growing town. The sight of hazy blue mesas through the early morning mist and the first shafts of light striking the golden prairies to the north of Trinidad took her breath away.

Loretta's reverie was interrupted when Ino pointed at the still snow-capped mountains ahead of them. "See how the first light turns the mountains red," he said. "That is how these mountains got their name. The Sangre de Cristos, the Blood of Christ. Those two mountains ahead are called the Spanish Peaks. The ranch is near them."

Loretta smiled. Ino said the name in a way that was almost reverent. "They're magnificent," she agreed.

The weather warmed slightly as the sun crept farther into the sky. It was nearly noon when Ino pulled the team over to rest them. Loretta unpacked small packages of snacks for her and Ino to eat. She drew the skirt to her simple dress up slightly and sat down on a rock outcropping. As soon as the horses were settled, Ino joined her.

"What is that flat-looking mountain over there?" she asked, pointing to the south.

"That is Fisher's Peak. Beyond is the pass the Santa Fe and the

New Mexico Territory." Ino looked around as he ate. "There are many markers for travelers here. Fisher's Peak to the south, Spanish Peaks to the north. The Indians believe the Spanish Peaks are the home of some of their gods who guard them. Sacred mountains."

"Indians?" Loretta asked.

"Not many in this part of Colorado Territory now." He allowed his eyes to scan the horizon. "All this belonged to them once."

By the time Ino announced they should resume their trip, Loretta was amazed by the beauty and quiet around them. She could easily see why someone like Clare McIlhenney would choose it as her home and be willing to fight not to lose it.

The horses seemed to know where to go on their own and a few hours later Loretta saw wisps of white smoke curling up against the dark green trees just over a rise in the road. She stretched her body up as far as possible to get her first glimpse of her new home. Home. That was a word she never thought she would be able to say without being afraid. She had no idea what to expect from Clare McIlhenney or her ranch hands, but it couldn't be any worse than what she'd already survived.

When the clearing in front of the house came into view, Loretta smiled. It was larger than she'd thought. A sprawling single-story home of creosote logs with white chinking gleaming in the dappled sunlight filtering between tree branches. It was well shaded for the summer months and semi-protected from snow in the winter. Everything around the house seemed neat. A corral and a stable weren't far from the house and there was a large stack of split wood between two tall trees near the house. Tall stands of aspen and evergreens seemed to extend endlessly a few yards from the rear of the structure, running up the low-lying foothills.

Ino reined the horses in and jumped from the seat to jog around the wagon to help Loretta down. "It's lovely, Mr. Valdez," Loretta said as she placed her hands on his shoulders and stepped off the wagon.

"Uh, there's a stream and a couple of pools not far from here where we get our water. There's fish in them if you're inclined to fish."

"I'll go exploring after I get settled," Loretta said with a smile.

Nodding, Ino went to the back of the wagon and lowered the tailgate. Loretta looked around the grounds once more while Ino climbed into the back of the buckboard and pushed her luggage closer to the tailgate.

"Your room is not far from Clare's room," Ino said.

"You said I would have a home of my own," Loretta said, a little disappointed.

"You will, but it ain't quite ready for anyone to live in just yet," he grunted as he slid a large valise toward the back. "It'll take some fixin' up, but the roof is solid."

He pushed the main door to the house open and led her to a small room near the back of the house. As Loretta entered, she glanced around and nodded. It was small, but there were two windows that gave her a wonderful view. On one side tall trees cast shade, but the other let her see the mountains and the small valley they'd traveled through on their way to the homestead. The room was furnished with a small bed big enough for one and a small chest of drawers. A washstand sat under the rear window and held a porcelain pitcher and wash basin.

"You can see the small cabin back in those trees," Ino said as he set the bag down at the foot of the bed.

"This is very nice, Mr. Valdez," Loretta said. "For now."

"I'll get your other bag," he said. Loretta followed him outside and reached into the front of the buckboard to get her travel valise as he pulled a second bag from the bed of the wagon. Just as they were entering the house, Ino heard the sound of hooves approaching. "Might be Clare and the hands," he said, taking a deep breath.

Loretta placed a hand on his back. "Are you sure it will be all right that I'm here?" she asked.

"It'll be fine, ma'am," he nodded. He set the bag down and waited for Clare to come into view. "Why don't you take your valise to your room, Miss Loretta. I'll bring this one in a few minutes."

Loretta started to protest being sent to her room like a child, but thought better of it. She walked into the main room of the house and watched through a front window as Ino greeted two riders on horseback who were followed by a small buggy. Two younger-looking men swung off their horses and were on the ground before the animals came to a complete stop. One of them grabbed the bridle of the horse pulling the buggy while the second moved to the side of the conveyance to help someone out. Loretta recognized the passenger as Clare McIlhenney, who held a hand gingerly across her abdomen and moved slowly as she got her feet beneath her. Clare patted the cowboy on the shoulder and limped toward Ino, pushing her wide-brimmed hat back on her head while the men led the horse and buggy toward the stable. Loretta saw the frowning, angry look on Clare's face and turned away.

"I see you finally made it back," Clare snapped. She shifted her weight uncomfortably.

"Yeah, we just got here. There was a real bad storm last night so we didn't get as early a start this mornin' as I hoped," Ino said calmly as he shoved his hands into his jacket pockets.

"Must've been the same fuckin' storm that spooked our herd over half of southern Colorado during the night," Clare said loudly as she stepped toward Ino, glaring at him. "Me and the boys been out since before sunup roundin' them up. Sure as hell could've used another hand."

"I got back as soon as I could...," Ino began.

Clare brought her face so close to his that their noses nearly touched. "It wasn't goddamn soon enough!" Clare seethed.

"Clare..."

"I told you I don't need anyone else up here. I can handle it without the assistance of some woman we barely know," Clare spat as she poked Ino in the chest. "She can pack up her shit and you'll take her back to town in a couple of days. You hear me?"

"We need her here, Clare," Ino said. "Why're you bein' so damn stubborn?"

"I don't want strangers in my house. Why is that so hard for you to get into that thick Mexican head of yours?"

"My but it's chilly out here," Loretta commented lightly as she approached Clare and her foreman. "And I'm not referring to the weather," she added with a glance at Clare. "You sound much stronger than the last time we spoke, Miss McIlhenney. Would you care for a cup of hot coffee?" Clare and Ino had been so busy glaring at one another that neither saw Loretta come out of the house carrying a small tray of cups and a steaming pot of coffee. "I don't know yet how you take your coffee, but I hope black will do for now," Loretta said nonchalantly as she handed a cup to Clare and another to Ino, who was staring at her rather stupidly. She used a piece of checkered cloth to pick up the battered pot and pour. "You could use a new pot, by the way," she said with a smile. "Washing it daily will cut back on the bitterness."

Clare grabbed her hat from her head and accepted the cup. "Thank you, ma'am," she said, softening her voice. The subtle scent of perfume struck Clare's nose, surprising her with the way it triggered her memories.

Loretta nodded. "I'll just take these to your hands."

Clare stared after her as she walked toward the stable and handed the other cups to the cowboys who were unsaddling their horses. Rather than returning to the house, she picked up a saddle and helped put the tack away, chatting with the cowboys as she did so.

"She's a pretty little thing, ain't she?" Ino leaned closer and asked quietly.

"I reckon, but that don't change nothin'. Goddamn it, what the hell were you thinkin'? Or did you let your pecker do that for you?"

"I already told you. We need someone who can cook and clean while you're laid up. I hired her so's I could have more time to help you and the boys with the herd without wonderin' what kind of cold meal was waitin' for us back at the house. I'm gettin' kinda tired of jerky and beans. Ain't you?"

"What're you payin' her?" Clare asked, taking a sip of coffee.

"I told her *you* would pay her twenty dollars a month. If it don't work out, you can take it outta my pay."

"I'll give her until right before the first snowfall, but I don't think she'll make it that long. You know how it is out here," Clare said. "Ain't no place for a decent woman."

"You live out here."

"No one's mistaken me for a decent woman since I left Pennsylvania when I was barely an adult," she said. She gulped down the remainder of her coffee. "Damn good coffee though."

"Musta washed the pot," Ino mumbled.

After Loretta returned to the house, Ino finished his coffee and handed the cup to Clare before turning back to the buckboard. As Ino leaned down to unhook and remove the horses' harnesses, Clare saw Caleb join him. He patted the hind quarters of the nearest horse.

"Pretty girl," Caleb commented with a glance toward the house.

"Yeah," Ino grunted. "Guess so."

"I wouldn't mind tappin' a little of that sometime," Caleb said with a grin

Clare didn't like what the young cowboy implied, but she was surprised when Ino dropped the reins to the team and grabbed the front of Caleb's shirt, pushing him roughly into the side of the buckboard.

"You lay a hand on her I'll kill you myself, boy. She's here to help out until Clare's back on her feet. She don't need some worthless piece of shit like you pantin' after her ass. *Comprende?*" Clare heard Ino threaten.

"I got it, I got it!" Caleb hissed. "I didn't mean nothin' by it."

Clare dropped her head and smiled as Ino shoved Caleb away and led the horses toward the stable. She reached for the handle of the front door to her home, but hesitated. Maybe she should wait for Ino. She suddenly felt ill at ease, remembering the lively hazel eyes she had seen at the doctor's office. She wasn't sure she wanted to be alone in the house with her new housekeeper. There was something in Loretta's eyes that made Clare nervous. What had she seen? Defiance? Fear? Whatever it was made Clare uncomfortable.

CLARE TRIED TO ignore Loretta as much as possible over dinner, limiting her conversation to yes and no whenever possible. Loretta had managed to find enough food to prepare a decent dinner, but chattered on about getting seasonings for their food the next time she was in Trinidad. Loretta and Ino carried on a lively conversation over dinner while Clare kept her eyes on her plate as if she was afraid someone might steal it, refusing to participate in the conversation. When dinner was finished, Clare watched Loretta clear the table and prepare to wash their dishes. Ino took a bag of loose tobacco from a bowl in the middle of the table and rolled a cigarette. He struck a match, inhaled a lungful of smoke and exhaled it silently as he glanced at Clare.

"I thought I'd watch the herd tonight," he said. "They might still be a little spooked from the storm."

"Good. I could use a full night's sleep," Clare said as she packed tobacco down into the bowl of a pipe and lit it. She stood slowly and limped to a chair in front of the fireplace and lowered her body gingerly. She felt more relaxed now that there was a reasonable distance between her and Loretta. Clare picked up a book lying on the table next to her chair and slid a pair of reading glasses on.

"Which meadow are they in?" Ino asked.

"Upper. We saw some animal prints this morning not far from there so keep your eyes open."

"Bears?"

"Too small. Probably a couple of wolves wandering down looking for easy prey among the calves."

Clare watched over the top of her glasses as Ino stood up with his cigarette clenched between his teeth and grabbed his hat and coat. It was still early enough in the spring that the nights were chilly. He picked up his gloves, took a rifle from its place over the mantle and checked it. Then he opened a cabinet near the front door and pulled out a dozen rounds.

Clare had returned to her reading when Ino's shadow fell over the book, blocking her light. "Um...listen. I...uh...promised Miss Loretta a hot bath soon as we got here. You know, instead of the stream out back. I'll get one of the boys to heat the water and...."

"She can do it herself," Clare interrupted brusquely and glanced to where Loretta stood washing dishes. "Last thing I need is some horny cowboy traipsin' in and out of my house. Just try to stay awake out there tonight."

LORETTA FINISHED WASHING the dinner dishes. The sun had dipped behind the mountain, casting the homestead into a quiet blue-gray. Above the homestead the last red and orange rays of the day curled around the side of the mountain like gnarled fingers, trying desperately to hold on for a few more minutes. Loretta was intrigued as the fingers of light slowly lost their grip and slipped away. She had never seen anything like it. Sunsets had always been beautiful to her, but the colors were more vibrant now than they had been in the city. She wiped down the kitchen counter and dried her hands on a small towel, gazing out the kitchen window. She saw Ino swing onto the back of his horse and settle into the saddle. When Loretta's eyes met his for a moment he nodded almost imperceptively in her direction and turned the horse away. With a sigh, Loretta walked toward Clare.

"Would you like another cup of coffee before you turn in?" Loretta asked. Clare hadn't heard her approach and the unexpected sound of her voice startled her, sending a stabbing pain through her side.

Clare pursed her lips and thought about it for a second before nodding. "Just one. Daylight comes early here."

Loretta poured two cups and set one next to Clare, who resumed smoking her pipe and reading a book.

"May I join you?" Loretta asked.

"Suit yourself," Clare muttered.

Loretta sat down across from her. "I was hoping you could answer a few questions for me," she said.

Clare looked over the top of her reading glasses. "About what?"

"I don't know much about you, or Mr. Valdez. I like to know about the people I work for."

"Why?" Clare asked, removing her glasses and setting them on the table next to her chair.

"It makes working together more interesting, don't you think?"

"Never thought about it. What other people do is none of my business. My life is no one else's business."

"That seems rather unfriendly," Loretta observed.

Clare closed her book and set it on the table. "How old are you, Mrs. Langford?"

"Twenty."

"Got any family?"

"I guess my mother and her husband are still alive, but I haven't seen them in years. Other than that I don't have any family."

"Isn't the preacher your brother-in-law?"

"He's not my real family. I married into his," Loretta answered after some thought.

"What happened to your man?"

"Uh...Charles was killed in an accident...last year," Loretta said between sips of coffee. She and Cyrus had never discussed the particulars of their lie. She needed to remember everything she said to warn him when she was in town again.

"Apparently you're no longer in mourning," Clare said. "I don't mean to sound cruel, Mrs. Langford, but since I'm old enough to be your mother, I figure I owe you the truth about life out here. If you came here to start a new and exciting life I suggest you keep moving west or return to your home. This is a cold, unforgiving place. I don't just mean Trinidad. This part of the west is still trying to decide whether it's civilized or not. Hell, it's not even a part of the United States yet even though I expect it will be soon. Life here isn't easy for a woman, especially one without a man to see after her."

"If it's so bad here why did you come to Trinidad?" Loretta asked.

"I was about your age when I arrived here...alone. My parents and brother were killed about two days ride from here. My father bought this land from an agent back east and sold everything we owned to make the trip. There was nothing for me to go back to."

"I'm sorry about your family."

"Long time ago.

"And Mr. Valdez?" Loretta asked, settling comfortably in her chair. For all the gruffness and seemingly unwelcome attitude, she was finding Clare McIllhenney an interesting woman to talk to. If you could get her started, she would talk.

"Ino came here on a cattle drive up from Texas about twenty years ago. He saved my life when my family was attacked and tended me until I recovered. Been with me ever since like a stray dog."

The two women drank their coffee companionably.

"Life is difficult here, Mrs. Langford," Clare said. "We don't get many chances to make mistakes. We're a long way from town."

"Ino said you were going into town in a few days. Is that true?"

"Yeah. The doc wants to check my ribs."

"Would it be possible to get some chickens there?"

"Chickens?"

"Fresh eggs would be wonderful and chicken makes a delightful meal from time to time."

"I haven't had a chicken dinner in years," Clare reminisced.

"If I paid for them, would you allow them?"

"I don't see why not, but you'd have to take care of them. My men and I don't have time to herd chickens as well as cows."

"I know it's late spring already, but I'd like to plant a garden. Fresh vegetables would be good for the men as well," Loretta added. A vegetable garden and perhaps a few flowers to brighten up the area around the house, she thought. It could be everything she had ever dreamed of as a girl. A real home.

"It's calving time. I can't spare the men to sew and tend a garden, no matter how good an idea you think it is."

"I worked on my parents' farm, Miss McIlhenney. I know what to do."

"Stop calling me Miss McIlhenney. No one calls me anything but Clare, even the men."

"Thank you. You may call me Retta, if you wish. Everyone does."

"You do know your stay here is only temporary, don't you, Mrs. Langford? I'll be up and around good as new in a few weeks and your services won't be required. I wouldn't plan on getting all nested in if I were you."

The bluntness of Clare's statement took Loretta aback somewhat. "I realize that," she said. *But I plan on changing your mind.*

EARLY THE NEXT morning, Loretta stood in the doorway and waved as Clare and her men left to relieve Ino. She made the best breakfast she could with what was available. The variety wasn't very good, but she would take care of that as soon as she got a few chickens and some seed for planting a garden. No one could live on beef and elk jerky forever and it was a wonder to her that Clare and her men didn't suffer from health problems.

Loretta smiled as she realized that for the first time in nearly five years she would be living a normal life. Perhaps in the future she would find a nice man who respected her and marry. But for now she had to remember she wasn't a whore any longer. She set about cleaning up the kitchen and making her bed before she took on the rest of the house. With Clare's limited mobility the house had fallen into some neglect.

While she scrubbed, she thought about the things Clare divulged about her life the night before. It hadn't been much and certainly not girl talk. It must have been difficult for her to build her ranch up alone. Clare had the calloused hands of a ranch hand and broad muscular shoulders, but the brightest eyes Loretta had ever seen. They were almost mesmerizing when Loretta looked into them and their color reminded her of the melted chocolate her mother prepared for cakes when she was a child. Clare McIlhenney was a quiet, unassuming woman who worked hard to live a simple life. There wasn't much more than that anyone needed, Loretta decided. It seemed to Loretta that Clare wasn't accustomed to having lengthy conversations. But she had a sense of humor and a gentleness about her which was covered by toughness and bravado. Loretta found her unexpectedly attractive.

By noon Loretta had thoroughly cleaned the inside of the house and wandered outside to have her first real look at the grounds surrounding it. About a hundred yards from the main house she spotted a much smaller cabin. Tall trees canopied over the roof to provide a cool spot during the heat of the day. The door to the cabin opened with a loud creaking noise and she stepped inside to look around. It was undoubtedly the original cabin Ino had told her about. He said it hadn't been used or cared for since the big house was completed a few years earlier. Now it would be Loretta's home. A thick layer of dust and dirt covered the puncheon floor and cobwebs draped from every available nook and cranny. Loretta smiled broadly as she surveyed the three room cabin. It would take a while and a considerable amount of cleaning, but once Clare and her hands left every day to tend the herd, Loretta would have nothing but time on her hands until they returned for meal times.

Along the side of the small cabin, Loretta located what must have once been a root cellar. It had fallen into disrepair as well, but was salvageable. If she was successful in growing a vegetable garden she would need a dark, cool place to store what she grew. The more she looked around the property, the more her excitement began to take control of her and she couldn't wait to get started. She picked up small rocks and began laying out an area where she could house chickens. She didn't know much about building chicken coops and only remembered the ones on her parents' farm. She would have to make a list of supplies she would need and hope Clare would agree to buy the materials. Her mind raced with all the ideas she came up with for the area between the cabin and the main house.

It was almost noon when Loretta heard the sound of a rider approaching the house. She walked around the side and saw the buggy approaching, an obviously pregnant heifer following behind. Clare eased down from the buggy seat and, using a homemade cane to steady her gait, slowly led the heifer toward a three-sided lean-to where hay had been stored. Loretta went into the main house and began preparing something for her employer to eat.

Clare led the heifer into the small building next to the stable and made sure she had food and water. As soon as she'd arrived at her men's campsite one of the heifers began acting as if she was going to give birth at any moment. Clare decided it would be best to have the animal closer to the house where mother and calf wouldn't be easy pickings for predators. When she was satisfied the heifer was comfortable, she ambled across the open area toward the house. She took a deep breath and wiped her forehead with the back of her gloved hand. She scraped the bottom of her boots before opening the door to the house and removed her gloves. She looked around the front room as she hung her hat on a peg inside the door. It seemed lighter than usual for some reason and a slight smile flickered across her thin lips. She couldn't remember the last time the house looked so clean.

"You'll be wanting something to eat," Loretta's voice said. Clare hadn't noticed the woman who was partially obscured by a dish cabinet. "I'll pack up some food for you to take back out to your men."

"Thank you," Clare said quietly. "It looks nice in here, Retta."

"It just needed a little cleaning and window washing," Loretta said. "Wash up and I'll get your plate and a cup of coffee."

Clare felt rooted to the floor, unable to make her legs move as her eyes took in the remainder of the front room. Everything seemed to be in its proper place, but there was something different about it all. She grinned when she finally realized that the layers of dust and soot from the fireplace that had coated everything was gone, revealing the true texture and color of the floor and furniture.

Clare walked into the kitchen and pumped water into the sink, filling her hands with the cold water, and rubbing them over her face. She felt as if there was an inch of dirt on it. She needed to spend time in the tub soaking her entire body and hoped she didn't smell as bad as she felt. She leaned against the sink to dry her hands and face as she watched Loretta busily preparing a plate.

"Are you going to join me?" Clare asked softly.

"I've already eaten," Loretta said over her shoulder as she drew a pan full of biscuits from the clay oven. "Please. Sit down," Loretta said with a smile as she carried a plate to the table. Clare could have made a whole dinner out of the biscuits sitting in front of her. The only thing missing was her mother's gravy. Now there was a meal she hadn't tasted in more years than she could remember. When Loretta set a small bowl of white gravy on the table, Clare could have jumped up and kissed her. For a moment, she couldn't do anything except stare at the food in front of her. Her mother had made the best biscuits and gravy in the whole world. The vague memory of her mother, a beautiful, delicate woman with the gentle strength of ten men, flooded Clare's mind. She thought she might break down in tears over biscuits and gravy, but managed to gather her emotions as Loretta set a cup of coffee next to her plate.

Clare's voice was barely audible as she said a simple 'thank you'. She savored each bite and the gravy made even the familiar jerky taste better. By the time she finished eating she felt a satisfied contentment she hadn't known in years.

"That was good," Clare said. "Almost makes me regret my earlier opposition to having you here."

"Well, I'm here now. We'll have to make the best of it while it lasts, I suppose."

Clare cleared her throat. "I...I should apologize for my behavior when you first arrived," Clare said.

"Does that mean you should apologize or you do apologize? We should do many things, but often don't," Loretta said with a smile.

"My parents did teach me manners, but I haven't had a need to use them for a long time," Clare said. "I do apologize for my bad behavior yesterday."

"You're forgiven," Loretta said. "While you're here perhaps you can suggest a place that would be suitable for a garden and yet be out of the way of work on other matters."

Clare brought her cup to her lips. "There's a small clearing behind the cabin out back that would make a decent garden area. It's too small for much else and is near enough to the stream to allow easy access to water."

"I may require some assistance with constructing a coop for the chickens as well. While I know how they should be constructed, I confess that I am not overly proficient with a saw or hammer."

"I'm sure one of the men will be glad to make the time to assist you," Clare said.

"I don't relish being left alone here without some protection. I'm a tolerable shot with a rifle. I would appreciate it if there was one available I could use."

"I will see that you have a rifle while you're here alone. Is there anything else you require?" Clare frowned as she looked at Loretta.

"No," Loretta said cheerfully.

"I better check on that heifer," Clare said as she stood up.

Loretta was heating a pan of water and stacking the few dishes Clare had used when she heard her name, somewhere in the distance. Looking around she didn't see Clare until she opened the front door of the house. Clare was on her knees next to the heifer that was now lying on its side in the lean-to. Hiking her skirt up, Loretta ran across the space between the house and shed.

Slightly out of breath, she stopped next to Clare. "What's wrong? Are you hurt?"

Clare was struggling to get the heifer on its feet. "She's ready to deliver, but something's wrong. I have to get her on her feet."

Loretta joined Clare and together they tried to move the heifer's hooves back under her. As Clare turned and put her back against the weakened animal to hold her in place, she said, "Tie the rope around her neck and loop it over the top rung of the stall. Then pull as hard as you can while I push."

"What about your ribs?"

"Fuck 'em," Clare snarled.

"What if we can't get her up?" Loretta asked as she repositioned the rope.

"She'll die and so will her calf," Clare grunted. Under her breath she said, "C'mon. Get up, dammit." Clare dug the heels of her boots into the dirt in front of the lean-to and moved her shoulders as far under the heifer's side as she could. "Take up any slack when I push," she ordered.

"She'll hang herself!" Loretta said.

"She'll get up before she does that...survival instinct," Clare said between pushes. She gritted her teeth against the pain shooting along her ribs. Slowly the heifer got her front hooves under her body and began to move. Clare rolled toward the rear of the heifer and used her shoulders to raise the hind quarters. Although she was already exhausted, as soon as the animal stood, Clare took the rope from Loretta and tied it securely to the top rail. She rolled her right shirt sleeve almost to her shoulder. "I need some lard or soap...anything slick," she said as she returned to the heifer's hind quarters. She lifted the tail and patted the animal's hip. Then looking at Loretta she said, "Move, woman, before she goes down again."

Loretta blinked and nodded before running back into the house. She returned a few minutes later with a large can of lard. Breathlessly, she stammered, "Now what?"

"Slather that on my arm. Ever birthed a baby before?" Clare asked as Loretta dipped her hand in the lard and began spreading the slippery off-white substance up and down Clare's right arm.

"No," Loretta said, looking at Clare with wide eyes. "What do I do?"

"Just talk to her and keep her calm if you can," Clare said quietly. "She's in trouble. Calf must be in the wrong position. If I'm lucky I can move the calf so she can shove its ass out."

"What if you can't?" Loretta said as she stroked the heifer's side.

"Then I reckon we'll have to try something else," Clare shrugged. "Or have fresh beef for dinner."

Loretta gasped as she watched Clare push her hat back and rest her head against the heifer's flank. She watched in disbelief as Clare inserted her hand into the heifer's ass, followed by her arm. Loretta slammed her eyes shut, glad she hadn't just eaten. She turned her head away and breathed through her mouth to fight off the feeling twisting her stomach into a knot.

"She's ready all right," Clare grunted. "I found a leg, but can't tell which one it is."

"Is it breathing?" Loretta asked.

Clare managed to smile at Loretta over the heifer's rump. "It can't do that until it's out."

Loretta felt more than stupid at her question, but nodded solemnly as she turned her attention back to the heifer.

"Ow!" Clare said loudly. "Shit! Shit! Shit!"

"What wrong?" Loretta asked, alarmed.

"C'mon girl. Relax!" Clare said as she gritted her teeth. "Damn that hurts," she muttered. She looked at Loretta and grinned. "Contraction."

"Oh. Are you all right?"

"C'mon baby, I know you got four legs. Where the hell is the other one?"

Loretta felt helpless as she watched Clare struggle with the calf for what seemed like an eternity. She whispered to the heifer and rubbed her sides and belly waiting for something to happen. "Should I go find Ino?" she finally asked.

"No time. Get a rope from the stable. Do you know how to make a slip knot?"

"Yes."

"Get a rope and tie the knot, then give it to me and saddle my horse. Can you do that? And hurry. I don't know how much longer this calf can last."

Loretta ran down the walkway of the stable and found a coil of rope. Quickly making a slip knot she ran back to the heifer and handed it to Clare, who had removed her arm from the heifer. Blood, mixed with slimy-looking mucus covered Clare's arm as she flexed her fingers and shook circulation back into her arm. She applied lard to her arm again and rubbed it on the rope. "I found the back legs," she explained. "I'm gonna put this rope around them and use my horse to pull this baby out of there. It might already be dead, but I can't afford to lose the heifer, too. I'll be ready here real quick, so get the horse."

She reached out with her cleanest hand and squeezed Loretta's shoulder. "You're doing good. Okay?"

Loretta nodded and returned to the stable. She found a saddle and stood on a bale of hay to get it onto the horse's back. It took her a few more minutes to get the bit and reins on and she hoped she had done it correctly as she led the horse toward Clare. As soon as she saw them, Clare withdrew her hand from the heifer and looped the end of the rope around the saddle horn.

"When I tell you, back him up real slow. I'll guide the calf out." Clare returned to her place behind the heifer and inserted her arm once again. "Slowly," she said with a nod.

Loretta backed the horse up and watched Clare for a signal. A few seconds later, Clare stopped her to adjust the calf's position. When Loretta resumed backing the horse, she watched as a wet red blob suddenly appeared and fell to the ground, covered with the same bloody, gelatinous substance she had seen on Clare's arm. Clare removed the rope from the calf's back legs and tossed it aside as Loretta wrapped the horse's reins to a pole near the lean-to. Loretta fell to her knees and wanted to cry when there was no sign of life from the calf. Clare pulled a rag from her hip pocket and wiped the sticky substance from its head. To Loretta's horror, Clare lowered her face and placed her mouth over the calves' nostrils and sucked out a disgusting looking substance, first from one nostril and then the other, and spit it on the ground.

Clare stood quickly and grabbed one hind leg and one front leg. "Grab the other side," she ordered as she looked at Loretta, who did as she was told, despite her paled expression. "I can't take a deep enough breath to suck it all out because of my damn ribs, but we have to clear more of this shit from its lungs. We'll have to pick him up and try to sling it out. If that doesn't work there isn't anything else we can do."

They swung the calf's lifeless body in an arc front to back. "The next time his head is up, swing him backward with all your might," Clare instructed calmly.

They repeated the swinging motion two or three times before Loretta saw fluid running from the calf's nose. "It's working!" she laughed.

Loretta's arms felt as if they might fall off her shoulders and she knew Clare had to be twice as exhausted as well as in pain. The heifer watched them intently as they swung its baby forcefully twice more. Its legs began to move slightly while Clare wiped it down and cleared as much mucus from its mouth and nostrils as possible. She untied the heifer, which immediately nudged the calf to get up and began licking it body to remove the remainder of the sticky substance from its body.

Clare limped to a barrel of rain water next to the lean-to and plunged her arms and head into the barrel, scrubbing off the blood and afterbirth. Her arms ached and she was certain she had re-damaged her ribs. She also knew she would fall asleep as soon as she found a horizontal position anywhere. Hell, at that point the ground looked pretty damned inviting. She rubbed the muscles of her right arm that had been nearly crushed by each of the heifer's powerful contractions as she led the animal into an empty stall in the stable. She was a mess and knew she smelled horrible. She ran a hand through her wet hair and released the heifer into a stall. Loretta carried the wobbly calf and set it down carefully next to its mother. She found another rag and spoke softly to the calf and its mother while she cleaned more of the slimy substance from the calf's face. She giggled as the calf tottered around on new legs and tried to keep from toppling over. Clare smiled at the scene and rested her chin on her hands as she leaned against the top rung of the stall. She knew the calf couldn't have survived without Loretta's help.

Loretta glanced up and saw Clare. "Isn't he beautiful?" she said, casting her a brilliant smile.

Clare couldn't remember the last time she'd seen that kind of excitement and joy on someone's face. "Yep. I'll leave them in the stable for a night or two so they can rest. Then they can join the rest of the herd."

"Already? Most women don't recover that quickly."

"It's a heifer, Retta. Not a person."

"Are you sure she's all right?"

"We'll know by morning. I'll have Ino check on them when he gets in." Clare looked down at herself and sniffed. "I have got to get a bath. Looks like you might need one, too. I'm afraid your dress is ruined," she said, glancing at Loretta.

"It'll be all right. What are we going to name him?" Loretta asked as she patted the calf that had begun to stumble comically around the stall.

"We don't name our animals," Clare said. "But if you want to, I don't guess anyone would mind." She made her way slowly outside, untied her horse's reins, and began leading him back to his stall. Clare unsaddled her horse and checked his food before closing and latching the stall. She was brought up short by the sight of Loretta hugging the calf and speaking softly to him. In its own way it was sweet and Loretta reminded Clare of a child who had been deprived of gentleness and kindness.

"They'll be all right," she said to Loretta.

Loretta stepped away from the calf and helped Clare spread hay on the floor of the small stall. She patted the heifer that seemed grateful for a chance to rest. As the heifer chewed a mouthful of hay, her calf found its own nourishment as he nuzzled against his mother's udder. Just like a man, Loretta thought, but kept it to herself.

Clare shuffled out of the stall and latched the gate. When she turned to leave, Loretta grabbed her by the arm. "You're bleeding," she said.

Clare looked down and saw the bright red stain across her upper abdomen. "Must have torn a stitch out. It'll be okay."

"Go inside and let me check it. If it isn't cleaned up you could get an infection."

"I'll take care of it later."

"No. Now!"

"You don't give orders here, Mrs. Langford."

"Why are you so damn afraid of letting someone help your sorry ass, Miss McIlhenney?"

"Oh, for Christ's sake," Clare mumbled. "Make it quick. I have work to do."

Loretta heated a pot of water and found a reasonably clean cloth to wash Clare's wound out. When she carried the water and cloth into Clare's bedroom, Clare was sitting on the edge of her bed.

"You'll have to remove your shirt and lie down," Loretta said.

"For what?" Clare reached down and pulled the tail of her shirt up, revealing her abdomen below her breasts.

"Because I can't see the cut or all the stitches." Loretta smiled. "Believe me, you don't have anything I haven't seen before. So don't be afraid."

"I'm not afraid," Clare grumbled. "Certainly not of you."

"I'm tougher than I look," Loretta said. She placed her hands on Clare's shoulders and pushed her down. She unbuttoned Clare's shirt and pulled the right side away from the injured area of Clare's abdomen. She soaked the cloth in warm water and squeezed out most of the excess water before folding it and laying it across the cut. She moved to the end of the bed and began tugging off Clare's boots.

"There's nothing wrong with my feet or legs," Clare protested.

"You need to change these filthy clothes and take a bath. It will be easier if I help you undress."

"I can undress myself! Just clean the damn cut."

Loretta removed the damp cloth from the stitched area of Clare's abdomen and dipped it in the warm water again. Gently she began wiping away the blood from around the injured area. She rested a hand on Clare's lower abdomen and examined the stitches.

"It looks like you pulled more than one out and the bleeding is coming from the new torn skin. Let me get some scissors."

"For what?"

"I should remove the pulled stitches. Then I'll clean out the wound and bandage it. Since it's partially healed that should hold it until you see Dr. Wayne."

Loretta left the room and returned a few minutes later with a small pair of scissors. She placed her thumb and index finger on either side of the line of stitches and clipped away three of them. When she was satisfied, Loretta lightly patted Clare on the stomach.

"I'll get a tub of hot water ready while you undress. Soak for about fifteen minutes and then I'll put a bandage on. Call me when you're out of the tub."

Clare nearly screamed when the hot water in the bath hit the re-opened wound, but eventually the stinging sensation on her raw skin faded away. As she soaked away her aches and pains she tried to think of a way to avoid Loretta's soft touch in the future. She couldn't afford to enjoy the sensations Loretta's gentle finger created. Those feelings had never led to anything but heartache.

TWO DAYS LATER, Clare sat on Dr. Wayne's examining table and through gritted teeth endured his poking and prodding. When he snipped the final stitch below her breast he said, "I would've thought your ribs would be a little further along than they are. Have you been resting and not putting any unnecessary strain on them?"

"Yep," Clare answered.

"Somehow I don't think that's the total truth, Clare."

"It's a ranch, Doc. Things happen that can't always be controlled."

"If you keep doing whatever it is that can't be controlled, you'll still be healing when Christmas comes. I want to see you again in about a month. Maybe by then you'll be able to take a deep breath without grimacing so much," he said as he patted her on the shoulder. "Keep the ribs wrapped for support. You can put your shirt back on now."

Clare slipped her arms carefully into the sleeves of her shirt and stood up. She refused to use her cane to walk and tried to appear as normal as possible. She stepped onto the boardwalk outside the doctor's office and strolled toward the dry goods store. By the time she made it down the street to the store she saw Ino carrying a large, squawking crate which he set carefully into the back of the buckboard.

"What the hell is that?" she asked when she was closer.

"A bunch a chickens, wire, some provisions, seed, and a few other things Miss Loretta needs for her cabin," Ino said as he shoved the crate onto the bed of the buckboard.

"How much longer before we can leave?"

"We'll be ready after we grab a beer."

Clare nodded and wandered into the dry goods store. She looked around until she saw Loretta near the back of the store looking through bolts of fabric. When Loretta saw her approaching she smiled.

"Did you get everything you need?" Clare asked.

"Yes, and thank you. What did Dr. Wayne say about your ribs?"

"They're healing."

"Did you tell him about the calf? I'm sure you re-injured your ribs."

Clare shifted her weight uncomfortably. "No need to tell him about that. It couldn't be helped." She reached across Loretta's body to feel a piece of fabric between her thumb and index figure. "Nice fabric," she managed, distracted by her closeness to Loretta's body.

"When I get paid I'll get some and make a lighter weight skirt for summer."

"Summer will be over in another couple of months. Get what you need. I owe you for ruining your other dress with that calf anyway."

"You don't owe me for that. I was just doing my job," Loretta protested.

"I don't pay you to tend cattle." Clare looked at the other bolts of fabric and picked one up. It was dark blue with gold and silver stripes. "This would work well for curtains. Maybe you should get this to cover the windows in your cabin. I trust my men, but they're human." Clare picked up the bolts and carried them to the front counter. Horace stared at her when she dropped them on the cutting table. "It's for my housekeeper," she explained brusquely. "Get whatever else you need and we'll wait for you at the saloon," she said to Loretta.

Chapter Twelve

LORETTA WIPED HER forehead with the back of her hand and readjusted her straw hat. She leaned on the handle of her hoe and surveyed the long rows that made up her fledgling garden. After nearly a month, the seeds she'd planted had broken the ground and were stretching toward the sun. She picked up a nearby canteen and took a long drink of cool water. Every day after Clare and her hands ate their noon meal and returned to work, Loretta donned her hat and grabbed her hoe, determined to keep unwanted grasses and weeds from invading the garden.

She squatted down and closed her hand around a fistful of warm dirt. She brought it close to her nose and inhaled its scent, smiling. Memories of working with her father in the rolling fields on their Ohio farm seemed as fresh as they were when she was a child. Those had been the most uncomplicated, happiest days of her life. Until now. For the first time since leaving home she felt at peace.

She hiked her skirt up slightly and carried the hoe to a small shed located behind her cabin. When she finished her work and had a little free time, Loretta enjoyed exploring more of the property surrounding the main house and outbuildings. She walked through her garden, looking around to make sure she hadn't missed any stray weeds and set off across a grassy area toward the stream that ran behind the cottage. Although the stream couldn't be seen from the house, Loretta heard the water tumbling over rocks and boulders long before she saw the falling water itself. She remembered the spring house her father built to cool the butter her mother churned along with other perishables.

Loretta shaded her eyes with her hand and followed the course of the stream. It ran from much higher in the Sangre de Cristos and while the flow of water was steady, there were sections where the land flattened out allowing deep pools of water to form. If she could find a pool relatively close to the main house that was deep enough, Loretta was sure she could make a spring box. When the snow melted at the higher elevations, the water would become much colder. In a deep enough pool, deeper water would remain cool even though the surface temperature was warm.

Loretta was careful as she stepped over rocks along the sloping bank of the stream. She wasn't in a hurry and still had time before she needed to return and prepare the evening meal. She slipped her hand into the pocket of her skirt and withdrew the butt end of the loaf of bread she had baked the day before. Since she was a child, the ends of bread loaves had been her favorite part. The thick, brown, crusty ends seemed filled with flavor that lasted longer than the softer insides. She took a bite and returned the rest to her pocket, chewing slowly and savoring the full flavor.

A few yards downstream, the water flattened out just below a natural waterfall. Loretta looked up and down the bank and spotted an area littered with large and medium-sized rocks that were flat enough for stacking. She sat down on the bank and removed her shoes and stockings. Looking around to make sure she was alone, she pulled her skirt hem up and tucked it into the waistband before wading into the cold water. Goosebumps shot up her legs and she shivered. She felt along the bottom of the stream just off the bank and began pushing and rolling rocks into the water. Satisfied with the rock bottom of about two by three feet she'd created, she began lifting stones to build the side walls.

Even though she worked steadily, she had only moved half the rocks she needed when she began to feel fatigued. She climbed onto the bank and pulled her legs up to rest her head on her knees. She took deep breaths and gazed at the work she'd begun. She had no doubt she would feel the effects of the lifting and carrying the next day. After resting a few minutes, she pushed herself up. The water in the pool appeared glassy on the surface, but she had felt the steady current around her legs. It was the perfect place for a spring box.

As she started to turn away and pull on her stockings and shoes again, she noticed movement in the water just beneath the surface. She bent over and looked more closely, smiling when she saw dozens of small black fish swimming near the edge of the pool. She reached into the pocket of her skirt again and removed the chunk of bread. She pulled off a small piece and stretched out on the bank and slid her hand into the water. The fish fled a safe distance, but returned cautiously within a minute and began nibbling at the water-soaked bread between her fingers. Each time Loretta withdrew her hand for more bread, more fish appeared. She giggled as the fish tickled her skin.

She watched the fish nibble at the bread and the lazy movement of the water combined with the warm sun beating down on her back began to make her drowsy. She brought an arm up and rested her head on it. It wasn't long before she drifted off into a nap.

CLARE SAT COMFORTABLY astride her horse as she rode behind the main house. She hadn't found Loretta inside and didn't see her working in her garden. She had spotted the large paw prints of a bear earlier and returned to warn Loretta the animal might wander closer. She became concerned when her housekeeper was nowhere to be found. In spite of her best efforts she felt drawn to the amber-haired woman. She reminded Clare of a time when she had been young and looked forward to life. It was a dream that vanished in a hale of gunfire many years before.

Clare moved her horse toward the stream a few hundred yards away in case Loretta had decided to relax and catch a few fish for dinner. When she reached the stream, there was no sign of Loretta, but she saw the roughed up area near the bank and became worried. She looked up and in the distance she saw what appeared to be a body lying face down on the bank and partially in the water. She spurred her horse forward, reining it in when she reached the body. Dread filled her and she pulled her rifle from its case and looked around as she dismounted. She didn't see any evidence of the bear as she ran toward Loretta's prone body. She knelt down and pulled the unconscious woman into her arms.

Loretta's hand flew up, knocking the straw hat off her head.

"Are you all right?" Clare asked as she noticed how the sunlight glittered off Loretta's golden hair.

"What?" Loretta answered, shaking her head to fully awaken.

Clare released her and Loretta scrambled to her feet and wiped her wet hand on her skirt.

"I'm sorry," Loretta said.

"For what?" Clare asked, taking a step forward.

"I must have dozed off. I didn't realize it had gotten so late. I'll have dinner ready soon."

"It's not time for dinner. I came back early and got worried when I didn't find you at the house. We saw some bear prints earlier and I thought I should warn you. What were you doing?"

"I found a good spot for a spring box," Loretta said, pointing to spot farther downstream where she had begun stacking rocks. "The water is cold and deep enough to keep butter and cream all year round."

"Good idea. Is that why you were laying on the bank?"

"Oh, that. No. I was just...it's silly. I'll get back to work."

Clare looked exasperated. "You're not a prisoner here, Loretta. No one's going to beat you if you take a break. Have I given you the impression I expect more from you than you're already doing?"

"Of course not! I just want to do a good job."

"You're doing a good job. Certainly better than I expected when Ino brought you here over my objections. Guess that proves that even I can make a mistake. So why were you laying on the bank playing in the water?"

"Come see," Loretta said.

"What is it?"

Loretta took something from her pocket and motioned for Clare to join her at the edge of the water where she handed her a small chunk of bread.

"Puny snack," Clare mumbled.

"It's not for you. Just lie down and do what I tell you to do," Loretta directed.

Clare's mouth curled upward in the beginning of a grin. She wiggled her eyebrows at Loretta. "Right here in front of God and everyone?" she asked with a laugh, unable to resist the opening Loretta had left for her. Loretta blushed furiously at Clare's unexpected flirtation.

"Just watch," Loretta finally said as she stretched out on the bank once again and slowly lowered her hand into the water, a portion of the bread between her fingers. In less than a minute small fish began to appear and swim just beyond her hand. Finally curiosity and hunger overcame them and they began nibbling at the bread as it softened in the water. Clare smiled and lay down next to Loretta. As her hand entered the water the fish fled.

"They'll be back," Loretta said softly. "You have to be patient."

"In case you haven't noticed, patience isn't my strong suit," Clare said. When the fish returned she watched them cautiously, mesmerized by the growing number.

"They're nibbling my fingers," she whispered to Loretta.

Loretta smiled as she saw the childlike awe in Clare's eyes. "Sort of tickles, doesn't it?"

"It's wonderful," Clare smiled back at her. "Thank you."

As Loretta's hazel eyes met hers, Clare felt something she hadn't felt in years. Loneliness. The need to be close to someone. She cleared her throat and stood up, offering her hand to Loretta to pull her up. When Loretta took Clare's hand and started to stand, the pebbles along the riverbank began to slide under her feet. Clare grabbed her around the waist to keep her from falling into the stream.

Clare liked the way Loretta felt in her arms and held her for a moment longer than necessary to make sure she had regained her balance. At least that's what Clare told herself. Loretta's body was warm from lying in the sun and Clare soaked up the warmth.

"Thank you," Loretta said as she got her feet under her again and noticed that Clare was blushing.

"You're welcome," Clare managed over the lump growing in her throat. Even as she spoke she couldn't drag her eyes away from the rich color of Loretta's hazel eyes. She released Loretta and stepped away from her.

Loretta frowned and, taking a step closer, placed a hand lightly on Clare's chest. "Are you all right? You look flushed."

The touch seemed to burn straight through Clare's shirt as she looked down at the young woman. She swept her gaze over Loretta's face. The closeness between them sucked the breath from Clare's lungs. She longed to feel Loretta's lips against hers. Would they feel as soft as Annalee's? It had been twenty years since that first kiss which had changed her life forever.

Loretta seemed to have stopped breathing. She brought her fingertips to Clare's mouth and gently touched her lips. "You're lips are so soft." Loretta said.

Clare lowered her head and brushed her lips against Loretta's, not knowing what to expect.   The moment Loretta's lips parted slightly, Clare deepened the kiss and slipped her tongue inside. Loretta stepped away from her quickly and brought her hand to her mouth.

"I'm sorry. I didn't mean to offend you," Clare said.

Looking up at her, Loretta said softly, "I'm not offended. It's just that a kiss like that...it's what...lovers do."

Loretta stepped toward Clare once again and ran her hand from Clare's shoulder to the back of her neck, pressing lightly to guide her mouth into another kiss. She wondered what it would be like to feel Clare's calloused hands travel over her skin and found the idea...stimulating. Her lips parted as they met Clare's again, inviting her to explore. Tentatively, Clare moved her lips against Loretta's, her tongue sliding unopposed into the welcoming warmth. She smiled through the kiss as their tongues met and pirouetted around each other before wandering off to find the other miracles within the dark recesses. This was the kiss she had longed for with Annaleee and never had. This was a kiss worth dying for.

Loretta was surprised at the desire she felt in the deepening kiss and slid her arms down Clare's arms, pulling their bodies more closely together. She had only kissed one other woman, but Clare, for someone who acted so rough, was so gentle Loretta couldn't help but be drawn to her.

"Where did you..." she started to ask when the kiss ended. Her eyes shifted to a sudden movement over Clare's shoulder.

"You bitch!" Ino seethed as he grabbed Clare by the shoulder and spun her around. His fist found her jaw and she stumbled back from the blow. Her boots slid down the bank. She tried to catch her balance, but couldn't. She landed in the stream, the icy water sending shocks through her body. She saw Ino wading into the water after her and fought to stand up to defend herself from another blow. Ino grabbed her by the front of her shirt and pulled her up while drawing his arm back.

"Stop it!" Loretta cried out as she joined them in the stream. She wrapped her arms around Ino's fisted hand and hung on. Clare used Loretta's distraction to tear Ino's hand away from her shirt and push him away. Without a word she climbed out of the stream as quickly as she could and strode to her horse. She grabbed the saddle horn with both hands and swung into the saddle without using the stirrups. Loretta watched as the horse galloped away. She turned back to Ino and pushed him away.

"What the hell were you doing?" she demanded. The coldness of the water made her shiver slightly.

"Did she hurt you?" Ino asked. His face was red with anger and his breathing was heavy and ragged.

"Of course not. Why did you do that?"

"I should have warned you about Clare," he said. He shook his head and waded out of the water.

"Warned me about what?" Loretta demanded. She stood in the middle of the stream, small droplets of water dripping from her disheveled hair onto her cheeks like tears.

"Clare's a good woman. My friend. But...well...sometimes she ain't right in the head," he said, tapping his index finger again the side of his head. "I figured maybe she wouldn't do nothin' since she was so much against havin' you here. But I was wrong. I can take you back to town tomorrow if you want to pack up your things tonight. I'd appreciate it if you didn't never say anything to your brother-in-law or anybody else about what Clare did to you."

"She didn't do anything to me," Loretta insisted.

"She kissed you. I been watchin' how she looks at you. It's not right."

Loretta angrily snatched up her shoes and stockings. "I have to get dinner ready. And I won't be going back to town tomorrow or any other day."

"Looked to me like maybe you wanted her to kiss you," Ino shot as Loretta started to push past him. He took her by the arm and pulled her closer. "Somethin' like that could get you killed," he hissed.

"Is that a threat, Ino?"

"A warning. It's one thing for townspeople to think there's somethin' sinful going on between Clare and me because I'm a man and she's a woman. She's not the woman she appears to be. I've seen her at her worst and I know what she's capable of if she's pushed." His hand loosened its grip and his face softened slightly. "I like you, Retta. I wouldn't want to see anything bad happen to either one of you. If Garner found out you two were doin' something two women shouldn't be doin' he'd kill you both and take Clare's ranch. Is it worth riskin' your life and Clare's for?"

CLARE'S CLOTHES WERE still damp when she dismounted in front of the Cattleman's Saloon. She felt humiliated by her inability to control her emotions. The memory of Loretta's lips against hers remained strong. Her lips felt as if they were throbbing for everyone to see as she pushed through the door of the saloon. She signaled for a drink as she approached the bar, her eyes scanning the room. She closed her eyes, feeling the shot burn a path down her throat.

"I didn't expect to see you back in town so soon," Peg's silken voice said.

"Didn't expect to be back so soon," Clare said as she motioned for a refill. "Busy night?" she asked, praying it wasn't.

"Deader than a wake after the liquor's run out," Peg said with a grin. She rested her hand on Clare's shoulder and squeezed it lightly. "Your clothes are wet," she stated the obvious.

"Had an accident. Can I stay with you tonight?"

"You know you're always welcome, sugar. We'd better get you into a tub of hot water before you catch your death. Go on up and I'll be there in a few minutes."

Clare nodded and motioned for another refill to take with her. The lack of food combined with the fast shots Clare downed made her light-headed. Peg ran a supportive arm around her waist. "Let's get you cleaned up and under the sheets before you freeze to death." Clare managed to maneuver her way across the open room, hearing the chuckles of the men playing poker at a nearby table.

"Ignore them," Peg said quietly when she felt Clare hesitate.

In the time it took Peg to prepare a tub of water, Clare managed to get half undressed. Her shirt was unbuttoned and she had one boot off. She struggled to dredge up enough coordination to pull the other boot off, finally dropping her foot to the wooden floor, defeated.

"Maybe I should just go to sleep, Peg," she said, the room spinning slightly as she tried to focus on the other woman.

"No one's sleeping in my bed in damp, musty-smelling clothes," Peg said. Standing in front of Clare, Peg turned her back to her. "Give me your foot and use your other foot to push against my ass so I can get this damn wet boot off," Peg ordered.

Once the boot was off, Peg reached down and pulled Clare to her feet, struggling to push the damp shirt off her shoulders as it clung to her skin.

"You're real pretty, Peg," Clare slurred as she swayed slightly.

"No one's bothered to call me pretty since the last time you were here needin' some tender care" Peg snorted. "That why you're here tonight?"

"I can take care of myself," Clare insisted.

"I know you can, but there's only so much you can do for yourself, cowgirl. Now shuck those wet pants off." Peg smiled as Clare pushed her jeans down, holding on to Peg's shoulders to step out of them. "Ain't you got no proper underwear?" Peg asked as Clare finally stood naked in front of her, except for a pair of gray woolen socks.

"Can't wear bloomers under the pants and my last binder fell apart. Reckon I need to get a new one."

Clearing her throat, Peg said, "You best get in that water while it's still warm. Otherwise you'll be taking a cold bath."

Peg slipped an arm around Clare's bare waist and urged her into the tub. Small wisps of steam floated above the water. As Clare finally brought one leg up and stepped into the water, her foot slid on the bottom. She grasped Peg tightly to keep from losing her balance. As Peg reached for her, her hand inadvertently found its way to Clare's breast. Clare gasped and stared at Peg, unsure what to make of the jolt that shot through her.

"Sorry," Peg mumbled as she moved her hand away and helped Clare settle into the warm water.

Peg knelt down next to the tub and stroked Clare's hair back, brushing her thumb across her cheek. Clare shook her head. "I'm sorry for showing up like this, Peg," she said, covering Peg's hand with hers.

Peg patted her on the shoulder. "Something wrong you want to talk about, sweetie?"

"Nope. Just felt a little lonely."

"Finish cleaning up so you can get some sleep."

While Clare finished bathing, Peg removed a few stray articles of clothing from her bed and fluffed the pillows up to make them more comfortable. When she turned around, she was surprised to find Clare standing behind her, a towel wrapped around her body. Clare stepped closer and hugged the woman. Warmth spread through her body and Clare wished it could have come from Loretta's embrace. "Thanks for being my friend," she whispered. "For understanding."

As she began to pull away Peg stopped her. They stood staring at each other for a few moments in uncomfortable silence before Clare said, "You feel real good, Peg."

Peg brought her face closer to Clare's. "So do you, sugar. I know what you need tonight." Her lips lightly brushed over Clare's before she stepped back.

Not often, but occasionally, when the need to connect to another person, a woman, became overwhelming, Clare had gone to town and sought out Peg's company. Peg never judged her and never told anyone, not even Mavis, what they did together. The kiss between her and Loretta earlier in the day had unsettled Clare. She needed to relieve the frustration she felt when she was near the much younger woman. She should tell her to leave the ranch and not return. Clare moved closer to Peg and leaned down to kiss her again, this time with more pressure. Peg responded by running a hand up Clare's bare back and the rancher smiled down at her. "It's been a long time."

"You need to find someone to be with all the time, sweetie," Peg sighed.

"I don't want anyone who will leave me alone again," Clare said through clenched teeth. "I didn't want to go bumping around in the back of a wagon halfway across the country. I didn't want my folks to be murdered, leaving me to fend for myself in the middle of nowhere. I didn't want to be riding around day and night staring at the asses of a bunch of cows. But that's the hand I was dealt. I'm doing the best I can, Peg," she muttered as her fingertips drifted down the brunette's bare arms. With a smile, Peg leaned closer until their lips met. Clare felt her body react and she grasped Peg's shoulders, drawing her closer, inhaling the amazing scent that was uniquely Peg's.

"Come on to bed and get some rest now, sugar," Peg whispered. "I'll be there in a minute."

A moment later Clare felt Peg slide back against her and draped her arm around the woman's warm body. She liked the feel of Peg's naked body pressed against hers. She frowned as she wondered if Loretta's body would fit as well against hers and feel as soft.

THREE DAYS PASSED and there had been no sign of Clare. Loretta was becoming concerned even though work around the ranch seemed to be progressing as usual. Ino hadn't mentioned the incident at the stream again. He spoke to Loretta as he always had and shared dinner with her in the big house in Clare's absence. If he was worried about Clare's disappearance it wasn't evident to Loretta. That night over dinner, Loretta fidgeted with her food, pushing it aimlessly around on her plate. Periodically she glanced at the empty chair where Clare usually sat.

"She's okay," Ino said between bites.

"You've seen her? Talked to her?"

"She works the herd every day, same as always."

"But she hasn't been back to the house in days. Not since last week."

"Clare's fine. Just not eating as good as we are right now. I told her to come on back, but she won't. Says she can't."

"She's staying away because of me, isn't she? Because I'm still here."

"She doesn't trust herself."

Loretta gently set her fork on her plate and pushed away from the table. She took a deep breath and tilted her chin up slightly. "I won't leave until I speak to her."

Ino took a deep breath and puffed his cheeks out. "There's much you don't know about Clare McIlhenney. No one does."

"Except you."

"*Si.* I see many things." He wiped his moustache with a napkin and studied Loretta for a moment. "What have you heard?"

Loretta laughed. "Everyone thinks Clare is having sinful relations with not only you, but all of the men who work for her. That seems to be the most widespread rumor."

Ino nodded and smiled. "Also the oldest. It is true that I once offered to live with her as man and wife. To protect her property. She said no, but told me to tell the man at the Land Office I was her husband to get the property boundaries of her papa's land after he was killed. She was with me and I guess we convinced the land agent. As for the other men who work for her, there is nothin'."

"Someone told Cyrus she's killed people," Loretta said.

"That is true as well, but if you tell the sheriff or anyone else I will say you are lyin'."

"Surely she only killed to protect herself or her property."

Ino picked up his coffee cup and took a long gulp. He reached for the package of tobacco in the bowl in the center of the table and rolled a cigarette, striking a match before answering.

"Life here can be very hard. It was harder twenty years ago. If you're a woman it's twice as hard. What has Clare told you about what happened to her family?"

"Just that they were killed."

"Their wagon was alone and it was attacked by a group of riders who hoped to steal their horses and whatever else they would be able to get money for. I heard the shots, but arrived too late to help anyone except Clare. I patched her up the best I could." He rubbed his forehead. "You seen that scar on her head? She's got a worse one on her shoulder where I dug a bullet out. She wanted to hunt down the men who murdered her family. She could shoot a rifle, but not that good."

"When did you and Clare move here?"

"Soon as she could sit a horse. One day when she was mostly recovered, she went inside the wagon to get dressed. When she came out she was the Clare you see now. Put on her papa's pants and shirt. His boots, hat, and coat. Ain't dressed any different since then except to buy new pants or boots. Far as I know, I'm the last one who's seen her in a dress. She looked like a real lady back then. Kind of fragile. She decided to use her papa's old Henry rifle and practiced until she could hit a gnat in the ass at fifty paces. And real quick, too. We rode to town and got the boundary lines, then pulled the wagon here and got to work. Her papa had some money hid in the bottom of the wagon that got us started."

"What does that have to do with killing anyone?"

"Clare used to go to town at least once a month. I taught her to play some poker and she got pretty good. Wish I never taught her 'cause it wasn't long before trouble showed up."

INO AND CLARE rode into Trinidad to pick up a few meager provisions they could afford just ahead of a thunderstorm that was making its way over the mountains behind them. It was too late to stop at the dry goods store and they headed for the Cattleman's Saloon. A chill was in the air and a few drinks would warm them up. Ino went straight to the bar and ordered a drink. He turned around to see Clare join four men at a poker game.

Early in the morning they would saddle up and return to the ranch. He sipped from a shot glass of whiskey and felt the liquid burn its way to his stomach and hoped the cold rain that had started falling would let up by morning.

It was still early evening and the rainy weather kept the number of customers at the Cattleman's Saloon small. Ino heard the sound of horses outside and watched as three men, strangers in town, wearing slickers pushed their way into the saloon. Rain ran down the slickers and off their slouched hats. The spurs on the men's boots jingled lightly as they made their way to the bar and ordered drinks. Ino didn't recognize them and turned his attention back to the card game.

Once the men consumed a few shots and apparently felt warmer, they drifted toward the ongoing game. Between hands the players scooted their chairs around and invited the strangers to join them. Within a few minutes the slickers and hats were strewn across chairs at a nearby table and all but one of the strangers had anted up. It didn't take more than a few hands to wipe most the newcomers out. Ino had taught Clare well and she had paid attention. She knew the regulars in the game and was familiar with the way they played. Ino hoped she'd win a few dollars from the strangers. He picked up his drink and sauntered closer to the table and rested his shoulder against a nearby post to watch the action.

By the tenth hand and fifth round of drinks, money in the center of the table was stacking up as some of the players attempted to win back their losses in a single hand. From the look on his face, one of the new players must have believed he had a winning hand. He reached into his pocket and pulled out a small, red draw-string pouch and tossed it into the center of the table. An older man, one of the locals, reached out and picked up the pouch. He pulled out a gold necklace. Hanging from the necklace was a cream-colored cameo set against a dark pink background. Clare leaned forward to get a better look at the piece of jewelry. Ino saw her eyes narrow slightly stare at the man who had tossed it in.

"I won it in a poker game about six months ago," the stranger said with a friendly smile. "It must be worth somethin'."

Another player picked it up and examined it before passing it around the table for each player involved in the hand to look at. When it was passed to Clare her fingers seemed to caress the fragile filigreed gold chain. She turned the cameo over and looked at the back. Her fist tightened around it before she placed it back in the pouch and tossed it to the center of the table. When the hand played out the stranger who thought he had a winning hand was wrong. The winner scooped the chips and necklace from the middle and pulled the pot in front of him as the strangers stood and wandered back to the bar.

"I'll buy it from you," Ino overheard Clare say when the winner started to stuff the pouch into his shirt pocket. "Fifty dollars."

"Might be worth more than that," the man said.

"It's not," Clare said. "My mother had one like it."

Ino hoped the man would turn down Clare's offer. They really couldn't afford to waste the money. He held his breath as the man thought about it for a moment and then slid the pouch toward Clare. She picked it up as she stood and slipped it carefully into her pocket.

"Let's go," she said as she picked up her rifle and walked past Ino. A heavy mist settled in over the town as they wordlessly left the saloon and walked toward the livery where their horses were stabled for the night. Clare paid the stable boy and began saddling her horse.

"What's the rush?" Ino asked, belching from the drinks he'd consumed in anticipation of eventually falling into bed with one of the saloon girls.

"Something's come up," Clare answered. "If you're too drunk to go with me I can handle it alone."

"Naw. I'm good. Just need to take a piss is all."

"Go out back."

By the time Ino returned, the heavy mist had become a steady downpour. He pulled his slicker over his head and followed Clare into an alleyway near the saloon and waited. It was less than an hour before the strangers left the saloon and got back on their horses. They rode away with Clare and Ino following at a distance.

"Where we goin'?" Ino asked when they were out of town.

"Depends on how far they go," Clare answered without further explanation.

DESPITE THE MISTY, cold weather the cowboys eventually found a shallow overhang in the foothills outside Trinidad and started a small fire. Clare and Ino tied their horses in a grove of trees and silently made their way toward the campsite on foot. Ino heard the sounds of the men's laughter and cursing as they crept up on them. From behind a stand of brush Clare and Ino watched the men, although Ino still had no idea why.

"You sober enough to shoot?" Clare whispered.

"Yeah," Ino said with a nod.

"Then go over to that clump of bushes and wait for my signal," she said.

As the men began to settle down, Clare stood and brought her rifle to her shoulder. Ino stood a few feet to her left. "Don't move!" Clare called out.

One of the men reached for his rifle and she rapidly fired two rounds into the ground close to him, forcing his hand back.

"What do you want?" one of the men yelled back. "We ain't got nothing."

"Where'd you get the necklace you gambled with tonight?" Clare demanded, taking two steps closer.

"Won it in a poker game about six months ago," he answered.

"You're a liar!" she screamed and fired another round so close to his head that dirt flew up and struck his face.

"Who the fuck are you?" he hollered as he jumped back slightly.

Rainwater streamed from Clare's hat as she moved closer. "You stole it from my mother after you murdered her, my father, and my brother," she said *calmly. The coldness in her voice sent a shiver down Ino's spine.*

"That's impossible," another cowboy said. "Everyone there was..."

"Obviously not," Clare said in a hard voice.

"So now you're going to arrest us all?" the leader of the group laughed.

"No," Clare said. "Who was your leader? Tell me and you'll die fast."

When no answer came, Ino asked, "Now what?"

"If it takes all night, I'll get an answer. My parents and brother deserve justice," Clare spat. "Can you handle this?" she asked when she saw Ino rub his hand over his face.

"Yeah," he answered softly.

"Then stake them out," she ordered. She held her rifle on the men. When one of them reached into his jacket Clare shot him without hesitation. Ino ran to the man's body and rolled him onto his back. He pulled out a pistol and tossed it into the brush.

"Anyone else feel brave?" Clare snapped.

While she kept the remaining two covered, Ino tied them down spread eagle on the ground.

"You don't have to stay if you don't want to," she said when he rejoined her.

"What you gonna do?"

"One of them will tell me who their leader was that day even if I have to peel the skin from his body one strip at a time to find out."

"Let's take them back into town and turn them over to the sheriff," Ino pleaded. "You can't just murder them. It won't make you feel no better, Clare."

"I'll sleep like a baby. Did you take any other weapons off them?"

"Just this pig sticker."

She took the knife from him and anchored it in her belt. He grabbed her arm as she started to walk away. "What if you're wrong and these ain't the guys?"

"My mother's initials were engraved on the back of the necklace. I'm not wrong."

"He said he won it in a poker game."

"He said six months ago. In fact, he said it twice. When did you find me?" When Ino didn't answer she said, "Four months ago."

Without another word she strode to where the men were staked out. She stood over the first man and looked down at him. "I'm your judge and jury tonight. Who led the attack against my family?"

"Go to hell, bitch!"

A single rifle shot shattered the bone below the knee of his right leg. He screamed in pain as she chambered another round and brought the rifle to her shoulder once again, aiming higher on his leg. His arms strained against the rope holding him down. "Who led the attack against my family?" Clare repeated.

"Leave him alone!" the second man yelled. "He don't know nothing."

Clare turned and fired down at the second man, striking him in the thigh. "Shut up! It'll be your turn soon enough." She swung back to the first man. "Who was it?"

"I don't know. I only joined up with these men last month."

Another bullet ripped through his upper leg just above the knee, followed by another agonized scream. Ino was watching and beginning to feel sick to his stomach. He came up beside her and took a deep breath. "Stop," he said.

"Go stay with the horses," she ordered. "This might take a while."

"You're not any better than they are if you keep this up," Ino said through gritted teeth.

"No! They had a choice! Now go!"

She looked back down at the man who was now crying in pain. "I can shoot you lots of places that won't kill you right off, but you'll suffer. Tell me what I want to know."

"I...I don't know his name." Clare chambered another round. "I swear to God! I don't know his name," he begged. "He headed out on his own afterward and we ain't seen him since."

Clare turned the rifle on the other man. "What's his name?"

"TJ is all I know. Never knew his last name."

"Do you regret what you did?"

"You was easy pickings. All alone out there. You were asking for it," he sneered defiantly.

Ino saw Clare's face turn red with rage as she brought the rifle to her shoulder. "My brother was only eight-years-old. All he was asking for was a chance to live." Without another word Clare pulled the knife from her waist and knelt between the two men. She ripped open each man's shirt and drew the blade across their chests. Blood oozed to the surface of their chests and traveled down their sides. "I won't kill you, but you'll die soon enough," she said. She stood and looked down at the bleeding men before she strode away without looking back. Ino followed her a few seconds later.

"SO YOU SEE, *senorita*, Clare's not the woman people think she is. She can be kind, but, like everyone else, she has a dark side," Ino said with a sigh. "There are times when she can't control her anger."

"That's...horrible, Ino. And you never told anyone about that night?"

"No. Someone found them, still staked out, half-eaten by vultures and coyotes, and told the sheriff. But many days had passed. What could he do?" Ino said with a shrug.

"If they murdered her family then perhaps they deserved to die."

"Perhaps. But it is not my place to judge. She still looks at strangers wondering if they're the leader, TJ. I don't know what she'll do if she ever does find him. It's all she seems to live for sometimes."

"How did you find out that Clare liked, you know, other women?"

"By accident. Clare don't drink much, but one night a long time ago, maybe about twelve years now, we'd had a very hard month. Almost out of money, barely payin' the hands. About all we had left was a couple of bottles of whiskey we used mostly to clean out wounds on the cattle and horses. We was both tired and thought a few drinks would help us sleep. Next thing we know we drank just about all that rotgut. Sometimes too much whiskey can make you feel kinda sorry for youself. Next thing I know Clare is bawlin' like a baby about her folks, her little brother, their home in Pennsylvania, and some gal named Annalee. I wasn't feeling much pain by then myself and didn't think much of it. I already knew about her family and she told me a little about the farm they owned. Sounded real nice. Then she started telling me about how she was the reason her folks was dead. All because of this Annalee. Said the kiss didn't mean nothin', but I could tell in her eyes that it did to her. She said they was caught by Annalee's mama doin' something respectable girls didn't do. Guess Annalee's mama made a fuss and that's when Clare's folks up and moved west. Women who do something real shameful could be killed or at least run out of town. So I guess in Clare's head, whatever happened between her and Annalee made her folks move. Then they were killed and she survived. Been punishin' herself for it ever since."

"It wasn't her fault those men attacked her family."

"She don't see it that way. Don't want nothin' like that to ever happen again. Made me promise I would make sure she didn't fuck up. That's what I been doin' ever since except when we go to town and she stays with Peg."

"Peg?" Loretta was surprised, but remembered what the storekeeper had said about the only friends Clare had. Saloon girls and whores.

"Peg's been here almost as long as me and Clare. Clare likes her and I reckon Peg feels the same way about Clare. When we go to town I stay with Miss Mavis. So who am I to say anything if Clare spends time with a prostitute?" Ino shrugged. "That Peg. She can keep a secret better than anyone I know."

Loretta frowned. Clare spent time with a prostitute and that made it all right with Ino.

"If you don't see anything wrong with Clare spending time with Peg, a prostitute, then does that mean it's only all right as long as the other woman is a prostitute?" Loretta fumed.

"Whorin's a sin, being with a whore's a sin, what Clare does is a sin, so I guess if she has to do what she does, then it might as well be with a whore. Everybody has needs and Clare sure ain't no damn nun. I don't meddle in her private life."

"As long as it's only with a whore."

"Peg won't tell to save her own skin, so I don't interfere."

"So, if I was a prostitute, a relationship between me and Clare would be acceptable to you."

"Yeah, but you ain't."

Loretta wanted to throw her head back and laugh at the irony. She thought all her problems would be solved if she left her life as a prostitute behind and started a new life.

"Clare won't mean to hurt you, but she will," Ino said solemnly. There was a touch of sadness in his voice. "Clare's my friend and I would be happy to see her happy. I'll protect her with my life, but she can shut you out in a minute and you'll never know why. Then she goes away for a few days and comes back and acts like the same old Clare."

"Do you think she'll eventually come home, knowing I'm here?"

"Can't say. She's damn stubborn. If she don't want to see you or talk to you, she won't, and there ain't nothin' you can do about it."

Chapter Thirteen

ONCE BRANDING SEASON was in full swing, Clare and her men were out with the herd from dawn to dusk. When the men returned to the ranch at night they were almost too tired to eat, regardless of how wonderful the meal was. The herd was growing at a faster rate than anyone anticipated. The new fence between her property and the Garner ranch had made the herd much more manageable. That, along with using fence riders and night riders, kept the herd from being plundered.

Clare grabbed the lariat around the neck of a large calf and strode closer to the animal, then reached down and grasped its legs, lifting it slightly until it fell onto its side. She dropped her knee onto its flank and held it while Ino took the branding iron and pressed the design into its hide. Smoke rose lazily from the animal's skin as Clare stood up and released it to rejoin the herd. She wiped her forehead with the back of her gloved hand and waited for the next calf.

"Rider comin'!" Frank called out.

Clare bent down and picked up her rifle when she saw a trail of dust moving in their direction. Her nerves kicked into high when the wagon came into sight and she saw the woman handling the reins. "Take a break," she ordered.

Clare grabbed the traces of the two horses pulling the ranch wagon as Loretta drew the reins back. "What are you doing here?" Clare asked.

Loretta stepped carefully from the wagon seat and dropped to the ground. "My job. I thought you and your men might be getting hungry. And since you haven't seen fit to come home to eat for over a week I brought lunch to you."

Loretta walked swiftly to the back of the wagon and lowered the tail gate. "It'll be ready in a few minutes," she called out.

Once everyone had eaten their fill of Loretta's hearty beef stew, they drifted off to work again. Clare lifted the large cast iron pot onto the back of the wagon and secured it for the trip back to the main house.

"Thanks for bringing food out here. The men appreciated it," Clare said as she slipped a rope through the handle of the pot. Her eyes darted around searching for anything to avoid looking at Loretta.

"We need to talk," Loretta said as she wiped her hands on the skirt of her dress.

"Nothing to talk about. I need to get back to work."

"Nothing... I can still feel your lips on mine, Clare," Loretta said in a low voice. "Do you expect me to forget that? Have you forgotten?"

"It was a mistake, Retta. You shouldn't have come here and I shouldn't have let you stay. I knew what could happen."

"Please come home, Clare. I'll stay in the cabin until you leave each day. I promise you'll never see me."

Clare shook her head. "Don't you understand that I can't," she said, her voice cracking. Satisfied everything in the wagon was sufficiently tied down, Clare closed the tail gate and turned away to rejoin her men. Ino was right, Clare thought. Even if she allowed Loretta to stay, what could she offer her? A life spent hiding away from everyone, living in fear?

CLARE GUIDED HER horse up the incline of the low hills lying along the foot of the Sangre de Cristos. She was exhausted. The sky had turned a purple-gray as the sun sank behind the mountains, leaving only its shadow behind. A cool evening breeze drifted down the mountain from the higher elevations and she inhaled the scent of the trees around her as she moved higher into the foothills. She had once looked forward to being alone in the mountains, but now she made the journey with a heavy heart. Her feelings for Loretta, a woman half her age, had intruded on the stable, secure sameness of her life. What was it in Loretta's smile or laugh that made her feel warm inside? When their eyes met, even while working, Clare could never hold her gaze more than a few seconds, long interminable seconds. If she met Loretta's eyes longer than that she knew she would drown in them and be lost.

Clare shook her head and mashed her hat further down on her head, stopping her horse and gazing over her shoulder to the valley below. Far in the distance she could see wispy trails of smoke coming from a chimney, her chimney. She and Ino had picked every stone and set them in mortar to create the massive fireplace to warm them on the frigid winter nights. Now Loretta was there, humming some nonsensical tune while she prepared dinner. The humming brought a feeling of home to Clare and she secretly listened, almost expecting Loretta to burst into song any moment. Bringing her to the ranch had been a mistake.

Clare had to get away from the house to save her sanity. She had been so close, too close, to doing something she knew could never happen. Only Ino and Peg knew her secret and neither of them would ever tell. Now, Loretta knew as well and Clare wanted her to leave, to take her infectious laughter and leave.

She was exhausted and couldn't wait to fall onto the small bunk in the line shack where her mind wouldn't spend time thinking about hair the color of the richest honey, questioning hazel eyes, or anything else that reminded her of Loretta Langford. How had she let this happen? Her jaw was still tender where Ino had struck her, but he had only been protecting her from herself. She dragged the saddle and blanket from her horse and threw them over a railing in front of the shack. She released the horse into a small corral partially covered by a lean-to containing feed and water.

After seeing that the horse was fed, she brushed him and left him to rest before stumbling into the shack for rest of her own. Clare took in the interior of the shack. It only served to keep a person from freezing to death and offered no creature comforts other than the fireplace and a small bed with a straw-filled mattress. A bowl of water for washing up sat next to the bed. A lantern hanging from an overhead beam provided a dim light. Aside from the table and two chairs, there were no other furnishings. There were still dimly glowing embers banked in the small fireplace hearth. She set two logs over the embers and poked them to bring them back to life. While she waited for a meager meal of beans and jerky to heat, she washed her hands and face and pulled a book from the small table next to the bed. She stretched her legs out in front of her and took a deep breath. As soon as she ate something to stave off her hunger she was certain sleep would quickly follow.

The sound of a horse's hooves striking the packed ground in front of the shack brought Clare to her feet, reaching for her rifle near the front door. She leaned toward the front window and peeked out. A single rider. Maybe it was one of her hands letting her know there was a problem. She gripped the rifle in her hand and lifted the latch securing the door. She stepped outside and was surprised to find Loretta looking down from the prancing horse.

"What the hell are you doing here?" Clare snapped. "I almost shot you."

"I know you want to get rid of me, but that seems a little extreme even for you."

"Who told you where this shack is?"

"Ino."

"You're lying. He knows I don't want to see you."

"And he knows I'm not leaving. Are you ready to spend the rest of your life in this shack simply to avoid me?"

"You're fired! Now get the hell off my property. Or do I have to get the sheriff out here to remove your fuckin' ass?"

Loretta ignored Clare's rant and slid off the saddle. "I really need some pants if I'm going to ride a horse much." She bent her knees slightly to work her muscles back into the right place. "My crotch hasn't been this sore since..." she started. Her face flushed and her eyes avoided Clare's. "Well, in a long time. Got any coffee?"

"You're not staying. Head back to the main house before it gets any darker."

"Come back with me, Clare."

"I can't. Go back to town so we can all get on with our lives."

"You know that old saying about once a clock strikes, it can't be recalled?"

"What about it?"

"Lots of things are like that. Once a kiss has been given and accepted, you can't take it back. It's still there. I still feel it when I close my eyes," Loretta said.

Clare grumbled and opened the door to the shack. "Damn!" she said when she saw the burned remains of what would have been her meal. She dumped it into the fire.

Loretta took two cloth-wrapped packages from her saddlebags and carried them into the shack. She unrolled the packages and set out fresh bread and slices of beef and chicken, along with some fresh vegetables from her garden. She quickly set about heating the meat and vegetables over the fire. "I expect you haven't had much to eat since you decided to run away from home. You're thinner."

When Clare didn't respond Loretta looked over her shoulder and saw Clare standing in front of the main window, her hands shoved in the pockets of her denim pants. "Come and eat while the food's hot. If I have to bring your dinner out here every night I might ask for a raise in pay. You'd save money by simply coming home."

"I didn't ask you to come here so I don't know why I'd pay you extra for it. Maybe I should pay you extra to stay away from me." Clare picked up the plate of food and ate as if she hadn't eaten in a week, shoveling spoonfuls of food into her mouth. Loretta poured a cup of coffee and Clare washed the food down. She felt better. She missed Loretta's cooking. She missed seeing her face, her smile. And even missed that damn humming as Loretta worked around the house or in the garden. Unexpectedly, the temperature inside the small shack seemed much warmer than usual.

Now that she was alone with Loretta, Clare was at a loss for something to say. Following a few minutes of uncomfortable silence, Loretta stood up and looked down at her. Clare thought she saw a hint of sadness in Loretta's eyes and knew she was the cause of it. Loretta folded the cloth she had wrapped around the food. "Sleep well," she said. Her voice was so soft she wasn't sure she had really said anything as she walked to the door.

"Loretta," Clare said, needing to say something.

Loretta whirled around when she heard Clare's voice.

"Thank you," Clare finished.

"Just doing my job," Loretta answered.

Clare wasn't sure her knees would support her as she stood and moved toward Loretta. She brought her trembling hand up, hesitating briefly before daring to place it against Loretta's soft cheek. Loretta leaned into the touch of the rough hand as it stroked her cheek. The cloth in Loretta's hand fell to the floor between them as she leaned into the touch. Clare wrapped her arms around Loretta's waist, holding her tightly for a moment as warmth invaded her body.

Clare breathed in the scent of Loretta's hair and rubbed strands of the soft, amber hair between her fingers. The feel of Loretta pressed against her made her light-headed. It would be so simple to make the next move, to feel Loretta's lips against hers one more time. She shivered at the thought. Her thoughts were interrupted by the sound of horses rapidly approaching. She pulled Loretta's arms away and reached for her rifle. She motioned Loretta away from the door and peered out the window of the shack. She let out a long breath when she recognized the riders. She opened the door just as Ino was preparing to enter the shack.

"What's going on?" she asked.

"There's trouble. Dewey found where Garner's men cut the wire again. He started back to get some wire to fix it when old man Garner showed up with the sheriff and about a dozen men," Ino explained breathlessly. "Claims some of his cattle was grazin' near the fence and we cut it to steal his cattle."

Clare bolted from the shack and began saddling her horse. "Who's there?"

"Frank, Caleb, and the Burress boys. Zeke and me came to get you. Ain't been no shooting yet, but could be soon."

Clare swung into the saddle. Before joining her men she stopped briefly where Loretta stood in the doorway, outlined by the fireplace and lantern inside. "Can you make it back to the house alone?"

"Yes. Hurry and go," Loretta said.

FROM THE RISE overlooking the fence line separating her property from Garner's, Clare saw five small campfires along the boundary line. Kicking her horse in the flanks, she quickly covered the distance to her men and jumped off her horse, rifle in hand and strode to where her men were attempting to repair the break in the fence.

"Looks like you got some cheap barbed wire, Clare. Damn shit keeps breakin' on you," Thaddeus Garner said.

Clare picked up a strand of wire from the ground and examined it. She handed it to one of the Burress cousins. "It's been cut," she said. "Wonder who would have done such a thing?"

"Must be rustlers around." Thaddeus rocked back and forth from the balls of his feet to his heels. "My boys tell me a few head of my cattle wandered onto your side of the fence while it was down."

"And they know that because they just sat there on their asses and watched them without doing anything," Clare sneered. "Do you see any cattle?"

"No, but–"

"But what? Those same idiots sat there and watched one of my men drive your cattle through the fence and off to some unknown location without doing a fuckin' thing? I'd fire the whole bunch of 'em, if I was you. That is unless you're deliberately trying to start trouble."

"You gonna let that bitch talk to you like that, Pa?" Clement snapped.

"Tell that puke you call a son to shut the fuck up, Thaddeus," Clare said. She didn't want to start a fight, but knew she could provoke Clement. She also knew Thaddeus didn't hold his son in very high regard. The boy was a hot-head who started more trouble than he finished.

"Get on back with the men, Clement," Thaddeus ordered. "I'll handle this."

"Tell you what, Thaddeus, tomorrow when it's light, you and your foreman can come over here, through a gate of course, and check out any cows you see. If you find one with your brand that might have wandered onto my land, please feel free to take the poor lost baby home."

"And give you all night to hide them or alter the brand?"

"Look anywhere you want. You ain't gonna find a single steer with your brand. As soon as this fence is fixed we can all go home and get a good night's rest. I'll expect you early in the morning. This ain't worth fighting or killing over."

Thaddeus smiled. "You're right, Clare. We'll see you in the morning."

Clare watched as Garner and his men rode away. She turned to Ino and said, "Keep someone on the fence line all night, two if you think we need them. I don't trust that son-of-a-bitch as far as I can throw him."

IT WAS AFTER midnight when Clare unsaddled her horse and led him into a stall in the stable. She hadn't been back to the main house in over a week. She trusted Ino to take care of everything, but it felt good to touch the familiar walls of the stable. She walked into the main house and looked around. She'd missed her books and the comfortable chair she sat in to read in the evening. She wasn't sure how long she would have stayed away to avoid Loretta. She lowered her body into her chair and tapped tobacco into her father's old pipe. She loved the smell of the tobacco blend. She had helped her father mix it hundreds of times and although this blend wasn't exactly the same, it was close enough considering what she had to work with. She leaned her head back and watched the smoke from the pipe curl toward the ceiling and disappear. She reached onto the table next to her and picked up the book she had been reading when she began her self-imposed exile. She read until the tobacco in the pipe went out. Then she tapped the burned tobacco into the fireplace and got up. She made her way into the kitchen and stared out the back window. She could see the dark outline of the little cabin behind the main house from the light of a nearly full moon. She was tired. Tired of denying her feelings, tired of fighting herself, and tired of being alone.

Clare closed the back door of the main house quietly and walked toward the cabin. This was wrong. So wrong. She pulled the lever to the front door of the cabin up and opened the door far enough to step inside. She had lived in the cabin for ten years until the new main house was completed and knew it like the back of her hand. The small bedroom was in the right rear of the cabin and the door was open. When she looked into the room, her breath caught in her throat. Loretta's hair was splayed out over the pillow. In the dim moonlight filtering into the room Loretta looked like a peaceful child. An angel. A very young angel. Clare wanted to go to her and feel the softness of her skin once more before she fell asleep, but her feet remained rooted to the floor and finally she turned away to leave.

"Please don't go," a voice behind her said. "You've come home."

There was something in the way Loretta said the word "home" that drew Clare into the room. A vision of home filled her and she crossed the small room in three steps. She marveled at how beautiful Loretta was, even half hidden in shadow. Clare's breath caught in her throat as Loretta propped herself up on her elbows and looked at her. She reached out and took Clare's hand in hers. "Is everything all right?"

"No," Clare said as she squeezed Loretta's hand.

Loretta's hair hung down behind her and the look in her eyes was seductive. Clare sat on the edge of the bed, still holding Loretta's hand. "This is so wrong," she said as if to convince herself.

"Holding my hand?"

Clare shook her head slowly and leaned forward until her lips met Loretta's. Would she be as welcome this time as she had been the last? she wondered. The answer came as Loretta deepened the kiss and brought her body closer to Clare's. When the kiss ended Clare's lips moved lower to Loretta's jaw line and neck. She had never tasted anything so wonderful. She felt her body react, a familiar desire rising within her. But she felt frozen in place, afraid to act on what she was feeling. This wasn't Peg. Peg satisfied a physical need, but had never touched her soul. Clare was afraid she might not be able to control herself. She might hurt Loretta if she acted on her every desire.

"I don't want to hurt you," Clare mumbled against Loretta's neck.

"What do you want to do that could harm me?"

"Consume you. Take your body and make it mine. It frightens me," Clare confessed. "I'm not an animal. Yet what's inside of me feels like a captive animal looking at freedom lurking just beyond its cage. So close yet so far away."

"Touch me, Clare. Let me feel your hands on me. Let me set you free."

"What...what if I can't stop. Even if you want me to."

"I know you won't hurt me, but you're driving me crazy right now." Loretta wiggled around on the bed until she could pull her nightgown over her head. She ran her fingers through her hair and away from her face.

Clare's breathing came in gasps as her eyes took in Loretta's supple white breasts. They were there for the taking, the nipples puckering into hard dark knots in the cool air of the small room. "I want you," she rasped. "You're so beautiful."

"Then take what you want," Loretta whispered as she reclined against her pillow.

CLARE STOOD AT the window gazing out into the darkness. She rubbed a hand over her face as the memory of Loretta's hands on her body ran through her mind. It had been everything she'd dreamed it could be and more. It had been tender, yet raw. The sound of her name on Loretta's lips as she gasped with pleasure, the hunger in her eyes as she pulled Clare to her, the gentle fingers buried in her tangled, sweaty hair, the intoxicating scent of Loretta's body as she gave herself to Clare. How would she stand not knowing those feelings again? Buried in her thoughts, she was surprised to feel arms wrapping around her body.

"Go back to sleep," Clare whispered.

"Come back to bed with me. It's cold without you," Loretta said between kisses along Clare's back.

Clare closed her eyes and turned around. She took Loretta in her arms and kissed her roughly. "The sun will be up soon," she said when she released her. "I can't be here."

Loretta stepped back, the look in her eyes asking a question Clare couldn't answer.

"I'll get dressed and start breakfast," Loretta said.

Clare nodded and reached for her clothes. "You should go back to town," she said.

"I had planned to go into Trinidad for a visit next week."

"No. I want you to pack and stay in town."

"You can't be serious," Loretta said with a short laugh. "After last night I–"

"I want you to leave."

"Why? Did I displease you?"

"No. Of course not. What we had last night was beyond anything I have ever dreamed of. But it was all we could ever have. Don't you understand that?"

Loretta adjusted the blouse she'd slipped on and moved closer to Clare. "Look at me, Clare," she said. The look in Clare's eyes was anguished, begging Loretta to understand. "If what we had last night is all there ever is between us, it was still the best experience of my life. Don't you understand *that*?"

"I can't ask you to wait out here for me every night like some guttersnipe. That's all I can ever offer you and you deserve more."

"You don't have to ask. I know we can't be together any other way. It's what I want. To be here for you. Please don't send me away now."

Clare pulled her into her arms and held her. "When you decide it's not enough and leave, I'll understand. I'm sorry I can't give you everything you want or need."

"You've given me a home and yourself. I don't need more than that to be happy."

"I wish I could touch you outside of this cabin," Clare whispered into Loretta's ear, sending a shiver through her.

"I know you'll be touching me in your mind."

"Every minute of every day," Clare said with a smile. "Better get breakfast going. I seem to have worked up quite an appetite."

"Oh. And Clare?"

"Yeah," Clare said as she pulled on her boots.

"Next time you go into town, don't stay with Peg."

Clare's head jerked up, staring at Loretta with a shocked expression.

The corners of Loretta's mouth turned up in a seductive smile. "Did I forget to tell you I don't share well with others?"

Chapter Fourteen

EXCITEMENT AND A sense of celebration rippled through the growing town of Trinidad as the first of August, 1876 approached. Banners proclaiming it the "Centennial State" were beginning to appear along Main Street. On that date Colorado would cease to be a territory and would be welcomed as the thirty-eighth state in the Union. The fortunes of Trinidad were looking up. The railroad was inching closer every day and, when it was completed, cattle ranchers would be able to load their cattle and ship them to points north and east without the need for long and dangerous cattle drives. New businesses would come to town and, with them, new citizens.

Cyrus and Hettie had urged Loretta to make her monthly pilgrimage into town in time to join in the celebration. Reluctantly, Clare had given her hands a weekend off to join in the festivities, but remained behind alone on the ranch. Even though Loretta enjoyed the time she spent with her "family" in town, she hated being away from Clare. It had been a month since Clare came to her cabin the first time. Clare didn't come to her bed every night and still lived in fear one of her men would notice the time she spent with Loretta. But the times they spent together were indescribable.

With periodic help from the ranch hands, Ino, and occasionally even Clare, Loretta's chickens were laying. She brought fresh eggs into town for Cyrus and Hettie and even a few for Rosario. Her vegetable garden was producing and needed constant tending to keep out varmints and the ever-present unwanted weeds. It had been a dry summer and water had to be carried from the stream to keep her plants alive. It wouldn't be long before she would begin the process of storing food to get them through the winter.

While this trip should have been a happy one, Loretta couldn't get Clare and their new relationship out of her mind. As soon as Ino brought the buckboard to a halt in front of Cyrus' house, Amelia flew outside to greet her. The teenager danced around on the porch while Ino helped Loretta down and carried her valise and eggs up the walkway.

"Thank you, Ino," Loretta said. "I will see you after church on Sunday. Please give my regards to Mavis." She watched Ino blush as he nodded and hurried back down the porch steps.

"Oh, Loretta, it's going to be such an exciting weekend," Amelia exclaimed as she hugged Loretta tightly. "Hettie and I have been cooking for days. There's going to be a huge church social this evening. You've never seen so much food. There's even going to be a carnival. I've never been to one. Have you?"

Loretta could barely get a word in through the girl's prattering and she desperately needed a drink of water. Hettie swept out of the kitchen, drying her hands on her apron. She smiled when she saw Loretta and greeted her with a light hug and a kiss on the cheek.

"Living out there must agree with you. You look like you're simply glowing," she said.

"Actually, I'm quite tired even though all I've done all day is sit on my ass in that damned buckboard."

Hettie looked momentarily startled at Loretta's language. Loretta apologized and untied her bonnet when she saw the look on her friend's face. "It's awfully warm and I've had the sun beating down on my head for hours. I'm a little irritable."

"Amelia, dear, please bring Loretta a glass of that fresh lemonade we made." She placed a hand in the small of Loretta's back and guided her into the living room. "You'll feel much better once you rest a little and cool off."

"I'm sure I will. Is Cyrus home?"

"No. He and the elders of his church are setting up tables for the party this evening. All the churches in town have gotten together for the biggest party this town has ever seen."

"Amelia said you'd been cooking for days."

"It only seems that way to her. We only baked yesterday and today. Your friend, Mrs. Manning, and her husband are graciously providing most of the meat and preparing it."

"I'm glad the churches let them help."

"It was the Christian thing to do."

"I'm sure that's how they see it as well. When do you expect Cyrus home?"

"Not for a few more hours. If you need to speak to him about something urgent you can find him at the church."

"No. It can wait. I should help you prepare whatever you have left to do."

"You seem a little listless. Perhaps it was the sun. Why don't you go up to your room and take a nap. I'll wake you up in a couple of hours."

"Thanks, Hettie. I appreciate that."

Loretta drew the curtains closed and lay down on the bed. She rested her arm across her eyes. She didn't know what to do. How would she ever be able to explain? She was finally settling into the little cabin and thinking of it as her home. She loved where and how she was living. Clare was not the hostile, unsmiling woman everyone thought. Far from it, in fact, she thought with a smile. Rather, she had surprised Loretta with her tenderness and passion. When she and Loretta talked about books and the complexities of the stories, Loretta had been intellectually stimulated for the first time in years. Clare was a natural teacher, patient and open to Loretta's ideas and opinions.

Loretta smiled to herself. She had even seen Clare McIlhenney smile once or twice. In fact, Loretta was the one who made her smile. How would she be able to explain her feelings for the taciturn rancher to Cyrus? He already disliked Clare based on the rumors he'd heard about her. What would Clare think of her if she knew of Loretta's past? She was still deep in thought when she drifted off into a nap.

THE FESTIVITIES ON the grounds of the new city park in Trinidad were worthy of the event being celebrated. Loretta sat on a bench set beneath a wide tent and watched young children scamper over the grounds, trailing ribbons tied to sticks behind them. Women wearing colorful bonnets and long aprons stood behind makeshift tables which bowed in the middle slightly from the weight of the food they held. She couldn't help laughing at the antics of Willis and Rosario's three children. Each carried small bowls while their parents made repeated trips between the café and the park, their arms loaded down with platters of meat. Despite the alluring scent of Rosario's cooking Loretta had eaten very little. Hettie's fresh lemonade kept her body reasonably cool.

Loretta watched several men load bales of hay onto a wagon and hitch up a team of horses. Children began gathering nearby, but were sent away until the sun set. Then they could have a moonlight hay ride and watch the fireworks the city had brought in from Denver just for this special occasion.

"Are you enjoying the party?" Cyrus asked as he sat down next to Loretta and took a deep breath.

"It's wonderful, Cyrus. You've all done so much hard work," she answered with a smile.

"You haven't eaten much." He glanced at her plate.

"It must be the heat, added to the excitement. I'll eat more once the sun begins to go down."

Cyrus reached up and ran his fingers down Loretta's cheek. "Are you all right? You seem rather quiet."

Loretta looked down at her hands. "Actually, there is something I need to discuss with you. Perhaps tomorrow when everything has calmed down."

"Is something wrong at the McIhenney ranch? Have they done something to harm you?"

"No, no. Everyone has been wonderful to me, especially Clare and Mr. Valdez."

"I noticed that Clare McIlhenney is the only person who didn't see fit to attend our celebration."

"She was opposed to statehood so I can hardly imagine her celebrating it,' Loretta said.

"But the benefits cannot be..."

"Can we not discuss politics? It's such a wearisome topic for conversation," Loretta sighed.

"Of course, my dear, and certainly not a suitable topic for young women such as yourself."

"I have an opinion, Cyrus, but what's done is done. It's time to move on. People change, life changes, situations change. Often when least expected."

Cyrus took Loretta's hands in his and squeezed them. "So far everything has changed for each of us and all for the best it seems."

"Has it?"

"Of course! Coming to Trinidad has been the answer to all our prayers," he smiled benignly. "Let me find Hettie. We have something to tell you."

"As long as you promise not to pray for me any more."

"I cannot promise that."

"Then at least promise to pray silently."

LORETTA STOOD GAZING into the unused fireplace in the pastor's study on the second floor of the Trinidad Presbyterian Church. Dark walls shone from polishing. A small banker's lamp on the desk was turned on to provide some illumination. Loretta found the room oppressive and it matched her mood. While she waited for Cyrus and Hettie to join her, she moved to the window overlooking the park and opened the drapes a slit. What made her foolishly think she could leave her past behind? What was that old phrase her mother told her when she was younger? "Oh, what a tangled web we weave when first we practice to deceive." Until she left home, Loretta had never lied to her mother. There must surely be another proverb to explain what to do when your mother thought the truth was a lie. By not believing the truth, Mildred Digby had set her daughter on her future course.

When Hettie entered the study she smiled at Cyrus and moved to stand behind him at his desk.

"What was it you wished to tell me?" Loretta asked.

Cyrus gently slipped his arm around Hettie's waist and gazed up at her. "Hettie has honored me by agreeing to become my wife." Cyrus looked as giddy as a school boy.

"I wondered how long it would take you to work up the courage to ask her," Loretta said as she embraced each of them warmly. "I'm very happy for you both. Have you set a date yet?"

"The bishop has agreed to perform our ceremony, but he won't be able to make the journey from Denver to Trinidad until November," Cyrus beamed. "I hope you will join us on such a joyous occasion."

"I wouldn't miss it. Three months will pass quickly."

"I was hoping you would be my maid-of-honor," Hettie said.

"I'd be honored, Hettie," Loretta said with a smile. "Are you sure you wouldn't rather have one of the ladies in town?"

"There's no one I'd rather have stand as my witness than you."

"Who have you chosen as your best man, Cyrus?" Loretta asked.

"Elder Jessup. He has worked with me extremely closely while I was settling in and learning about my flock here."

LORETTA WAS QUIET during the ride back to the ranch Sunday afternoon. With the announcement of Cyrus and Hettie's upcoming wedding there hadn't been an opportunity to speak with Cyrus concerning Clare. Everyone else seemed listless as well, but she suspected their silence was due to an overabundance of alcohol and lack of sleep. When Ino helped her down from the buckboard, she carried her valise into her cabin and changed clothes. She checked her garden for weeds and fed the chickens before entering the back door of the main house to begin preparing supper. The house was unusually quiet and she wondered where Clare was. She still had a few hours before supper should be on the table and decided to make her favorite meal.

She walked outside and entered the wire enclosure Ino built for her chickens. She made soothing clucking sounds, waiting until she saw the chicken she wanted. It never strayed far from the feeding stations and as a result outweighed every other chicken in the coop. As a result its legs could barely hold up its body. She scooped the chicken up and carried it from the coop, away from the other chickens. "This is the price you pay for gluttony," she said as she twisted the chicken's neck, killing it instantly. Removing its head with a hand axe, she hung it by its feet to drain the blood and gathered wood to start a fire in a small fire pit behind the main house. She set a large black pot in the fire and made three or four trips to the nearby stream to fill it halfway with water. While she waited for the water to boil she went to the root cellar next to her cabin and found six large potatoes. She carried them into the house where she peeled them and placed them in a bowl of cold water.

By the time she returned to the fire to check the water, it was already boiling. She grabbed the chicken by the feet and immersed it in the hot water, holding it there several seconds. She rolled a short log closer to the fire and sat down to begin plucking the chicken. It wasn't long until her hands were covered with wet feathers and small down-like feathers floated in the air around her, catching in her hair. It was mindless work, but it gave her a chance to think. She loved the peacefulness around her. She dunked the chicken twice more to loosen the last of its feathers. She took a knife from her pocket and removed the feet and threw them into the fire. She pulled the innards from the chicken and disposed of them the same way. When she was satisfied the chicken was properly cleaned, she dipped her hands in the water to wash the blood off.

Inside, she rinsed the chicken carcass off again and placed it in a large pot on the stove to begin cooking. She was kneading dough for biscuits when the front door opened. She heard footsteps crossing the front room and then receding down the hallway. She smiled and hoped Clare liked chicken and dumplings.

A few minutes later Clare wandered into the kitchen and leaned against the door frame. "Did you enjoy your stay in town?" she asked.

"Yes, thank you. After being out here though, it was noisier than I liked."

"That's what happens when you go to town, I guess."

Loretta pumped water into the sink and washed her hands. Then she turned to look at Clare. "I brought you a present," she said.

"Why?"

Loretta was momentarily shocked by Clare's cool reception to her return, but shrugged it off. "Actually, it was a prize at the church raffle. A cowboy won it, but didn't want it, so I gave him the cost of his ticket and bought it from him," Loretta answered. It was a lie, but she didn't think Clare would accept it if she thought Loretta spent much money for it. "I'll get it," Loretta said. She saw the uncomfortable look on Clare's face as she moved past her and into the front room. She returned a moment later with a flat package tied with a yellow bow and handed it to Clare.

Clare untied the bow and removed the wrapping. Loretta watched her anxiously, looking for some sign that Clare appreciated the gift. Clare ran her fingers over the cover of the book in her hands. When she couldn't stand the silence any longer, Loretta said, "I saw other books by the same author on the bookcase near your chair and thought you might like this one. Have you already read it? Hettie says it's a very good book."

"It is," Clare responded in a soft voice. When she looked up, she said, "My mother had this book. It was lost when we came west. I've been wanting to replace it for years. Thank you, Loretta. I don't know what to say."

"Thank you is good enough." Loretta was touched by the look in Clare's eyes and turned back to her food preparation. "Perhaps after you read it, I could borrow it. Supper will be ready in about an hour."

Loretta glanced over her shoulder and Clare was gone. She wandered through the house until she found Clare lying on the bed. "Is something wrong, my love?" Loretta asked as she sat on the edge of the bed and rested her hand on Clare's chest.

"I had time to do a lot of thinking while you were gone, Retta. I want to make you happy, but I don't think I can."

"Why would you think that?"

"I want to live with you and love you as freely as any other couple would. Instead, we spend our time casting a glance here and there, sneaking a touch when no one is looking, while pretending to be something we aren't. I don't want to live that way. Do you?"

"Of course I don't, but what other choice do we have? I love you and if this is the only way I can do that, then I am contented. Is that why you seem so melancholy?"

Clare took Loretta's hand and kissed it. "All my life I haven't been able to live the way I've wanted to. I want that now more than ever, but I don't want you to be hurt. You could still find a good man who could show his love openly and without fear."

"I don't want a good man. I've already found the person I want, so you're just stuck with me."

Clare sat up on the bed and leaned in to taste Loretta's sweet lips once again. "Forever?" she whispered.

"Forever," Loretta whispered in return.

FOR THE NEXT few weeks work continued at the ranch at a steady pace. Loretta took care of her chickens and tended her garden. Occasionally she would find worms in the soil of her garden and save them to go fishing, serving fresh fish every two or three weeks. The fresh mountain air made Loretta feel healthier than she ever had. She picked and preserved the vegetables from her garden and dried fruit she had gotten from Hettie or one or two neighboring rancher's wives. Clare still came to Loretta most nights and their lovemaking was as passionate as ever, but clearly there was something unspoken on Clare's mind. Despite Loretta's best efforts, Clare refused to talk about what was bothering her.

One evening as Loretta finished preparing their evening meal, she noticed Clare pacing restlessly in the main room as if looking for a way to occupy herself.

"What's wrong, Clare?"

"Nothing," Clare answered. "I invited Ino to join us tonight for dinner. We need to talk about a few things concerning the ranch."

"Then I'll set another place at the table."

"I'll get it," Clare volunteered. Loretta had never seen Clare this nervous about having Ino join them for dinner before. When the knock came at the front door, Loretta saw Clare jump a little, almost dropping the plate in her hands.

Loretta caught the plate and said, "I'll get the door. Why don't you pour coffee for all of us," she said with a tender pat on Clare's back as she walked to the door.

Loretta took Ino's coat and gave him a brief kiss on his stubbly cheek when he entered. Clare approached him and handed him a cup of coffee.

"Why don't you both take a seat?" Loretta said. "I'll get

everything on the table."

Clare cleared her throat as she followed Ino into the dining room. "Smells good," Ino said.

Once the food was on their plates, there was no talking. Ino and Clare seemed grateful to have a way to fill the silence between them. Loretta looked back and forth between them and frowned. These very old friends sitting on either side of her could suddenly find nothing to chat about.

Clare finished her meal first and leaned back in her chair, wiping her mouth with a napkin. "I got a telegram from Pueblo a few days ago," she said. "About the herd."

"We gonna drive them north soon?" Ino asked.

"We won't have to. The army's sending an agent down to have a look at them. If he can contract enough cattle from this area, the army will drive the combined herd north with their own men."

Ino smiled. "It beats eatin' dust for a week behind a bunch of cows."

"I was worried about leaving the ranch unprotected while we were gone," Clare said as she glanced at Loretta. "I don't trust Garner."

"Wonder what the old man's up to," Ino said as he reached into the bowl in the center of the table and began rolling a cigarette. "Ain't seen hide nor hair out of him since that night at the fence line."

"Whatever it is, you can bet it's not anything good," Clare said as she finished off her coffee. She cleared her throat and added, "I'm moving Loretta into the main house before winter sets in."

Ino's eyes squinted as the smoke from his cigarette left his mouth and drifted over his face. "Think that's a good idea?" he asked.

"The cabin roof is sound, but when the snow is heavy it's cut off from the main house by deep snow for long periods of time. I've had to dig my way out many times in the past. She'd be safer in the main house."

"You're the boss," Ino said with a shrug. "Your decision, as long as you're ready to face the consequences." He look from Clare to Loretta and added, "Both of you."

Loretta's face reddened slightly. With Clare's announcement the room had become suddenly uncomfortable. "I have to go into Trinidad in November," Loretta said to change the subject.

"You go every month," Clare said.

"I might stay in town a little longer then. Hettie and Cyrus are getting married and I'm the maid-of-honor. You're both invited to attend with me."

"Congratulations," Ino said. He looked pointedly at Clare and added, "Maybe one day we'll celebrate your marriage, too, Miss Loretta."

Clare started to say something, but Loretta stood up and asked,

"Who's ready for some dessert?"

AFTER INO LEFT and the kitchen was cleaned once again, Loretta joined Clare who was sitting in her chair in front of the fireplace. Smoke from her pipe curled lazily above her head as she closed the book she had been reading and removed her reading glasses. She smiled when she saw Loretta. Although Loretta would return to the cabin soon, having her sit with her in front of the fire created the peaceful feeling of a real home. She would enjoy winter evenings alone with Loretta, no longer facing the solitude that had been her life for so long. It left her too much time alone to contemplate the twists and turns her life had taken, none happy until recently.

Even after twenty years the citizens of Trinidad still regarded her with distrust. She hadn't done much to encourage their friendship. She couldn't let go of the fight she had faced at every turn when she had tried to claim the property she believed was legally hers. Now the battle for control of her father's property continued more subtly, especially since the arrival of Thaddeus Garner ten years earlier. It seemed the minute he arrived in Trinidad he was after Clare's land.

"I finished reading *The Scarlet Letter* today," Loretta said as she set a cup of coffee next to Clare.

"Did you like it?"

"It was a very interesting story. I felt sorry for Hester and Reverend Dimmesdale, however."

"Why? They sinned and were caught. Do you think their punishment was undeserved?"

Loretta leaned closer to the fire and stared into the flames. "It seemed unfair."

"Hester committed the sin of adultery."

Loretta laughed, but there was no joy in it. "But she didn't know her husband was alive. Everyone sins. Whether being in love and expressing that love is a sin, I don't know. The story reminded me of being here."

"With me?"

"In a way." Loretta left her chair and lowered herself to the floor in front of Clare. "If what I feel for you is a sin according to some, then I am a sinner indeed. I have chosen gladly to be with you."

"There will always be those who break the rules of civilization. I suppose it all depends on how one handles what they've done," Clare said. "I've sinned many times and felt little remorse afterward."

"Did you feel like a sinner when you killed those men who murdered your family?"

"You and Ino must have had a very long talk," Clare said with a frown.

"We did."

"It felt like sweet revenge when I let those men die. But it didn't bring my family back to me. I hope they at least rested more easily in their graves knowing they weren't forgotten."

"Would you kill their leader, after all these years, if you found him?"

"Without a second thought. As bad as people think I am, I would never kill a helpless woman or child who could do me no harm just for the sake of a few coins."

"And what about your sin with me?"

"I would gladly suffer any punishment to continue sinning with you." Clare cradled Loretta's face in her hand. "Unlike Reverend Dimmesdale, I don't have a need to reconcile my actions with my beliefs."

Loretta smiled. "Perhaps next time we should read a book with less weighty moral issues. Will you join me later?"

"Of course."

Chapter Fifteen

THE ONE HORSE buggy topped the final rise before reaching Clare's ranch on a sunny, but brisk Saturday morning in mid-October. Clare was assisting Frank Carson re-shoe two of their horses. She heard the sound of the buggy approaching and looked up.

"Take a break, Frank," she said patting him on the back. "Looks like the agent from the army is finally here."

She walked slowly across the packed dirt between the stable and the main house, arriving in time to greet a man and a woman. She helped the woman step out of the buggy while the man stepped down from the opposite side.

"Thank you," the woman said in a soft voice with a slight southern drawl as she dusted her gloved hands over her dress and looked around.

"Carter Jamison," the man said as he approached Clare, hand extended.

"Clare McIlhenney," she replied as she shook his hand.

"This is my wife, Amanda. You certainly are a long way from town," Jamison commented as he brushed his hands together as if cleaning dirt from them. "Nice house."

"Thanks. Can I offer you a cup of coffee or something else before we get down to business?" Clare asked.

"We'd appreciate that. It's a dusty trip out here," Jamison said as he and his wife followed Clare toward the house. She opened the front door and held it as the two entered.

"Loretta!" Clare called out. When there was no response she said, "My housekeeper's probably tending her garden out back. I'll be right back. Please make yourselves comfortable."

Clare exited the back door off the kitchen and spotted Loretta, stooped over, turning the soil in her garden into hills with her familiar hoe. Clare stepped carefully to avoid stepping on anything that wasn't a weed.

"The army procurement agent and his wife have arrived," she said. She allowed her hand to linger a heartbeat longer than usual on Loretta's shoulder.

Loretta smiled up at her. "I baked a cake this morning hoping they would be here. I'll be right in."

A few minutes later, Loretta entered the back door and removed her straw hat, hanging it on a hook inside the door. She pumped water into the sink to wash her face and hands before taking cups and small dishes from a cabinet in the dining room. She cut a generous portion of cake for each dish and set the cups and dishes on a serving tray and carried them into the living room. She set the tray down and returned to the kitchen to get the coffee pot. She handed a dish and fork to Mrs. Jamison, then filled a cup with steaming coffee and set it on the table next to her. She repeated the same motions with the cattle buyer, but when she looked at him as she handed him a dish, her hand froze and her face blanched. By the time she was ready to pour his coffee, her hand had begun trembling. Jamison reached out and took the cup from her to prevent the coffee from spilling. Her eyes met his briefly and there was no misinterpreting the lascivious look she saw in his eyes. Carter Jamison was a portly man in his forties and fancied himself a great lover. Although Loretta had done what she needed to do to please him as a customer, Jamison had only been interested in taking her in ways she was certain his wife would never have allowed. His preferences bordered on the sadistic. He always requested Loretta and she had never been able to convince Jack that she was afraid of the man. His money had simply been too good for Jack to turn down. She may have been Jack's favorite, but like his other girls, she was replaceable and disposable.

Loretta handed Clare a dish, followed by a cup of coffee. "Is there anything else you need?" she asked.

"Won't you be joining us?" Jamison asked. "I'm sorry, my dear. I don't believe we've been introduced." He looked across the room at Clare.

"This is my housekeeper, Loretta Langford. You can stay if you wish, Retta," Clare said.

"I should get back to the gardening. Just leave your dishes when you're finished and I'll come back in for them later. It was nice to meet you both."

As quickly as possible, Loretta hurried from the room and went out the back door. How was it possible she would meet a former customer so far from St. Joe? Perhaps she should have kept moving west until she ran into the ocean. Perhaps she should have taken the train east instead. She tied her hat under her chin and leaned against the house, covering her eyes with her hands. God, what if Carter Jamison told Clare who she really was? No, he wouldn't do that. His wife was with him. What if he came back again alone while Clare and the men were away from the house? She should have told Clare everything about her past, about the prostitution that had kept her alive before it nearly killed her.

"How long will you be in the area, Mr. Jamison?" Clare asked.

"A week. I've already signed contracts with three other ranchers to take their herds. If you and I can come to an agreement my quota will be filled. Then my wife and I can perhaps take a day or two to see more of this beautiful area. How long have you been here, Miss McIlhenney?"

"Twenty years. It's taken a long time to build my herd up. If the army will drive the herds north itself it would be much faster than waiting for the cattle to be driven by each individual rancher."

"How many head do you figure you have?"

"A couple hundred," Clare said. "I don't want to deplete my herd. By next year I should have at least that number again. A steady supply. We can ride out and you can see them whenever you're ready. Mrs. Jamison will have to stay here, however. The cattle are still in the higher meadow and I'm not sure the buggy would make it. There aren't any real roads farther up."

"That's fine," Amanda Jamison said. "This cake is delicious. Perhaps I can get your housekeeper's recipe while y'all are gone."

"Yes," Jamison added. "Please offer her my compliments as well. She is obviously quite a talented young woman."

"I'll get a horse saddled for you. We should get back in time for you to return to Trinidad before dark."

BY EARLY NOVEMBER Clare's herd had been picked up by the army and driven north. Clare and her men began driving the remaining cattle into the lower pastures while Loretta put up the last of the vegetables from her garden and finished filling the root cellar. Ino and Clare slaughtered two of their herd for winter as well as deer and elk. Work would continue around the ranch through the winter, but at a slower pace.

Two nights before Hettie and Cyrus' wedding, Loretta snuggled down under the quilt covering Clare's bed. A light snowfall had begun earlier in the day and the smaller fireplace in the bedroom kept the room comfortable. There was always the danger that something might happen during the night that required Clare's attention, but it had become a risk both women were prepared to take.

"What are you thinking about?" Clare asked as she spooned closer to Loretta and draped an arm over her.

"How good you feel against me. How much I crave your touch."

Clare's hand tightened slightly around Loretta's waist, pulling her closer. "Close your eyes," Clare whispered.

Loretta smiled when she felt Clare's hand begin to roam over her body, teasing her nipples lightly and then moving on. "I'd much rather that was your mouth," Loretta breathed.

Clare's response was kisses along the back of Loretta's neck and down her back while her hand caressed Loretta's buttocks, kneading the soft skin. Loretta pushed back against her, encouraging Clare's hand to explore farther. Clare's breathing grew heavier when she found the wet warmth between Loretta's legs. Loretta groaned as the fingers teased her.

"Does this hurt you?" Clare asked, stopping her movements.

"I wish I could see your face. The way you look at me takes my breath away."

Clare rested her head against Loretta's and said, "I love you, Retta," as her fingers slid slowly inside. Loretta's hips began to move, forcing Clare's fingers deeper with each thrust. Loretta turned her head and buried it in her pillow to muffle the scream that erupted as she orgasmed. When her body began to settle down she rolled toward Clare and kissed her with all the passion she felt.

As the kiss ended, Clare brushed Loretta's hair back from her face and gazed up at her tear-stained face. "I knew I would hurt you," she said. "I'm sorry."

Loretta caressed her face. "You didn't hurt me. It was wonderful."

"Then why the hell are you crying?"

"That was the first time you've said you loved me. I never expected to hear that."

"I wouldn't be here with you, like this, if I didn't love you, Retta. I guess I thought you knew."

"I love you, too, Clare."

"I see it in your eyes every time you look at me."

"It's still good to hear it."

"I'll say it more often then."

"When we're alone."

"Then I can show you as well as tell you," Clare said with a smile.

"I DON'T KNOW why I have to practically lynch myself just to go to a wedding," Ino groused as he rode next to the buckboard Clare was driving.

"You look very dapper, Ino," Loretta said. "Mavis will be impressed."

"You think so?"

"I have no doubt."

Clare rested her elbows on her knees, leaning forward as she held the reins to the team of horses. "Clare looks quite attractive as well," Loretta added. "And you can both change into something more comfortable after the ceremony and reception." She leaned closer to Clare and whispered, "That's why I packed your work clothes in my valise."

Loretta pulled the quilt over her lap tighter around her. Certain no one could see her gloved hand move onto Clare's thigh and run dangerously close to Clare's crotch.

"Thank you," Clare muttered with a smile as Loretta giggled at her lover's reaction.

Nearly an hour later Clare drew back the reins and jumped down to help Loretta off the buckboard.

"Are you all right?" Clare asked as she gently lowered Loretta to the ground.

"Just dandy," Loretta said, rubbing her butt. "I think there were more potholes in the road this time."

"It only seems that way in the winter because the ground is frozen," Clare said with a smile. "Maybe you can borrow a pillow to sit on for the trip home. I can probably borrow one from Peg."

Loretta cast her a nasty look and slapped her on the shoulder. "I'm sure Hettie or Amelia will have one."

"That hurt, you know," Clare said with a chuckle as she rubbed her arm.

"Serves you right. You'll recover," Loretta mumbled.

"While you get settled I'll pull the buckboard around back and unhitch the team."

Clare watched Ino shove a finger into his shirt collar and wiggle it around. "You gonna need the buckboard to pick up Mavis?" she asked.

"Thought I'd get a buggy from the livery. Easier to get in and out of."

"Save me a seat in the church. Soon as Retta's fixed up and ready to go, I'll join you and Mavis."

"You sure it's all right if Mavis goes with me?"

"No one will start a fuss at a wedding. You staying with Mavis tonight?"

"Probably. I'll see if this get up works like Retta says."

"If you don't show up for the wedding we'll all know it worked," Clare said with a laugh.

A TALL, OLDER man with bushy, reddish-orange muttonchop sideburns and small glasses perched near the end of his nose stood at the front of the church, rocking back and forth slightly on the balls of his feet. His purple robe hung to the floor, a gold embroidered cross decorating the front of the garment as organ music filled the Presbyterian Church of Trinidad. His arms were folded across his chest cradling a large white *Bible*. The music, which had been playing as guests were seated in the sanctuary, stopped and the sound slowly echoed away.

"Please rise," the man at the front intoned. Clare, Ino, and Mavis rose from their seats. Everyone turned their heads toward the back of the sanctuary as the music resumed. Between the heads of other guests, Clare saw Loretta standing at the entrance, a large bouquet of flowers clasped in her hands. Her eyes scanned the filled church and a smile spread across her lips when she saw Clare. Loretta took a step forward and made her way toward the front, pausing after each step. She had almost reached the front when a side door opened and Cyrus and his best man walked to the altar and stood to its right side. Clare thought Cyrus looked nervous. He fidgeted with his hands as Loretta smiled at him and took her place to the left of the altar. When she turned to face the rear of the church, the music paused before beginning a majestic sounding anthem Clare recognized as familiar organ music she had heard at weddings as a girl announced the arrival of the bride.

Hettie stood for a moment at the back entrance to the church before stepping forward. Clare hadn't seen the demure school teacher more than a few times, and then only briefly, but today she looked radiant. Her white gown trailed on the floor behind her. The neckline sat halfway up her slender neck and was trimmed with what looked like tiny pearls. The same was true for the long sleeves that hooked over a finger on each hand to hold them in place. The veil that fell past her shoulders made it appear that she was walking out of a mist. Her face was solemn until Cyrus stepped forward to take her hand. Then she broke into a smile that lit up the room.

Clare didn't remember much of the ceremony once the man at the front began speaking. She spent most of her time staring at Loretta. Cyrus and Hettie exchanged rings and vowed to love one another and no other for as long as they lived. Cyrus gave Hettie a chaste kiss when they were finally declared husband and wife. Clare waited until all of the guests had departed for the reception before she made her way to the front to escort Loretta out of the church.

Loretta wrapped her arm around Clare's, grateful it was over. "Did that man talk longer than necessary or was it just me?" Loretta asked.

"I wasn't listening. I was watching you. You look beautiful." They made it to the entry of the church and Clare wrapped a warm cloak around Loretta's shoulders.

"I'm tired," Loretta breathed.

"Perhaps you should go back to Cyrus' house and lie down for a while," Clare suggested.

"If I lie down now, I'll never get up again. All I want is to go home and lie down in our bed…with you," Loretta said in a low voice. "But I have to make an appearance at the reception. I saw Ino and Mavis. Mavis looked lovely. Did she like Ino's clothing?"

"I don't think they'll make anything more than a brief appearance at the reception if the way Mavis was looking at Ino is any indication. I can't tell you how jealous I am that I can't act toward you the way I want to." The tone in Clare's voice was sad. "I wish I could tell the world how much I love you and how happy you make me, in every way."

"We know and that's enough for me," Loretta said, giving Clare's arm a squeeze. "But I do wish we could dance. I love to dance."

They laughed together until they reached Rosario's café which was closed to host the wedding reception. Willis even closed and locked the door between the reception and the saloon for the night.

When Loretta and Clare finally arrived at the café, they passed Ino and Mavis leaving.

"Want me to bring you a shot from the saloon," Ino asked.

"Punch no good?" Clare asked.

"Punch no liquor," he said.

"No thanks. I'll find something," Clare said. "See you tomorrow."

CLARE LEANED AGAINST the back wall of the café, sipping a cup of coffee and chatting with Rosario and Willis Manning. She was only half listening, distracted by how lovely Loretta looked. A few couples were dancing to music played on the piano Willis had moved from the saloon. Loretta had been trapped into one or two dances with older men who attended Cyrus' church. Loretta was a graceful dancer and the men with her seemed at ease. A hand on Clare's elbow drew her attention away from Loretta.

"May I have a moment, Miss McIlhenney?" Cyrus Langford asked quietly.

"Of course, Reverend." Clare excused herself from Willis and Rosario and followed Cyrus to a table away from other guests.

"I...I wish to ask a favor, Miss McIlhenney. I know I should have already done this, but with the wedding preparations and all, it slipped my mind," Cyrus said.

"I'll be glad to help if I can, Reverend," Clare said. "If you'll stop calling me Miss McIlhenney."

Cyrus smiled thinly and to Clare it didn't appear to be genuine. The man was being forced to ask a favor from someone he didn't care for much. Clare was sure it was more than a little difficult for the man.

"So what can I do for you, Cyrus?" Clare asked with a smile. After all, he was Loretta's brother-in-law.

"Well, Hettie and I are leaving tomorrow morning to spend a week in Denver. I have church business there and, well, we thought the trip might serve as a honeymoon for us as well."

"Mixing business with pleasure," Clare observed.

"Yes, well, in all the preparations I let an important detail slip by me. Amelia will be here alone for the week or so Hettie and I are away. I cannot allow that. She's still a child. I was wondering if you would allow Loretta to stay in town with her while we're gone."

Clare stood up and glared at Cyrus, suddenly feeling insulted. "I don't own Loretta, Reverend. She doesn't need my permission. Whether she wishes to assist you by staying with Amelia is up to her."

Loretta had been watching Clare and saw Cyrus approach her. They chatted for a moment and then Clare's demeanor seemed to change. Loretta excused herself from the group she was talking with and made her way across the dining area.

"Beautiful wedding, Cyrus," she said as she stepped up to stand next to Clare. "What's going on?"

"I was simply asking Miss McIlhenney if she would allow you to stay in town with Amelia while Hettie and I are out of town. She seems to have taken my request as a personal affront," Cyrus explained.

"Perhaps it was the way in which you phrased your request. I will be happy to spend more time with Amelia. I've missed her since I began my work at the ranch. But I would much rather bring her to stay with me than come into town. I can use her help decorating for the holidays and cooking."

"What about Mrs. Manning?" Cyrus asked. "She is Amelia's employer, after all."

"I'll speak to her, Cyrus," Loretta said, patting him on the back. Then she turned to Clare, her eyes sparkling. "Clare, I just had the most wonderful idea!"

When Clare just stared at her, Loretta continued, "By the time Cyrus and Hettie return from Denver, it will nearly be Thanksgiving. We should invite everyone to the ranch for dinner that day. Amelia can help me clean the main house and then with the cooking."

"Well, I don't..." Clare started.

"I'm not sure..." Cyrus sputtered.

"As you keep reminding me, Cyrus, this is a new life. That means new friends," she said looking at Clare, "for all of us."

"Please assure Miss Amelia that she will be welcome at my...our...home, as will you all," Clare said, feeling slightly overwhelmed.

Loretta mouthed a 'thank you' when she left to find Amelia.

Life as Clare had known it for the last two decades was changing quickly. Possibly it was changing into what it should have been. Yes, Loretta Langford had changed everything, she thought as she rested against a wall at Rosario's café. The people around her, guests at Cyrus and Hettie's wedding reception all seemed happy for the minister and the school teacher. They had been welcomed into the fabric of the town in a way Clare never had been. She frowned as she watched guests dance, laugh, and seem to enjoy one another's company. Overwhelmed by her own bitterness had she pushed them away, isolating herself from everyone. She didn't have much time to dwell on her lonely past before an enthusiastic voice next to her asked, "Don't you just love this time of year, Miss McIlhenney?"

Clare smiled when she turned and saw Amelia standing next to her, bouncing lightly on the balls of her feet, keeping rhythm with the music.

"I used to," Clare answered. "It's happier when you're with your family."

"Or when you start a new family," Amelia beamed.

Clare thought about it for a minute before nodding. "You're right,

Miss Amelia. When your family can't be with you, you can create a new family of friends. Do you miss your family?"

"Yeah, sometimes." Amelia's face turned solemn for a moment before brightening again. "I lost my family, but found a new one with Loretta, Cyrus, and Miss Hettie."

"I thought Cyrus was your brother."

"What? Oh, I meant our parents. Cyrus is a step-brother from our father's previous marriage," Amelia said quickly.

"Funny how you can feel closer to a friend sometimes than your own family."

"You mean the way you love Mr. Valdez?"

"I suppose. He saved my life and puts up with all my bullshit...I'm sorry."

Amelia leaned closer to Clare. "I've heard that and worse a thousand times," she said with a giggle.

"Have you been drinking, Miss Amelia?"

"Rosario and I had one shot to celebrate," Amelia said, holding her fingers up to show how much liquor she had imbibed.

"Well, don't get carried away. I'll pick you and Loretta up tomorrow morning."

LIGHT SNOW BEGAN to fall again before they reached the ranch again. Loretta showed Amelia the room she would be staying in while Clare got a fire going in the fireplace.

"Coffee will be ready in a few minutes," Loretta said as she joined Clare next to the fireplace. "I'm glad to finally be home."

Clare smiled at her. "I'm glad you regard it as your home. What did you tell Amelia about where you'll be sleeping?"

"Just that I would be sharing your room because it's closer to the kitchen and I have to get up very early to feed the men."

Clare looked around to make sure they were alone. She leaned down and kissed Loretta softly. "Not too early, I hope," she said.

Amelia and Loretta prepared a Thanksgiving feast that amazed Clare. She couldn't remember the last time she had looked forward to celebrating a holiday, but this year, thanks to Loretta, she had something to be thankful for. With fewer worries about the smaller herd, Clare felt free to spend more time at home, with occasional trips to take hay to the herd. The winter was milder than Clare expected and they had been blessed with average snowfall. It left the ground white and sparkling clean, but still maneuverable on horseback. For the first time for as long as she could remember, Clare looked forward to walking into her house each evening. Ino had even stopped making comments about what others would say if they knew about the relationship between the two women. Clare was suddenly determined to live her life without worrying about what others might say. She personally invited Willis and Rosario Manning and their children, as well as the girls from the saloon who had befriended her, including Peg.

Cyrus and Hettie looked radiant when they arrived by buggy at the ranch. After dinner, which consisted of numerous trips back for seconds and thirds by most of Clare's hands, Loretta and Hettie threw cloaks around their bodies and took a walk together to let their dinner settle.

"That was a wonderful meal, Loretta. We have so much to be thankful for this year," Hettie said.

"It's the new life we were all seeking. Are you enjoying married life?"

"Very much, but this is only the beginning. Cyrus is anxious to have children."

"Is that what you want as well?"

"I love children, but Cyrus keeps talking about the Twelve Apostles. I don't think I'm quite ready for that," Hettie said with a blush.

"Does he make you happy? That's all that matters."

A broad smile, accompanied by reddened cheeks, crossed Hettie's face. "I'm embarrassed to even think about how happy he makes me, Retta. I didn't know it was possible to feel so...so fulfilled and," she lowered her voice, "so wanton. Anything that wonderful must be sinful."

When Loretta began laughing out loud, Hettie pressed a hand over her mouth before the sound could draw anyone else's attention. Soon both women were reduced to subdued giggles.

"I'm so happy for you, Hettie," Loretta finally managed.

"Someday you will know the same happiness."

For the first time, Loretta wished she could tell someone that she had found happiness. "I know I will," she said instead.

They walked back toward the main house slowly. Hettie looked up at the gray clouds that were beginning to drift over the mountains. "It's been a wonderful day," she sighed. "But it looks like more snow may be coming. We should start back to town soon."

"It's been wonderful having Amelia with us this week. She seems happy and I hope you'll let her visit us again soon."

Hettie nodded and pulled her cloak closer as a cold breeze blew around her ankles. Loretta opened the back door to the house, but before she could enter she ran into Peg. Peg smiled at her and Loretta couldn't bring her eyes to meet Peg's. The saloon girl stepped aside and made way for Hettie to enter the house.

"I wanted to tell you that I appreciated the invite, Mrs. Langford," Peg said as she stepped outside. "I hope I didn't make the day too uncomfortable for you."

Loretta stepped back a little. "I'm sure Clare was happy you could join us," she said.

Peg looked back toward the house. "It's good to see Clare happy. And I'm pretty sure you're the reason."

"What are you talking about?"

"I ain't blind, honey," Peg said with a smile. "I've known Clare a long time."

"I'm aware of that," Loretta said more harshly than she intended.

"She's a good woman. She needs another good woman to take care of her and love her. I ain't been a good woman in a long time. Just take care of her."

Loretta wasn't sure what to say. "I will."

Peg laughed. "Don't worry, sweetie. Clare and I have talked and your secret is safe with me." She extended her hand to Loretta.

Loretta paused for a moment before she took the offered hand and gripped it firmly. "Thank you, Peg. I know Clare regards you as a friend. That won't change."

"But no more kisses," Peg snickered.

"Not on your life," Loretta said with a genuine laugh.

Chapter Sixteen

THE STAGE PULLED to a halt in front of the Wells Fargo office on Commercial Street in downtown Trinidad after dark. Even though there were street lamps on every corner along the main street, they didn't make the town look any more exciting than it usually did.

The stage from Pueblo had hit every pothole for the last sixty or so miles and by the time Jack Coulter gladly stepped from the carriage his body felt as though it had been beaten in a barroom brawl. He removed his bowler hat and rubbed a hand over his face. He glanced around the main street as he waited for his single suitcase to be tossed from the top of the stage. The coach carried a maximum of eight passengers. It was a moderately comfortable seating arrangement as long as all the passengers were thin. However, at least two of Jack's fellow passengers hadn't pushed away from the feeding trough for any extended periods of time. Jack had been squeezed against the side of the coach for several hours and his clothing reflected it.

"Where's the nearest hotel?" Jack asked as he caught the suitcase tossed down to him.

"The Columbian," the driver said. "Two or three blocks that way," he added with a jerk of his head.

"How about a place to eat and get a drink?"

"Down this street a couple of blocks. Rosario's is next to the Cattleman's Saloon."

Jack looked down at his clothing and decided he needed one or two stiff drinks to ease the dry taste from his mouth before he settled in for the evening. He grasped his small suitcase while thinking Carter Jamison would have hell to pay if he was wrong about Loretta being in Trinidad. Jack glanced in a few store windows while making his way toward the saloon. He drooled over the food he saw on plates as he passed by Rosario's, but continued on until he pushed through the main doors of the saloon. He stepped up to the bar and dropped his suitcase with a thud. He slapped some bills on the bar and waited for the bartender to fill two shot glasses with whiskey. He gulped down the first shot and then looked around the saloon while he sipped the second. He watched four men at a table dealing cards and smiled. If nothing else, Jack was a veteran poker player. Maybe he could recoup some of the money he had expended thus far in his search for Loretta Digby.

"Don't let their looks fool you," a young man leaning against the bar said. "They're old, but you'll lose your underwear if you get dragged into a game with 'em."

"Pretty good, huh?" Jack asked.

"Been playing poker since the game was invented." The young cowboy stuck his hand out. "Clement Garner," he said.

"Jack Coulter," Jack responded as he took the outstretched hand. "So what's exciting to do in Trinidad?"

"Leavin' it," Clement grunted. "Where you from?"

"St. Joe. I'm looking for someone. Heard she'd moved here a few months ago."

"Must be a good friend for you to leave St. Joe and come to the ass end of Colorado."

"No. She used to work for me in St. Joe. Then the bitch stole money from me and lit out. If I find her sorry ass I plan to drag her back and have her arrested. Name's Loretta Digby."

Clement tossed is drink down and motioned for another. "What's she look like? Maybe I seen her."

"Short with long hair the color of fresh honey. She's about twenty and has hazel eyes that can convince a man to do just about anything."

Clement smiled. "Sounds like a right fetchin' looking woman. Wouldn't mind if I run into her, but she don't sound familiar. Might've gone on farther west. What kind of work did she do for you?"

"She's a whore. Actually, my best girl until she pulled that stunt about stealing my money."

"Is that right?" Clement asked. "The sheriff's office is across the street. Maybe the sheriff can help you locate her."

"I'd rather handle the matter by myself. I wouldn't want anyone to think I was made a fool of by a whore, no matter how good she was in bed."

"Who's your friend, Clement?" a pleasant female voice asked. Jack turned toward the sound and removed his hat.

"This here's Jack Coulter from St. Joe. He's looking for an old friend," Clement said.

"You got something against makin' new friends, Jack? I'm Carlotta."

"It's a pleasure, Carlotta."

"I can make it that way if you're looking for company," Carlotta said seductively as she batted her eyelashes at Jack.

"If I wasn't starving for nourishment I might take you up on a little hospitality." Jack flashed her a rakish grin.

"I'll be here all night," Carlotta said as she dragged her index finger down Jack's chest.

"I'll remember that."

"Friendly town," Jack said as he watched Carlotta sashay slowly across the room.

FOR TWO DAYS Jack asked everyone he met about Loretta Digby

and no one seemed to know the name. Jack had taken Carlotta up on her invitation. While she was a whore, she wasn't Loretta. The more he thought about getting Loretta back and teaching her a lesson she'd never forget, the angrier he became, taking out his frustration and anger on Carlotta.

On the evening of his third day in Trinidad he returned to the Cattleman's Saloon. He saw Carlotta the moment he entered and gave her a smile. Carlotta quickly whispered to the older woman with her and made a hasty retreat upstairs. When Jack had his drink, the older woman approached him. No amount of makeup could hide the fact that she had been in the business well past her prime. From the looks of her she had probably been a heart breaker ten or fifteen years earlier.

"Ma'am," Jack said with a tip of his hat.

"Carlotta tells me you're a little...energetic when you're with her."

"I am a passionate man," Jack said with a wink and a charming smile.

"The bruises I saw on Carlotta's body don't suggest passion had anything to do with it."

"I suppose I did get a little carried away. I'll act differently the next time I'm with her."

"There won't be a next time. I won't ask any of my girls to put up with bad behavior," Mavis said, looking him up and down carefully. "And I'm sure they've all spoken to Carlotta by now. You should go back to St. Joe. Maybe they're more forgivin' there."

Jack grabbed Mavis' arm and pulled her closer roughly. "My girls never complain about how they're treated, especially by me. In fact, I'm only here long enough to find one of my former employees so I can charge her with theft. I don't suppose you know Loretta Digby? I'm surprised she's not working for you. My most popular whore until she took advantage of my good nature."

Jack saw something in Mavis' eyes briefly before she jerked her arm away. "Must have been passin' through town. You'll have to take your search elsewhere."

"Yeah. I'll do that.

Jack turned around and saw a young woman serving food at the café adjacent to the saloon. He smiled and walked away from the bar.

JACK COULTER WATCHED a slightly overweight woman leave the café, shepherding three young children, and lock the front door. From where he was standing in the alleyway across the street he would be able to see anyone leaving through the saloon doors. He had already checked the rear door to the café and found it locked as well. The door from the café into the saloon was the only remaining exit. He struck a match and lit a cigarette. Although he had seen Amelia, he was certain she had not seen him. Their reunion was likely to be a surprise, probably not a welcome one. One thing he was sure of was that if Amelia was still in Trinidad, Loretta wouldn't be far away.

By the time Jack finished his cigarette, the front door of the saloon swung open. Amelia turned and waved at someone inside before walking down the boardwalk. Jack dropped his cigarette and crushed it under his shoe. When Amelia crossed the street a block away, Jack stepped out of the shadows of the alleyway and followed her, staying in the shadows as much as possible. Gradually he closed the distance between them until he was a half block behind her. She paused momentarily at a street crossing before moving on.

Jack saw an alleyway a few feet from where Amelia was walking. She glanced down it before proceeding. In an instant Jack grabbed her from behind and pulled her into the alley, covering her mouth with his hand. She struggled briefly.

"Shut up or I'll break your fucking neck," he snarled in her ear. He turned her around and shoved her against the brick wall of the closest building. Although it was dark in the alley, Jack could see her eyes widen and saw the fear in them.

"Where's Retta?" he asked. "Don't scream," he added as he removed his hand from her mouth, but kept it close. "I just want to talk to her."

"You tried to kill her. I don't know where she is. She moved on and I stayed here," Amelia said between heavy breaths.

Jack slapped her. "I can hurt you in ways you can't even imagine, you little bitch. Retta wouldn't leave you here alone. Where is she!"

"I don't know, Jack."

"Retta's a thief. She stole from me. I can have you arrested as her accomplice."

"I didn't do anything."

"You're a whore, Amelia. No one will believe you." He curled his hand into a fist and slammed it into the girl's abdomen.

The blow took her breath away. When Jack grabbed her by the throat and pushed her forcefully against the wall again, tears filled Amelia's eyes. "Please Jack. Don't hurt me any more," she whimpered.

"Then tell me where Retta is! With just a couple of words everyone will know what you were in St. Joe and you'll lose this idyllic little life you've begun. Is that what you want?"

"No. Everything here is normal. Please."

"Where...is...Retta?" Jack asked again, emphasizing each word slowly.

"She...she doesn't live in town. She works on a ranch outside of town."

"Is she fucking the cowboys? Setting up her own little whorehouse?"

"No. She's a housekeeper at the McIlhenney ranch."

"Well, that's a total waste of a damn good piece of ass." Jack laughed. "If you never want to see me again go on home and don't mention our conversation to anyone." He took Amelia's face in one hand and squeezed it tightly. "Understand?"

Amelia nodded and left the alley as fast as possible.

LORETTA EXTRACTED HER hands from a new batch of dough for bread and washed her hands, preparing to get back to her daily household chores. Clare came down the hallway from the master bedroom. She grabbed her coat and picked up her rifle, pushing the lever-action to check the ammunition. Satisfied, she set it down and shoved her weathered hat on her head.

"Going out?" Loretta asked as Clare began buttoning her coat.

"Ino and me thought we'd see if we can scare up an elk. We saw a small herd near the lower meadow yesterday."

"Will you be gone long?" Loretta asked as she walked Clare to the door.

"I don't know."

Loretta grabbed the front of Clare's coat and pulled her down into a hungry kiss. "That's so you won't forget to come home to me. Will you return in time for supper?"

"I'll be especially looking forward to dessert," Clare said with a smile.

Clare stepped off the porch and made her way to the stable, where Ino was waiting for her. She shoved her rifle into its case hanging from the right side of the saddle before swinging herself up and settling into the saddle. Loretta stood on the porch and watched Clare and Ino until they disappeared over the top the hill leading away from the house.

Loretta's life with Clare had settled into a comfortable existence. She ran her hand across the back of Clare's rocker, her favorite spot each evening, whether she was gazing into the flames deep in her own thoughts or using the glow of the fire to illuminate whatever she was reading.

She had just checked her dough and begun cleaning when there was a knock at the front door. She hurried across the main room and pulled a curtain back to see who was at the door. Clement Garner stood on the porch with hands shoved in the front pockets of his heavy coat, looking around. Knowing how much Clare disliked the young man, Loretta leaned her back against the door, scarcely daring to breath.

A fist banged at the door. "I know you're in there, so open the damn door!"

Loretta unlocked and opened the door no more than a crack. "Can

I help you, Mr. Garner?" she asked.

"I'm sure you can," Clement answered with a smile Loretta didn't like. He placed a hand on the door and shoved against it with his shoulder. Loretta retreated slightly as he looked around the front of the house before stepping inside and closing the door.

Loretta looked at him. "What do you want?"

He smiled and licked his lips as his eyes moved slowly from her head to her feet. "I had an interesting conversation with an old friend of yours the other night."

Loretta grew increasingly uncomfortable with the way the cowboy stared at her. "You should leave. Clare doesn't like strangers in her house," she said.

"Well now, she ain't here, is she?" Clement took his hat off and hung it on a peg on the wall. "Besides, you let me in, just like any good little whore would if she wants to get paid," he said, stepping closer to her.

He reached out and took her wrist, pulling her closer to him. With one hand secured around her waist and the other holding the back of her head, he forced her into a bruising kiss. The stubble on his face rubbed abrasively against her skin and she pushed him away. When he tried to grab at her again, she slapped his face to bring him back to his senses. "Stop it!"

Faster than Loretta would have thought possible, Clement swung his arm and backhanded her hard enough to knock her down. As she wiped a hand across her mouth to check for blood Clement drop-kicked her in the ribs, knocking the breath from her lungs, bringing back frightening memories of Jack's beating. Clement rolled her onto her back, leering at her as he unzipped his pants and knelt on top of her. "Jack said you're the best ass he's ever had," Clement said. When she heard Jack's name she stopped fighting momentarily. She resumed struggling when he began pulling her dress up. He slapped her again and jerked her legs apart.

Even though her ears were still ringing from being hit, Loretta heard the sound of a rifle being cocked to seat a round. When Clement looked up, Clare was standing in the door, her rifle pressed tightly against her shoulder, aiming at him.

"Get your ass up!" Clare ordered through clenched teeth.

Loretta scooted from under Clement and pushed her dress down. Never taking her eyes off him, Clare said, "Take his gun."

Clare took a step into the room keeping the rifle leveled at him. Loretta removed Clement's revolver as he slowly got up with his pants halfway down his legs.

"Leave 'em!" Clare ordered as he reached down to pull his pants up.

"Come on Clare," Clement said with a smile. "She's a whore. Hell, I'll even pay her."

"The blood on Loretta's face tells me different," Clare said as she gripped the rifle tighter and took a step closer.

Loretta managed to get to her feet and wrapped an arm around her ribs. They ached, but she'd been hurt worse. She looked at Clare and then at Clement, anger building inside her. She straightened the skirt of her dress and walked toward him, stopping in front of him, glancing down. She smiled and leaned closer to him. "No wonder you have to pay for a fuck. You're pathetic," she laughed.

Loretta saw Clement's facial muscles twitch at her comment. Suddenly, filled with humiliation and rage, she grabbed his arms and brought her knee up solidly against his crotch. As his face contorted in pain and he fell to the floor grabbing his privates, Loretta leaned over him. "No one will *ever* rape me again and get away with it! The next time you come near me I'll kill you myself, you son-of-a-bitch!"

Clare was startled by Loretta's outburst, but kept a wary eye on the man writhing on the floor. She glanced at Loretta, who was breathing heavily and shaking with anger. Loretta looked up and saw the question in Clare's eyes before she turned away and made her way to the bedroom.

Clare snatched Clement's shirt collar and unceremoniously dragged him out the front door of the house, depositing him half-naked in the dirt. She saw Ino unsaddling his horse next to the corral and motioned him over. He trotted toward her and stopped abruptly when he saw Clement, still tenderly cradling his crotch.

"Get this piece of shit off my property." She leaned down and grabbed a fistful of Clement's hair and pulled his head closer. "That's the second time that woman has kicked you in the crotch, Clement. Next time I'll save her the trouble and shoot your dick off."

"She's a whore," Clement croaked. "And a thief."

"What the fuck are you talkin' about?" Clare asked. She clenched her hand into a fist and drove it into Clement's face to shut his filthy mouth.

"There's a guy in town lookin' for her," Clement said, spitting the blood from his mouth.

Clare released Clement with a shove, walked back in the house, and slammed the door. She leaned against the front door and took a deep breath. She made her way to the bedroom she had been sharing with Loretta for the past two months and cracked the door open enough to see Loretta. "Are you all right?" she asked quietly.

She saw Loretta's red-rimmed eyes when she glanced up and nodded. "I'm fine," Loretta said. "I'll be fixin' dinner in a little bit."

"Want to tell me what Garner was talkin' about first?"

Tears filled Loretta's eyes and she couldn't bring herself to look at Clare. "Before I came to Trinidad I worked as a whore for Jack Coulter in St. Joe. He beat me and raped me. Cyrus isn't my brother-in-law and Amelia isn't his sister. Amelia and I were prostitutes working for Jack.

Cyrus was one of my customers and saved my life after the beating."

"So everything you've told me has been a lie?" Clare asked.

"Only the part about my past." Loretta looked up, her eyes begging for Clare's understanding. "I wanted to start a new life and I couldn't if anyone knew about me."

"What are you planning to do now? Run again?"

Loretta shook her head slowly. "I'm tired of running, I can't hide forever. I need to speak to Jack." Loretta sighed and stood up. "I'll stay in town with Cyrus and Hettie."

"Is that what you want?"

Loretta spun around and glared at Clare. "Of course it isn't what I want! Now that you know the truth the best thing I can do is leave as quickly and quietly as I can. I didn't want to leave my home or work for Jack. I hated the life I had to live to survive. I didn't have a choice then. I don't have a choice now. If I stayed I'd only hurt the people I care about."

Clare stepped across the room and stood in front of Loretta. "No one would be hurt if you stayed."

"You don't think the people in Trinidad won't start wagging their tongues once they know what I am? Cyrus will be run out of his church. He and Hester will be forced to leave town. And what about Amelia? She's just a kid. But worst of all, you will always know you're sleeping with a whore."

"Don't say that. You're not a whore."

"But I was, Clare, I was," Loretta said softly. "Would you be able to put the thought of others touching out of your mind? Touch me the same way again? But I'm not a thief."

Clare's eyes squinted. "And I'm a murderer. Do you think they'd like knowing that any better? Are you afraid of me, knowing what I did to those men? Knowing what I'd do if I found their leader?"

"You had to do what you did to get justice for your family," Loretta objected.

"You had to do what you did to survive." Clare put her fingers under Loretta's chin and lifted it to look into her eyes. "I'll take care of it."

Loretta grasped Clare's forearm. "Don't get involved."

"I already am."

CLARE WAITED UNTIL dinner was over before saddling her horse and heading to Trinidad instead of riding out to check her herd. A man Clement had called Jack Coulter was in town looking for Loretta. It was after dark when she reined the horse to a stop in front of the Columbian Hotel. She was out of the saddle and approaching the door before her horse was fully stopped.

"Is Jack Coulter here?" she asked at the front desk.

"I think he's left to have dinner and visit the Cattleman's," an older man Clare recognized from past poker games answered.

Before he could respond further Clare ran out the door again. She vaulted onto her horse and turned toward Commercial Street. She pulled her rifle from its case as she stepped down from the horse once again and strode onto the walkway that ran in front of the saloon. Willis and Mavis looked up when she entered and nodded as she strode toward the bar. Clare motioned to Willis for a drink as she glanced around the tables.

"You lookin' for Jack Coulter?" Mavis asked as she sidled nonchalantly up to the bar.

"Word gets around fast," Clare answered before tossing her shot back and wiping her mouth with the back of her hand.

"What's he been saying?"

"He claims he's here to take Loretta back to St. Joe so she can be arrested for stealin' money while she worked for him," Mavis answered. Clare noticed, gratefully, that Mavis didn't mention what Loretta had once done for a living.

"Has he filed that bullshit with Sheriff Beutler?"

"He told Clement Garner he didn't want to involve the sheriff."

"I expect the sheriff will be looking for me later tonight anyway. I roughed Clement up some when he tried to force himself on Loretta this afternoon while I was gone. Thaddeus won't be happy with how he looked when he got home."

"Everybody knows Beutler works for Thad. What are you gonna do?"

"Nothin' yet."

"Maybe you should talk to Reverend Langford. They all came to town the same day and Amelia hasn't been to work at Rosario's in a couple of days."

"Maybe she's sick."

"Rosario's kids say she's been at school."

"What time does Coulter usually come in?"

"Later than this. Maybe in another hour or two." Mavis rubbed the bridge of her nose. "He's a rough one, Clare. I had to tell him my girls were off limits."

Clare pushed away from the bar. "I'll be back."

CLARE STEPPED UP to the front door of Cyrus Langford's home. She pounded on the heavy wood and waited for someone to open it. She knocked on the door twice before the door finally cracked open.

"You all right, Amelia?" Clare asked. "I heard you haven't been to work in a couple of days."

"Yeah. I just needed a few days off. Working and going to school is wearing me out," Amelia said softly, careful to keep her face in the shadows.

"Reckon you'll be rested up by the time Jack Coulter leaves town."

"What? How do you...," Amelia began.

Clare saw that Amelia's lower lip was cracked and there seemed to be small bruises on the teenager's cheeks. "Reverend Langford home? I need to speak to him...alone."

"Yeah. He's here," Amelia said as she opened the door. "You can wait in his study."

Clare removed her hat and walked into the study. She twirled the hat in her hands and stared into a small fire glowing in the fireplace. A few minutes later she heard the doors of the study slide closed.

"What can I do for you, Miss McIlhenney?" Cyrus Langford asked.

"I wanted to talk to you about Loretta. And Jack Coulter."

"I don't know anything about Jack Coulter."

"He's in Trinidad. Got here a couple of days ago. Right before Amelia took some time off work."

"She hasn't been feeling well." His demeanor didn't change although he did find something interesting to examine on his desk.

"I know you and Loretta aren't related," Clare said matter-of-factly.

"Not blood related, no."

"Not in any way except as a prostitute and her customer."

"What exactly are you implying?" Cyrus demanded.

"Loretta told me she was a prostitute who worked for Coulter and that you were one the men who paid for her services. And that you saved her life."

"It's not what you think."

"It's not my place to judge you. What about Amelia?"

"I have never been with Amelia. She's only a child, for God's sake!"

"Coulter plans to take Loretta back to St. Joe and have her arrested for stealing from him."

"That's ridiculous! Loretta never took anything from Jack. She wasn't even conscious after he assaulted her. He tried to kill her once and he'll do it again. We should go to Sheriff Beutler. If I know Jack, he got one his customers who's a judge in St. Joe to issue a warrant for Loretta's arrest."

"The sheriff won't do anything."

"I need to talk with Jack. His pride is hurt because he lost his most profitable girl."

It hurt Clare to hear Loretta described as if she was a piece of merchandise, but she managed to keep her demeanor calm. "I'll take care of it, but thought I should warn you there could be trouble."

CLARE SWUNG HER leg over the saddle and turned her horse back toward the saloon. She had no doubt that the evening wasn't going to turn out well for someone. It was possible she wouldn't make it back home alive.

She tied her horse to the railing outside the saloon and walked to the back of her saddle to get her rifle. She reached up, but before she could withdraw it from its case her arms were seized and a thick arm wrapped around her neck. Her horse danced nervously around when she was spun around and slammed into its side. A fist plunged into her abdomen that drove the air from her lungs. The strong hands released her and she fell to her knees, gasping for air.

She was finally pulled up by the collar of her shirt. She blinked her eyes open and stared into the face of Thaddeus Garner. She caught a glimpse of Clement's bruised face over his father's shoulder.

"You shouldn't have hurt my boy," Thad hissed.

"He tried to rape my housekeeper. He's lucky I didn't cut his balls off," Clare managed.

Clement Garner lunged at Clare and his fist snapped her head back. "She's a fucking whore!" Clement screamed at Clare as she spat blood from her mouth. "Ain't that right, Jack?"

A mustachioed man wearing a suit and vest and hat that rode low on his forehead stepped out of the shadows. "That's correct," he said. "As well as a thief."

"Then get Beutler and tell him so he can arrest her," Clare said.

"I'm taking her to St. Joe and let the sheriff where the crime occurred arrest her ass," Jack said.

"We got things to settle here first," Thad said. "You assaulted my son. I can't let you get away with that, Clare."

"He was trespassing on my property. Loretta can testify to what he tried to do to her."

"You ain't even got a title to that property and no one's going to believe the word of a whore. You must be getting' soft, Clare," Thad said with a chuckle. "Let her go. We'll take care of several problems at once. No one will be upset to see you gone, Clare. Now get your rifle!" he ordered. Thad pulled a pocket watch from his coat pocket and flipped it open. His eyes shifted up to see the look on Clare's face. "You been wondering why I wanted your property. I knew who you were the first time I laid eyes on you. If I could get your ranch, you'd go away. But you're too goddamn stubborn for your own good and now I'll have to kill you."

Clare stared at the watch in Thad's hand and then back up at her nemesis. "You're gonna die tonight, Thad. I've waited twenty years. I killed the others and now it's your turn." She brought her boot up and pushed him backward a few steps. Before he could react she pulled her rifle from its case and rolled under her horse's belly.

Thad reached for his pistol, but it didn't clear its holster before

Clare squeezed off two rapid shoots, striking him in the chest. Clare's shoulder and leg burned as bullets struck her. She forced her body up and fired over the saddle of her frightened horse, watching as Clement Garner and one of Garner's men fell to the ground.

"Clare!" Mavis' voice called out. "Behind you!"

Before she could turn to face the danger behind her, a shot rang out, the force of it knocking her to the ground. As she fell she saw the smoke from Jack Coulter's gun and fired a shot in his direction. The echo from her final shot sounded as if two guns had been fired. Clare scrambled behind a water trough in front of the saloon. Suddenly there was a flurry of activity and gunfire. She glanced around the trough. She didn't see Jack Coulter and looked around to find him. A block away she caught a glimpse of a woman's silhouette holding a rifle, a hint of smoke still curling from its barrel. By the time Clare blinked the woman had disappeared down an alley next to where she stood.

"Don't move!" Sheriff Beutler ordered. His pistol was aimed at Clare's head. She laid her rifle down, but was unable to stand up. Willis came out of the saloon and went to her side.

"Put that damn pistol down, Beutler," Willis said as he and Mavis covered Clare's wounds with towels to staunch the bleeding. "And get the damn doctor!"

Clare didn't remember much about the incident when she woke up the next day in the doctor's office, shackled to a bed. She hurt too damn much to do anything other than suck in her next breath.

While she shifted her eyes around the room, Mavis' face appeared over her. "How you feelin', sugar?"

"Like shit," Clare rasped.

"Coulter and Thad are dead, but Clement and their hand will recover. The others skedaddled out of there."

"Looks like I'm under arrest," Clare said with a glance at the shackle around her leg.

"We'll straighten it all out. I sent for Ino. He should be here soon."

All Clare could manage was a nod. "I'm tired, Mavis."

"Go back to sleep, honey. Beutler will want to talk to you later."

CLARE WAS EXHAUSTED. It had taken her twenty years, but the murder of her family was finally avenged. Now, as she lay in the bed of Dr. Wayne's clinic, she wasn't sure she had anything else to live for, but wished she had her father's pocket watch. What if it hadn't been his watch, only one that looked like it? Then she had killed Thaddeus Garner for nothing. Was she so wrapped up in her search for vengeance that she had gotten carried away? The door to her room opened and Sheriff Beutler walked in. His face was grim when he stopped next to her.

"Looks like you're gonna survive, Clare," he said, his voice deep and gravelly. "Enjoy it while you can. You're charged with two counts of murder for Thaddeus Garner and Jack Coulter."

"They were trying to kill me. I was defending myself," Clare said, refusing to look at Beutler.

"Thad's pistol never left his holster and Coulter was shot in the back. Don't sound like self-defense to me. If I was you, I'd find myself a lawyer. Even if the jury don't decide to hang you, prison won't be no picnic either."

"Get out," she responded. "I don't need a lawyer."

"Suit yourself. Soon as you can walk I'll take you to the jail until the trial starts. Probably in a few days. Doc Wayne can check on you there."

As soon as Beutler left, Doc Wayne stepped into the room. "Time to check your bandages," he said. "Can you sit up?"

"Yeah," she answered. Wayne placed a hand behind Clare and helped her up.

"It's only been a few days, but everything seems to be healing just fine," the doctor said as he listened to her breathing and changed the bandages on her leg and arm. "You were lucky the bullets didn't hit anything vital."

"They'll probably hang me anyway," she said as she released a breath. "Thanks for takin' care of me, but I probably would have been better off dyin'."

"Dying's never the best option."

"It is when there's nothin' left to live for."

"You have visitors again. You ever going to allow them in?"

"Nothin' to say."

"They're worried about you. Give them a break."

"I don't want to see anyone," Clare insisted.

Wayne nodded and held his hand against Clare's back as she lay down again. He left the room and she heard the sound of loud voices arguing from his office. A few moments later the door to her room burst open and Loretta stomped toward the bed.

"Why won't you see us?" Loretta demanded as she approached the bed.

"Got nothin' to say. You should stay with the reverend and his family."

"The men still have to be fed and they're all worried sick about you."

"Get out," Clare said without conviction.

"No! We need to get a lawyer to defend you."

"Nothin' to defend. I shot and killed Thad. He never had a chance. Then I shot Coulter in the back while he was trying to get away. Ain't much defense for that. Just leave me alone."

Loretta leaned closer and said, "What about me? What happened between us didn't mean anything to you?"

"It's only important that no one ever know. Then you can get on with your life."

"I don't want a life without you and I know you didn't shoot Jack in the back."

"You weren't there so you don't know shit! You don't know me as well as you think. I know what I did and will face the consequences for my actions. Now leave me the fuck alone!"

Loretta had tears forming in her eyes, but brushed them away before she turned to leave.

"Tell Ino the ranch is his. He should marry Mavis and give her a real home," Clare said softly to Loretta's back.

Chapter Seventeen

LORETTA PACED UP and down the boardwalk in front of the Wells Fargo Office. The telegram promised the attorney would be on the stage arriving in Trinidad that day. Loretta remembered her own journey into town less than a year before. The final sixty miles had been tortuous and she regretted having to ask anyone to make the journey. Especially in the winter. Snow had begun falling in earnest earlier in the day and there were no signs it would let up during the evening. Perhaps in another year or two the train would finally make its way into the growing town, although Loretta had to admit the train ride wasn't much more comfortable than the stage.

Loretta came into Trinidad as soon as she heard the news about the shooting and had been staying at Cyrus' house near the church. It seemed that everything had changed. Amelia and Cyrus were unusually quiet.

"Why don't you go inside and sit down?" Hettie asked. "Pacing won't make the horses run any faster and it's freezing out here."

"I know, but I can't stand the idea of Clare sitting in a jail cell not even trying to defend herself. She's tough, but she's not a cold-blooded killer."

"Does she know this lawyer is coming?"

Loretta bowed her head slightly and studied her hands. "No," she answered softly. "I told her I knew someone who might be able to help, but she refused. She won't talk about what happened that night with anyone. Including me."

"An attorney from St. Louis will be expensive. What if Clare refuses this attorney completely?"

"I'll find a way to pay the fee. I have some money saved up."

"How did you find this attorney anyway?" Hettie asked.

"We met in St. Joe," Loretta said. Before she could explain any further, she heard the crack of a whip and looked up to see the team of horses pulling the Wells Fargo coach turn onto Main Street. "They're here. I hope."

The two women stepped back from the edge of the boardwalk and waited for the driver to bring the team to a halt in front of the office. Loretta tried to remain calm as she waited for the driver and shotgun rider to climb from their seat atop the stage. The driver jumped down and opened the passenger door to drop the steps down while the shotgun rider began lifting bags from the rear baggage compartment.

A tall, handsome man, almost pretty actually, in his early thirties stepped from the coach and snow began accumulating on his hat and shoulders immediately. He removed his hat and thumped it against his leg. As he reseated it on his head with one hand, he extended his other to assist a second passenger from the coach. Loretta smiled when she saw a woman's head lean out of the passenger compartment and take in the surroundings of their final destination. A moment later the woman's eyes found Loretta. She broke into a broad smile as she stepped from the stage. She said something to the man and walked toward Loretta, engulfing the younger woman in a warm embrace.

"It's wonderful to see you again, Retta," she said softly, placing a light kiss on Loretta's cheek.

"I'm sorry it's under these circumstances, Jo," Loretta said. She stepped away from the handsome woman she had only met one other time and turned toward Hettie. "Jo, this is my friend Hettie Langford. Hettie, this is Josephine Barclay, the attorney I sent for."

The two women exchanged pleasantries and waited for Jo's luggage.

"I have a room for you at the Columbian Hotel," Loretta said. "I didn't know anyone would be with you."

"Ah, yes. This is my legal assistant, Mr. Ripley Sinclair," Jo said as the young man joined them on the boardwalk and sent their luggage down. A dazzling smile added to his attractiveness. He removed his hat, exposing a neatly trimmed shock of black hair.

Loretta and Jo walked arm-in-arm away from the stage office toward the hotel, followed by Mr. Sinclair and Hettie.

"Ripley and I can share a room," Jo said. "We've done so many times in the past. His presence has saved me from an embarrassing situation on more than one occasion. We'll need to be close so we can work on putting together the pieces of our case."

Loretta glanced over her shoulder at the people behind them. "He's very attractive."

"If you're interested in him, I'm sure I can arrange something, my dear," Jo grinned. "However, I should warn you that he has a penchant for gentlemen."

"Then he's going to be very lonely in Trinidad. Why is he here besides to carry your luggage?"

"Ripley is an excellent attorney in his own right and Colorado isn't exactly friendly toward female attorneys. He will be my voice in court while I direct him from behind the scenes."

"I hadn't thought of that," Loretta frowned.

Jo leaned closer. "Perhaps I might interest you in spending some time with me while I'm here," she whispered.

"As tempting as that certainly is, Jo, I asked you here only for legal assistance."

"A shame. I can hardly wait to meet the woman who won your heart."

"I haven't won her heart. I thought I had, but now she won't even talk to me except to tell me to get out. She doesn't know I sent for an attorney to represent her. Frankly, I was a little surprised you agreed to come."

"I have to admit this is a little off the beaten path, but I thought it was the least I could do for the woman who gave me such a memorable night. I think of it often."

"You paid well for that night. More than I was worth," Loretta said, blushing slightly.

"You're very attractive when you blush, my dear. Your friend must be a fool."

Loretta laughed. "She's concerned about my reputation if anyone in Trinidad discovers my past."

"What has she been charged with?" Jo asked as she nodded to a passerby.

"Two counts of murder."

"And who were the victims of such an obviously heinous crime?"

"Thaddeus Garner was a rancher whose property abuts Clare's." Loretta paused for a moment before speaking again. "The other was Jack Coulter. He found me and came here to have me arrested, presumably for stealing from him, which, by the way, I never did."

"I believe you," Jo said with a smile. "If anything, he stole from the customers his girls serviced. Quite exorbitant." She glanced at Loretta. "But I would have gladly paid twice the amount to be with you."

The party arrived at the Columbian Hotel and waited as Ripley registered and received their room key. He handed the key to a young man in a deep red jacket and blue pants. They followed him up a flight of stairs to their room and waited until he set their luggage at the foot of the bed. Ripley handed the bellboy a tip and flashed him a suggestive grin.

Jo removed her hat and placed it on the dresser across the room from the bed. When they were finally alone, Jo sat on an upholstered chair and stretched her legs out in front of her. Ripley opened a leather briefcase and took out a pad of paper and a pen before sitting in a straight-back chair next to a small table under the room's window.

"Okay, Ripley, we have a double homicide charge. I'll need you to find out everything you can about Thaddeus Garner, a rancher, and then everything you can about the movements of Jack Coulter after he came to Trinidad. I am already familiar with his business in St. Joseph. If I need to I can contact a friend in St. Joe for more details."

Jo turned her head and looked at Hettie, her expression benign. "Are you comfortable speaking in front of Mrs. Langford?" she asked Loretta. "I'm not sure of her connection with this situation other than being a friend."

"Hettie knows what I did for a living in St. Joe. Her husband was one of my customers when I first met her. She helped save my life. However, her reputation and that of her husband could be seriously compromised if the entire town knew about their past involvement with me and what I was."

"Hm. That could make things slightly more difficult. Mrs. Langford, have you and your husband discussed how you might be affected if you had to testify at the trial?"

"We have and while I wouldn't relish being forced to leave Trinidad, we will do what we have to to help Loretta."

"Loretta's not the one on trial," Jo said. "I'm more concerned with how you can help Clare McIlhenney."

"I...I don't know her very well, but I trust Loretta's judgment."

"Ripley," Jo said returning her attention to her assistant. "I don't yet know our client's opinion about having an attorney. Do you think it would be best for you to speak to her first?"

Ripley shook his head. "I will have to be there, of course, but I think she will respond more freely if talking to another woman."

"If she'll agree to speak to either one of us. Will she tell us the truth?" she asked Loretta.

"I'm not sure. I know what she's done in the past and I know why she shot Thaddeus Garner."

"And why was that?"

"Revenge. She believes Garner was the leader of a group of marauders who murdered her family twenty years ago. Anything else she knows she'll have to reveal to you herself. She admits she shot at Jack, but I don't believe she shot him in the back. Willis Manning and Mavis Calendar might have witnessed the shooting. I have no idea what they saw though."

"We might have to assist in a jail break to get this one off," Ripley quipped.

"Clare's ready to die if found guilty," Loretta said. "I don't know how much she'll assist in her own defense."

"Goodie," Jo exhaled. "We'll go to the jail after we've had a chance to change and rest a little. The road between Trinidad and Pueblo was damned bumpy. I'll feel much better after a hot soak. Why don't you come back in about three hours, Loretta, and accompany us to the jail. I'm sure Clare trusts you more than she will us."

RIPLEY SINCLAIR ENTERED the Trinidad jail followed by Josephine Barclay and Loretta.

Sheriff Beutler leaned back in his chair when they entered. His deputy, Monroe Hardcastle, leaned against the door leading to the prisoners' cells.

"What can I do for you?" Beutler asked.

Ripley removed his hat and dropped it on the sheriff's desk. "My name is Ripley Sinclair and I'm here to speak to my client, Miss Clare McIlhenney," he announced.

Beutler looked over his shoulder at Hardcastle. "Is that right? I didn't know Clare had hired an attorney."

"My associate and I need to speak to her privately."

"What about her?" Beutler asked, pointing at Loretta.

"Miss Digby is here in case we need a few points clarified," Ripley answered smoothly. "Otherwise she will remain here."

"You got any credentials?"

Ripley reached into the inside pocket of his coat and handed the sheriff a folded copy of his license to practice law as well as an order from a Denver judge which gave him permission to practice in Colorado. Beutler read over the two documents and handed them back to Ripley.

"Let 'em in to see the prisoner, Monroe."

Hardcastle pushed the door open and motioned them inside. "Can't miss her. She's the only prisoner," he said as he closed the door behind them."

As soon as they were alone, Jo stepped in front of Ripley and walked to a cell two down from the entrance. Clare was lying on a cot, her back to the cell door.

"Miss McIlhenney?" Jo asked.

"Go away," a voice answered.

"My name is Josephine Barclay. I'm an attorney from St. Louis. My associate is Mr. Ripley Sinclair. We've been hired to defend you."

Clare rolled over and stared at the two attorneys. "I didn't hire an attorney and I don't want one. You made a long trip for nothin'."

"Truthfully, we were hired by Loretta Digby to work on your behalf," Jo explained. "She's convinced you're innocent and wants you to receive a fair trial."

Clare launched her body off the cot and grabbed the bars of the cell. Jo was startled when she saw her client face-to-face for the first time. "I heard you had been shot. What happened to your face?"

"I tripped."

"And you fell on your face, apparently more than once." Clare's nose looked as if it had been broken without being reset and a puffy face surrounded two black eyes. Dried blood caked her split and swollen lower lip. "Ripley, we need to get the doctor here right away."

"He can't do nothin' for me," Clare snapped.

"Your nose is broken. He can reset it unless you want to spend the rest of your life breathing from your mouth." Jo looked at her associate. "Now, Ripley."

Ripley left the cell area quickly. When he was gone Jo said, "Now do you want to tell me what really happened?"

"I slipped and fell into the bars with my face."

"Who helped you do that?"

Clare gave her a lop-sided grin. "A couple of real pissed off, law-abiding citizens."

"Where was the sheriff when this attack occurred?"

"Makin' his rounds and havin' a beer over at the saloon, I suppose."

"He left you alone in the jail. For how long?"

"An hour or so."

"The doctor's on his way," Ripley said when he returned to the cell. "Miss Digby is upset and a little adamant about coming in."

"No!" Clare said loudly. "I don't want her in here. That's my right isn't it? Not to have any visitors?"

"Well, yes, but surely you want to see Loretta."

"No, I don't."

"Is there a photographer in this burg?"

"I think so. Why?"

"I need to have pictures taken of your face so I can press charges against the sheriff for negligence."

Clare laughed. "No judge will accept that case and you know it."

"Colorado is a state now, Miss McIlhenney. There are laws in place to protect citizens from assault, no matter the circumstances."

Doctor Wayne arrived at the jail and examined Clare's injuries, old and new. "I'll have to re-stitch the bullet wound on your leg, Clare."

"Please don't reset the nose until I tell you to, Doctor," Jo requested.

Jo and Ripley left the cell area and rejoined Loretta in the office. Jo whispered to Loretta, who nodded and left. She returned half an hour later accompanied by a middle aged man carrying a camera over his shoulder.

"What's this shit?" Beutler demanded.

"I believe this gentleman is a photographer with the local newspaper. He's here to photograph your prisoner, Sheriff. Apparently, she's the clumsy type. I want her injuries documented for the record, just in case she should accidentally run her face into the bars after we leave," Ripley explained.

The photographer, a man named Lester Pennington, looked nervously at Beutler as he followed Jo and Ripley into the cell area.

"All right, doctor," Jo said after Pennington was gone. "You can reset her nose now. Can you estimate how old the injuries to her face are?"

"Less than twenty-four hours I'd guess," Wayne said as he snapped Clare's broken nose back into alignment. "It'll be about a week before the bruising fades and the swelling goes down," he said. "She has numerous bruises on her torso as well and they weren't there when Beutler brought her here. She couldn't possibly have gotten them by tripping and falling. If you need me to I'd be more than happy to give a statement or testify to that."

"Ripley, take the doctor's statement while I confer with our client," Jo said in a low voice. "Use one of the empty cells."

Clare leaned back against the cell wall behind her cot. Jo pulled a wooden crate closer to the bunk and sat down. "Clare, I need to hear your version of what happened the night Thaddeus Garner and Jack Coulter were killed."

"I shot them before they shot me," Clare answered.

"Why would they want to shoot you?"

"I had a fight earlier that day with Garner's son. I caught him in my house where he was attempting to rape my housekeeper."

"Loretta Digby," Jo said rather than ask.

"I guess so. She told me her name was Loretta Langford and that she was Reverend Langford's sister-in-law when I hired her. I learned the truth that same day."

"Did you go looking for Garner?"

"No. I came to town looking for Coulter. Garner was a bonus."

"Did he attack you for fighting with his son earlier in the day?"

"He had a couple of his men rough me up some then told me to get my rifle. I'm not sure what he had in mind, but it probably wasn't getting killed."

"According to the report of the incident, Garner didn't have a chance to draw his weapon."

"That's right. Obviously he wasn't fast enough."

"Witnesses say you shot him twice before the others had a chance to open fire. Is that correct?"

"Sounds about right."

"So you don't deny you killed him?"

"No."

"Truthfully, Clare that isn't going to help your case."

"Thaddeus Garner was the leader of a bunch of marauders who attacked my family twenty years ago. They murdered my parents and my eight-year-old brother. He was carrying my father's pocket watch the night he died. I couldn't believe the damn thing was still working after all those years. When I saw it that night I took justice and I'd do it again in a minute. I gave him a better chance than he gave my family."

"You can't take the law into your own hands."

"Sometimes that's the only kind that works. Thad Garner was a powerful man around here. He's been trying to run me off my property since the day he came to Trinidad."

"What about Coulter?"

"He came to town a few days before I shot him looking for someone he said had worked for him and stolen money from him. He wanted to have her arrested and sent back to St. Joe to stand trial. Once he started asking questions around town, it would have destroyed Retta's reputation as well as that of Reverend Langford and his wife and the young girl living with them. At the very least they would have been forced out of town."

"What do you know about Loretta's past before she came here?"

"Nothin'. After she was attacked by Clement she told me she was a prostitute and worked for Jack Coulter, but had never stolen money from him. I believe her. No matter what happens to me, I don't want any of them dragged into it."

"They may have to testify at your trial."

"No! I'll plead guilty. If you want to waste your time defending me then fine. But the minute you ask them to be a witness, I'll stand up in court and confess. I admit I shot at Jack. But that was after he'd already shot me. At best my shot was a wild one."

"The record shows he was shot in the back."

"The bullet must have gone through him and the doctor was confused. No one else but me could have shot him."

"Without witnesses to the whole incident you haven't left me with much to work with," Jo sighed. "The prosecution will almost certainly call Clement Garner to testify against you. If Jack told him about Loretta's past the town will learn the truth anyway."

"Guess I should have killed him too instead of just wounding him."

"That sounds pre-meditated, Clare. Don't say that to anyone else. You've given me quite a few things to look into and I'll do the best I can to prevent a hanging. You sure you don't want to see Loretta?"

"Positive. Everyone in town thinks I'm crazy already. I can't think of any reason to change their minds now."

"Not even to save your own life?"

"I don't have a life any more. I thought I did for a while, but it was only wishful thinking."

"Do you love Loretta?"

Clare barked out a laugh. "If I admitted something like that, I'd be hung as a pervert and you know it."

"She's a beautiful woman."

"She's a *girl* and confused. She was temporarily led astray by an older woman who took advantage of her." Clare's voice was resigned and bitter. She lowered her eyes and rubbed them with the heel of her hands. "She'll find a good man to care for her when this is all over and live a normal life. I'm tired and would like to get some rest now."

"I'll be back tomorrow," Jo said as she stood up. "By the way, was there an inscription on your father's watch?"

"Some initials and a date. T. M. from A. M. 2/14/1856. It was a gift from my mother the year we moved west."

LORETTA WAS DISAPPOINTED when they returned to the hotel a few hours later. She hadn't been allowed to see or speak to Clare since her arrest. Jo placed her satchel on the bed and removed her hat.

"Ripley, would you be a dear and let me speak to Retta alone for a few minutes?"

"I'll look over the notes I took today and make of list of witnesses we need to speak to."

"Good. See if you can arrange meetings with them sometime this week."

Ripley gathered a few papers and stuffed them into his briefcase and left the hotel room.

Jo poured water into the bowl on the dresser and washed her face, drying it slowly with a small towel. "Clare doesn't want to see you, Retta."

"But why?" Loretta said, exasperated. "She knows how much I care about her."

"She's trying to protect you," Jo answered with a slight grin. "Or at least protect your reputation."

Loretta laughed bitterly. "It might not sound very lady-like, but I'd say that was already shot to shit. Jack's told everyone I'm a whore and a thief. I haven't been involved with anyone other than Clare since I arrived here last May."

" Jack's dead and he can't repeat it now."

"People will believe him. Hell, Clement Garner believed it enough to attempt to rape me and he's still alive to spread the rumor."

"Did he give you money or offer to?"

"Not this time. He tried to buy my services months before he met Jack. I turned him down then, but if Clare hadn't returned to the ranch when she did, he would have gotten what he wanted anyway after he'd spoken to Jack."

Jo stood next to Loretta and caressed her face. "You are a lovely young woman, Retta. Any man would want you. I can easily understand that." She removed her hand, leaving Loretta's face suddenly cold, and sat on the edge of the bed. She leaned forward and rested her elbow on her knees. "I have to be honest with you, Retta. I'm not sure I can save Clare and your reputation."

"I don't give a damn about my reputation!"

"Reverend Langford, his wife, and Amelia might be hurt as well. Clare doesn't want anyone to be injured by her actions. I'll need to speak to them. Clare has forbidden me from calling you as a witness. She'll confess to murder if I attempt it. She's tying my hands as far as her defense is concerned. I think we might be able to win on the murder charge involving Thaddeus Garner, but she'll probably be found guilty for murdering Jack Coulter. I can't defend her against that charge without involving you and the Langfords."

"Cyrus would be forced to leave Trinidad," Loretta said solemnly.

"It's an extremely complex case. No matter what I do, someone will lose."

"What can I do, Jo?"

"I don't know yet. Give me and Ripley a few days to investigate. I'll be pressing charges myself against Sheriff Beutler."

"Sheriff Beutler hates Clare. He worked for Thad Garner," Loretta said.

"I figured something was going on between them." Jo took Loretta's hands in her own and held them. "Beutler left Clare in her cell alone and the office unlocked. While he was gone someone went in and worked Clare over. Doctor Wayne has given us a statement about her injuries, none of which she had the day before. Ripley has sent a telegram to Denver requesting extra protection, but that might take a few days. Or it might never happen."

"I can get Ino or some of Clare's men to come into town and guard her."

"What exactly is your relationship with Clare? She refuses to discuss it."

"Suffice it to say it's of a personal nature."

"That's another subject of concern. If a jury learns you and Clare are intimately, sexually, involved, I can guarantee she won't have a chance at trial. She could get the death penalty for that alone. In a bigger city, I might be able to defend it, but that's unlikely in Trinidad."

"When you speak to her again, tell her I don't care about my reputation. If you can get her acquitted, I'll go anywhere so we can be together. I'll do whatever I have to to save her."

JO AND RIPLEY settled into hard wooden chairs at a table in the Cattleman's Saloon. Jo was tired and stretched her legs out and wiggled her toes inside her shoes while Ripley ordered drinks. He set the glasses of beer on the table when he rejoined Jo and removed his hat. Jo took a long drink and made a face as she set the glass back down. "I'd have to already be drunk to drink this," she said. With a smile she added, "It will make me glad to get back home and have a real drink."

"It's wet," Ripley said with a shrug. "The bartender is Willis Manning and that stunning redhead he's talking to is Mavis Calendar. She's responsible for the girls who work here."

"See if you can get them over here to talk to us separately."

Ripley strolled back to the bar and spoke to Willis and Mavis for a moment before returning to their table accompanied by Mavis. Mavis Calendar was obviously older than the other girls in the saloon, but that didn't detract from her attractiveness.

Mavis smiled down at Jo, who was in the process of appreciating Mavis' body from head-to-toe. "Something special I can do for you?" Mavis asked suggestively.

"Please, have a seat," Jo answered. "Can we buy you a drink?"

When Mavis declined, Jo leaned forward and lowered her voice slightly. "My associate, Mr. Sinclair, and I are representing Clare McIlhenney. We'd like to ask you a few questions."

"Fire away. I didn't see much, but will tell you what I can."

"Just tell us the truth without embellishing. Did you witness the shooting the night Thaddeus Garner and Jack Coulter were killed?"

"Didn't see old man Garner get shot, but I did see Coulter go down after he shot Clare."

"Did you see her fire at him?"

"He was mostly in the dark behind her. He shot first and she got a round off from her rifle in his direction. Can't say for sure she hit him even though she doesn't miss what she's aimin' at very often. Looked like she was trying to buy a little time to get out of the line of fire. Next thing I know Coulter fell."

"So Clare and Coulter were facing one another?"

"Yep."

"And she couldn't have shot him in the back."

"Clare wouldn't do that. Not her way."

"So you didn't see her get shot by anyone other than Coulter?"

"Nope. It was mostly over before I got to the door. How's she doin'?"

"Probably been better. What do you know about the problems between Clare and Mr. Garner?"

"All the Garners are trouble. Old man Garner's been trying to run Clare off her land as long as he's been here. About the last ten years or so. He claimed she didn't own her property legally and was always causing trouble. Especially after she began putting up barbed wire a few months ago."

"Were there bad feelings between Clare and Clement Garner as well?"

"Hell yeah! That little prick always thought he was some kind of stud. Made a move on Loretta when she worked at the café next door. Clare embarrassed him real bad in front of his daddy and a few of their hands."

"We've been told he offered her money to service him. Is that true?"

"That's what I heard, but I didn't see or hear him do it. Ino Vasquez might have though. Him and Frank Carson were eating dinner in the café, along with Clare, that night."

Jo cast a look at Ripley and saw him writing the names down. "Is there anything else you can tell us about either Clare McIlhenney or Thaddeus Garner?"

"Clare's a good woman. Garner was a born asshole."

Jo smiled. "If possible, I'd like to speak to Mr. Manning now."

"I'll send him over," Mavis said as she stood up.

"Check into the property thing, Ripley. See if there's a title at the land office," Jo told her assistant while they waited for Willis Manning to join them.

JO LIFTED HER skirt as she made her way through the snow to the front steps of Cyrus and Hettie Langford's home. Ripley leaned past her when they reached the door and knocked three times.

"Do you honestly think these people will be willing to destroy their own lives by telling us the truth?"

"You never know what people will do when they're stressed," Jo answered.

A moment later the front door swung open and the two attorneys were greeted by a smiling, friendly-looking man in his late thirties. "Yes," he said. "Can I help you?"

"My name is Josephine Barclay and this is my associate, Mr. Ripley Sinclair."

Cyrus nodded toward Jo and shook Ripley's hand. "What can I do for you?"

"We represent Clare McIlhenney and would like to ask you a few questions," Jo stated.

"I don't know anything about that unfortunate event. I wasn't there," Cyrus said, raising his chin slightly.

"I understand that, Reverend Langford, but I believe you knew at least one of the men who were killed."

"Actually, I knew them both, but...," Cyrus began.

"Let them in, Cyrus." Loretta stood on the bottom step of the staircase to the second floor. "It's rude to leave them standing on the porch like door-to-door salesmen while you look as if you're preparing to shut the door in their faces. I asked them to come to Trinidad."

Cyrus frowned, but opened the door farther and motioned Jo and Ripley inside. "We can go into my study for privacy," he suggested as he led the way.

Cyrus looked decidedly uncomfortable when he took a seat behind his desk.

Jo pulled a sheaf of paper and a writing instrument from her bag and leaned back in the chair she had taken in front of the desk. "In what capacity did you know Thaddeus Garner, Reverend?"

"I knew who he was and saw him in town, but we never spoke."

"He wasn't a member of your flock?"

"No. I have no idea what his religious affiliation was."

"And Jack Coulter?"

Cyrus' eyes shifted to Loretta and he hesitated.

"I've already given my statement, Cyrus. I told the truth," Loretta said.

"I knew Jack Coulter from the visits I made to his brothel in St.

Joe. Other than taking my money for services rendered, we never spoke much and certainly weren't friends," Cyrus said clearly in clipped wording.

"When did you learn Mr. Coulter was in Trinidad?"

"Amelia came home from work at Rosario's two or three nights before the shooting," he answered, looking down at his hands which were tightly clasped in front of him on his desk.

"What did she tell you about her meeting with Coulter?"

"She said he was telling everyone about Loretta. He tried to get Amelia to tell him where Loretta was, injuring and frightening her in the process."

"Amelia worked for Coulter in St. Joe, didn't she?"

"She's just a child!" Cyrus railed. "For God's sake, Loretta. Amelia can't be brought into this."

"Amelia helped you and a woman named Hettie Tobias rescue Loretta after Coulter tried to kill her, didn't she?"

"Yes. She knew I had been Loretta's 'client'," Cyrus said, his face turning red from embarrassment. "She found me at my hotel and took me back to Jack's place of business. Then she found a safe place to take Loretta. Hettie helped get Loretta and Amelia out of St. Joe and is now my wife."

"Congratulations," Jo said with a smile. "Since Mr. Coulter apparently told everyone he met about Loretta's past it's possible, in fact probable, you and Mrs. Langford will be called to testify at Miss McIlhenney's trial. Amelia, as well, about her assault by Coulter."

"I cannot permit Amelia to testify. She's a girl and has a new life here. We'd all be forced to leave town in the middle of the night."

"I understand the consequences, Reverend. That's why I am here today. Miss McIlhenney doesn't want you involved because she also understands the consequences. I'll do what I can, but cannot promise anything. Needless to say, you cannot leave town until this matter is cleared up by a jury."

"I warned you about associating with that woman!" Cyrus stormed. "We've had nothing but trouble since you insisted on living out there."

"Clare is willing to be hanged for these crimes so your reputation won't be tarnished, Cyrus," Loretta snapped back. "Think about that while you try to remember the chapter in your precious *Bible* that calls for extending Christian charity toward those in trouble."

CLARE LEANED BACK against the wall of her cell. The weakening light of the dusky afternoon filtered though the small window above her cot. Cold December air chilled the cell, but she barely noticed. In a few months her ranch hands would begin moving the herd farther into the foothills of the Sangre de Cristos to feed on tender new grass. For the first time in nearly twenty years, she would not be with them. Jo Barclay had checked the title to the ranch at the land office and soon the property her father had died for would be in the hands of Ino Vasquez. He'd worked hard and put up with Clare's moods long enough to earn it. She had spent most of her adult life making the ranch successful, but it had never been her dream. She wondered what would have happened if she'd left it years ago.

"Can I get anything for you, Clare?" Hall Burress, one of her men asked. Her hands had been taking turns sleeping on a cot in the sheriff's office since the night she had been left alone and beaten.

"No thanks. It'll be time to go to sleep soon," she answered.

Hall nodded and strolled back into the front office. Clare wouldn't have minded having someone to talk to, but she couldn't think of anything to say. She scooted down on the bunk and pulled a thin blanket over her body. She rolled over and stared across the small cell.

"Clare? Clare, are you awake?" a voice called out in a whisper from the alleyway behind the sheriff's office.

Clare threw the blanket off and pulled the crate she had been using as a chair and table under the window. She stepped up and looked outside. Her heart broke when she saw Loretta standing in the snow beneath the window to her cell.

"Go away, Retta," Clare whispered, "before someone sees you."

"You won't let me visit you, so this was the only way I could think of."

"I didn't want you to see me like this. Like a criminal."

"I miss you beside me at night." Loretta did her best to smile for Clare.

"I'm sorry that the last time you see me will be in jail or shackled. Take a good look now because I...I don't want to see you again."

"That's not fair," Loretta said, taking a step closer to the window.

"There's nothing I can offer you, Retta. I didn't want it to end like this."

"Jo's been talking to everyone and getting witness statements. She's very hopeful about the trial."

"She's wasting her time and getting your hopes up for nothing. I can't beat this."

"I never thought of you as a quitter."

"I have to be realistic. If I don't fight it, no one else will be hurt. Don't you understand how dangerous every path is? I won't take others down with me. It's good enough to know Garner and Coulter are dead. Garner can't hurt me any more and Coulter can't hurt you any more."

Tears sprang to Loretta's eyes. "They lived long enough to destroy both of us. I love you, Clare McIlhenney. I don't want to lose you."

"What kind of life could we have together, always hiding, afraid someone will discover our secret?"

"Jo told me you would sacrifice your life to protect me and my reputation. I forbid you to do that. I'll do what I need to."

"You don't own me, Retta. You'll destroy Cyrus, Hettie, and Amelia. Is that what you want?"

"It's better to tell the truth and be free than to spend the rest of my life living in the shadow of the truth. Now that I know what I can have, I refuse to walk away, even if you ask me to."

"Even if I told you I don't love you?"

"You'd be lying. You can't touch me the way you do without loving me."

"When you were with Coulter, men touched you every night," Clare said. She knew it was a cruel thing to say, but she had to convince Loretta to find a better life.

Loretta drew in a sharp breath. "No one has ever touched me the way you do. When you get out of jail we can go someplace new where no one knows us and start over. You've already turned the ranch over to Ino and there won't be anything here for you any more."

"Please, don't make me beg or say things that will hurt you."

Loretta covered her mouth with a gloved hand so no one would hear her chuckle. "I've already made you beg a time or two. You've already said things that hurt me. What are you going to try next before you realize you can't win?"

"I'm afraid, Retta."

"I'll be here waiting for you, no matter what, baby."

Clare heard the front door to the office open and the door slam shut. "Sheriff's back," she said. "Go get some rest."

Clare watched until Loretta disappeared from sight into the shadows of the alleyway.

JO BARCLAY AND Ripley Sinclair attempted every legal maneuver they could think of to delay Clare's trial, including submitting motions for a change of venue and a request for a mental evaluation. The only successful motion they made was their request to have a judge sent down from Denver to oversee the trial. Clare had decided not to participate in her own defense. Other than Jo and Ripley, she refused to see or speak to anyone. Jo couldn't remember the last time she'd had such an uncooperative client or one so willing to die.

"Perhaps you should piss her off some way," Ripley suggested. He and Jo were on their way to the final meeting with their client. A month in Trinidad, Colorado was more than enough for Jo. She would be glad to return to what she considered civilization. She doubted she would be able to save Clare's life and the emotional distress she saw on Loretta's face every day was heartbreaking. The change from the passionate, eager young woman she had met in St. Joe a little over a year ago was hard for her to watch every day. Jo wished she could find a way to bring the light back into Loretta's eyes.

As soon as Deputy Hardcastle checked the contents of their satchels, Jo and Ripley followed him into the back to Clare's cell. Before she stepped into the cell, Jo turned and asked, "Ripley could you please go to the café and bring back some coffee for us?"

Ripley set his satchel inside the cell and said, "Of course. Do you mind if I take time to order breakfast as well?"

"Enjoy," Jo said with a smile. "We have a lot to talk about before the trial begins tomorrow. Lots to do between now and then."

Clare sat on her cot with her legs drawn up and her arms wrapped loosely around them. "We don't have anything to talk about," she muttered.

Jo took a deep breath and turned to face her client. "You're right. You're going to be found guilty as hell in what will probably be the shortest trial in Colorado history, followed very quickly with you being strung up from the nearest tall object. Think about that for a second. Then think about seeing Loretta's face contort in anguish as she watches you kick and struggle to suck in even one more small breath. If you were hung right you'd break your damn neck when your body fell, but we're talking about a bunch of angry, drunken people living barely on the fringe of civilization. They would rather see you suffer. And you will. I've seen it happen and it's not pretty. Loretta will see your eyes bulge from their sockets while you gasp for breath. Your face will turn an ungodly shade of purple, and your tongue will begin to swell and protrude from your mouth. All that in addition to pissing and shitting on yourself. That's the vision you're willing to have Loretta live with the remainder of her life. All the while she'll be thinking about what she could have done to save you. Never knowing she couldn't have done a damn thing because you, the woman she thought loved her, didn't give a shit. She deserves better than that, Clare. I only spent one night with her, but it's not a night I'll likely forget. If I had a woman who loved me that way every night, I would be a happy woman."

"You spent a night with Retta?" Clare asked.

"Yes. A rather glorious one in St. Joe while I was passing through on business. I'm proud to say I was the first woman she had been with. You have me to thank for her sexual expertise when she's with you. In fact, now that I know you'll be gone, probably within the week, I might stay a little longer to…console her."

Clare leaped from the cot and grabbed Jo, shoving her roughly against the brick wall of the cell. "Don't talk about her like she's an object you can use and throw away!"

"Isn't that how you're treating her right now? Like what she feels doesn't matter?"

Clare's voice broke and her grasp loosened on Jo's arms. "I never meant to hurt her by loving her."

"Then do something about it, Clare. At least give her the hope you're willing to fight to stay alive for her. You're a lucky woman. Don't throw it away."

Clare's arms dropped to her sides and she half-stumbled back to the cot. "What do you want me to do?"

THE BALLROOM OF the Columbian Hotel buzzed with activity. The hotel management had been more than willing to set the large ballroom up as a court room for the trial of Clare McIlhenney. The buzzing grew louder as Sheriff Beutler pushed Clare toward the front of the room and shoved her down into a hard wooden chair behind the defense table. Ripley sat next to her with Jo sitting behind him, presumably acting as his assistant. Clare turned halfway in her chair and scanned the crowd gathering behind her. On the left side of the narrow aisle she saw Virginia Garner seated next to Clement, several of the Garner ranch hands surrounding them. Clare's eyes met Clement Garner's, the hatred in his eyes clear to anyone who looked. Apparently he had recovered from his injury in the month since the incident. There would be no sense in arguing with him about what had actually happened the night his father and Jack Coulter were killed. Clare was certain Clement Garner would reveal the truth about Loretta if called to testify.

Also seated in the left side of the main aisle were townspeople Clare had known for twenty years. She'd had disagreements with most of them.

Seated behind the defense table on the right side of the aisle, Clare saw that the visitors to her trial reflected the way people saw her. Most of her ranch hands, Ino, accompanied by Mavis, Willis and Rosario Manning and the girls from the saloon sat behind Clare. Not people the court would consider the most reputable in the world. Clare cast them a smile of sorts. Before she turned to face the judge's podium she caught sight of more people entering. Cyrus Langford, his wife Hettie, and Amelia stepped tentatively into the ballroom and looked around, finally finding seats near the back of the room. She didn't see Loretta and shifted in her chair to face the front once again.

Ripley tapped Clare on the shoulder and leaned closer. "Are you ready?"

"Never been readier. In case I don't get a chance later on, thanks," Clare said without meeting his eyes.

"THE PROSECUTION CALLS Clement Garner to the stand," Franklin Bucknell, the attorney for Las Animas County, called out.

The witnesses preceding Clement had been at best hearsay witnesses who hadn't actually seen anything or they were ranch hands who worked for Thaddeus Garner. Ripley tricked one or two into admitting they held Clare while Thaddeus and Clement physically attacked her.

Once Clement swore to tell the truth and settled into the witness chair, Bucknell hooked his thumbs into his suspenders and boomed. "Where were you the evening of December fifteenth?"

"In town with my father and a few of our hands."

"What was the purpose of the visit to town?"

"We picked up a few supplies and then relaxed with a few drinks. Nothing special."

"Did you see Clare McIlhenney while you were in town?"

"Sure did. She attacked us outside the Cattleman's Saloon."

"And what was the result of that premeditated attack?"

"Objection," Ripley said from his chair. "No evidence has been introduced to indicate anything pre-planned occurred."

"Mr. Garner, please tell us about the relationship between your father and Clare McIlhenney," Bucknell intoned

"Objection, your Honor. Hearsay. The witness wasn't present during every conversation between Mr. Garner and Miss McIlhenney. Furthermore, no evidence has been introduced to prove Thaddeus Garner is the father of this witness."

Clement shot out of his chair. "What the hell are you saying?!"

Ripley shrugged. "You could have been adopted for all I know."

Laughter rippled through the on-lookers. Clement's face turned red as the judge slammed his gavel down to restore order.

Questioning resumed when Clement was seated once again. "Were there any occasions, when you were present," Bucknell began, looking pointedly at Ripley, "that made you aware of the nature of the relationship between Mr. Garner and Miss McIlhenney?"

Clement glanced at Ripley waiting for his objection before he answered. When none came he said, "Every time I accompanied my father and he had a conversation with Clare, they always turned into arguments. Clare doesn't have a legal title to her property and..."

"Ob...ject," Ripley said wearily. "Whether or not Miss McIlhenney holds the title to the land she lives on has absolutely nothing to do with the charges against her in this court, your Honor. Can we simply get on to what pertains to the night of December fifteenth?"

"Mr. Bucknell?" the judge asked, looking over the glasses perched on the end of his nose.

"Was there an argument between your father and Miss McIlhenney the night of December fifteenth?" Bucknell asked.

"Yes."

"Were shots fired?"

"Yes."

"Who fired first?"

"Clare did. Got the drop on us and opened fire. My father didn't even have a chance to draw his pistol before she gunned him down."

Surprisingly there was no objection from the defense table. Ripley leaned back with a grin on his face, reading papers Jo handed to him.

"Were you shot that night as well?" Bucknell continued.

"Yeah. So was one of our ranch hands."

"Both of you were shot by Clare McIlhenney, is that correct?" Bucknell asked as he turned and pointed at the defense table.

"That's right," Clement said clearly.

"Objection," Ripley said. "The witness has no way of knowing anything other than he was shot. For all we know someone behind Miss McIlhenney fired the bullets that struck him."

"No one else could have shot me and Clyde," Clement snarled. "No one else was there to protect Clare."

Ripley smiled. "In other words, you planned to attack Miss McIlhenney and made sure no one was allowed to help her when she was attacked. Did that include Jack Coulter?"

"Objection," Bucknell bellowed. "The defense will have ample time to cross-examine this witness."

The judge admonished both attorneys and Bucknell returned to his questioning of Clement Garner. Bucknell asked a few more questions before handing him over to Ripley Sinclair for cross-examination. Jo patted him on the back as he stood up.

"Mr. Garner, who shot you?"

"Clare McIlhenney."

"You saw her pull the trigger?"

"Yes."

"Wasn't she standing behind her horse?" Ripley paused. "I'll remind you that four previous witnesses confirmed Miss McIlhenney was shielded by her horse."

"Yeah. She was behind her horse," Clement conceded.

"Then how can you be certain she's the one who fired at you?"

"Wasn't no one else there."

"Where was Jack Coulter during this altercation?"

"I don't know where he was once the shooting started."

"Well, when his body was found, he was laying a step or two off the boardwalk *behind* Miss McIlhenney. Therefore, isn't it possible he was the individual who shot you and your father and your ranch hand?"

"Had no reason to."

Ripley picked up a small package from the defense table and opened it. He reached inside and pulled out a gold chain. A gold pocket watch dangled from the end and slowly rotated. "Do you recognize this watch, Mr. Clement?"

"Of course. My father's had it as long as I can remember."

"Did he have it the night of December fifteenth?"

"He always carried it."

"Where did he get it? Was it a gift from your mother?"

"Said he won it in a poker game about twenty years ago."

"Really?" Ripley punched the button on the top near the chain and the lid flipped open. He looked at it intently.

"Can you tell me what's engraved inside?"

"Nope. He said it was probably the initials of the man who lost it."

Ripley held the watch up for everyone to see. "What if I told you this watch was stolen? That the real owner and his family were murdered by marauders. Nearly twenty-one years ago. How old are you, Mr. Garner?"

"Twenty. If you're insinuating my father murdered someone and stole that watch–"

"What was your father's full name?"

"Thaddeus James Garner. So what?"

"Well, isn't that amazing? The leader of the marauders twenty years ago was a man known as TJ," Ripley stated.

"I didn't hear a question there, your Honor," Bucknell objected.

"Simply thinking aloud," Ripley said. He opened the watch case and looked at the inscription inside. "To T.M. from A.M. 2/14/1856," Ripley read aloud. "Now that's quite a coincidence. Your father's initials are the same as those of the man responsible for the murders of Terrance and Agatha McIlhenney. T.M. and A.M." Ripley turned his head to look at Virginia Garner before bringing his attention back to the witness. "No further questions, your Honor."

Clement glared at Clare. He stepped out of the witness chair and walked slowly back to his seat next to his mother. He made sure he caught Clare's eye as he walked past the defense table before he smiled and brought his hand up and pointed his index finger at her as if it were a gun and pulled the imaginary trigger.

Before court adjourned that day the jurors heard brief testimony from Dr. Wayne, Willis Manning, and Mavis Calendar concerning what they witnessed either during or immediately following the shooting. Clare was relieved when she was finally escorted back to the jail by Deputy Hardcastle. Much to her surprise the judge temporarily relieved Sheriff Beutler of his duties until the charges that had been filed against him were sorted out. Once her handcuffs were removed, she sat on her cot rubbing her wrists while Jo and Ripley found a place to sit.

"I thought today went fairly well," Ripley said as he removed his jacket and draped it over the frame of Clare's cot."

"We'll have our chance when the prosecutor rests his case," Jo said. She pulled a stack of papers from her satchel and thumbed through them. "Now that we know what they're relying on as evidence we should be able to create enough doubt to sway the jurors."

Clare snorted. "I don't know how things work where you're from, but I saw the way the men on the jury were looking at me."

"Then we'll simply appeal and have the trial moved to a bigger city," Jo said with a shrug.

"I need to speak to Ino," Clare said, leaning back against the wall of her cell.

"We need to go over your testimony," Jo said with a frown.

"They don't care what I have to say. I appreciate everything you're doing, but I don't expect to live to see the end of this trial. Find Ino. We'll talk about my testimony later."

CLARE COULDN'T SLEEP that night. She was calm, but afraid. She knew something would happen soon and shivered. It was well after midnight when she was awakened by the sound of something heavy falling. She wasn't sure where the sound had come from. A moment later the door between the sheriff's office and the cells flew open. Five men wearing masks stormed into the cell area. Clare jumped from her cot and grabbed the closest thing she could find that could be used as a weapon. The ceramic water pitcher would probably break with the first swing, but she didn't have much choice. One of the men twisted the key in the cell lock and jerked it open while the others held their weapons on her.

"Drop the fuckin' pitcher!" a voice ordered.

"You afraid of one woman with a water pitcher, Beutler?" Clare asked while shifting her stance. "You fire any of those pistols and you'll wake the whole damn town."

One of the men motioned toward her with his pistol and the others rushed into the cell, ducking the pitcher Clare swung at them. One of the men managed to catch her jaw with a glancing blow, enough to force her off balance and allow the others to grab her. They wrestled her to the floor and held her down. A man stepped forward and glared down at her as he yanked the mask from his face. Sheriff Beutler knelt down over her and unleashed a savage blow to her face, knocking her unconscious.

THE SKY WAS dusky gray, shot through with light pink rays of light trying to break through the fog that covered everything. Wet snow seeped through Clare's clothing. She awoke with a shiver and moved her head slightly to the side. She was lying on the ground and tried to get up, but couldn't move, her arms were tied tightly behind her back and another rough rope was around her neck and tethered to a nearly tree. She was far enough away from a campfire that the heat couldn't reach her. She started to open her mouth and groaned from the pain in her jaw as she remembered what had happened a few hours earlier.

"Looks like she's finally awake," one of the men said.

"Good," Beutler smirked. "Wouldn't want her to miss her own party."

The men rose and tossed whatever remained in their tin coffee mugs into the fire. Clement strolled to where Clare was lying, nudging her with the toe of his boot. "About time you woke up," he growled, squatting down beside her. "We've got a present for you."

"Fuck you," Clare mumbled.

"Let's get this over with," Beutler said, rubbing his hands together.

"No hurry," Clement said. "No one's gonna find her out here until there's nothing left but bones. This is private property."

"We need to get back to town for the trial," Beutler said. "Soon everyone will know she's missing and we'll the first ones they'll be looking at. Just do it and let's get breakfast in town like nothing's happened."

One of the men untied the rope from the base of the tree and tossed it to Clement. "Reckon you'll want the honors," he said.

Clement caught the rope and looped it in his hands. "Get the horse," he ordered. "Now I'm going to do something even the great Thaddeus Garner couldn't. Get rid of Clare McIlhenney once and for all." He laughed as two of his men picked Clare up under the arms and held her, waiting for another hand to saddle a horse. She struggled when she saw the cowboy and horse approach. She kicked and twisted as they lifted her onto the saddle. She drove the heels of her boots into the horse's side, but men on either side of her held the reins. They followed Clement toward a tree with a low hanging sturdy branch. He stood beside Clare while he threw the rope over the branch. She brought her leg up and kicked him in the abdomen hard enough to knock the breath out of him. When he finally stood up, he held an arm across his stomach and jerked the rope down hard.

Clare felt the rope tighten around her neck and had trouble breathing as she stretched her body as upright as possible in the saddle.

"Stand the horse under the branch," Clement rasped. He looked up at Clare, hatred filling his eyes while he watched her vainly attempt to lessen the pressure of the rope around her neck. "Is that too tight, Clare? Well, it's going to get a lot tighter. This horse is real skittish so I wouldn't move if I was you."

"Just finish it," she managed and closed her eyes.

"I think I kinda like making you suffer," he said with a cruel laugh. "I could play this fucking game all day." He turned and looked

at Beutler with a smile. "How long do you figure it'll take her to choke
to death if I leave the rope real tight like this?"

"A few minutes maybe."

"I want her to suffer. To pay for killing my father. Real slow like."

"Then tie the damn rope to the tree tight with no slack and leave
her like this. Sooner or later the horse will spook and she can dangle
for a while."

"I can't wait to watch you die, bitch," Clement said.

Clement pulled the rope behind Clare and took it to the tree
trunk. While he was walking behind the horse the rope loosened and
Clare drew in as much air as she could through her mouth. She felt the
rope pull against her neck enough to lift her slightly out of the saddle
as Clement ordered his men to hold the rope while he tied it off. The
rope was drawn so tightly that only a small stream of air could get into
her lungs which felt as if they might burst at any moment.

"Her face is turning a little red," Clement laughed as he patted
her on the thigh. The horse under her moved, shifting its weight a
little. Clare felt her airway grow smaller with every movement. She
flinched when the horse moved again as the men walked away. White
dots of light sparkled and danced behind her eyes. She tried to sit
calmly, but the struggle to inhale a breath made her light-headed and
she wasn't certain how long she could remain conscious. If she lost
consciousness, she would hang herself.

CLEMENT GARNER AND his men strolled back to their campfire
and poured fresh coffee into their tin cups. They settled down
laughing and placing bets on how long it would take Clare to slowly
die from strangulation

"Hey, boss, how about we save her after the horse moves? Then
we can hang her again?" one of the men said.

"I like the way you think," Clement grinned.

They watched as the horse beneath Clare began to prance
sideways. A few minutes passed. Clement picked up a small stone
from the ground next to him and threw it at the animal, striking it on
its rear leg. For an instant, Clare's body dangled beneath the branch
before falling heavily onto the snowy ground as the rope snapped.

"What the fuck!" Clement shouted.

"Guess you get to try again," Beutler said. "I thought you tied
that damn rope good."

"I did goddammit!" Clement said as the five men stood and
walked toward Clare's body.

Ino stepped from behind the tree, his rifle on his shoulder and
aimed at them. Before they could react, he began firing. The men tried
to run to cover, but they fell to the ground one by one. Ino ran to
where Clare lay and loosened the rope around her neck. He shook her

arm and cut through the rope binding her hands. "Clare!" he yelled, continuing to shake her shoulders.

His face brightened when Clare began coughing and wheezing when she took a long shuddering breath and looked up at him. "It took you fuckin' long enough," she said in a whispering voice.

"I had to wait until they were away from you," he beamed.

"Are they dead?" she asked as she rubbed her throat. It felt raw and burned. Ino ran back to where he'd tied his horse. He vaulted into the saddle and rode quickly back to her. He jumped off and brought his canteen to her mouth. The cool water running down her throat felt good. She choked and started coughing. "Not so fast," Ino warned. "You feel good enough to ride?"

Clare nodded and sat up, with some assistance from Ino. Her legs felt boneless as he helped her to her feet. Her knees started to buckle and Ino ran an arm around her waist to steady her. "Your horse is close. I tied him in a grove of trees after I followed you here. There is food and money in the saddlebags, along with your rifle, coat, and hat. You hurt anywhere?"

Clare shook her head. "Thanks Ino. This is twice you've saved my life."

"You saved mine too, *chica*."

"Take care of the ranch."

"We will. I hope someday you'll come back."

"Not likely, *compadre*. We?"

Ino's face turned red and his white teeth shone beneath his moustache. "Me and Mavis is gettin' married. Now with the ranch and all, I need a new housekeeper."

Clare stopped and stared at her friend. She pulled him into fierce hug. "Take care of her, too."

CLARE GUIDED HER horse south, away from Trinidad. Snow had begun falling again, covering her tracks away from where she had been left to die. She needed to cover as much ground as possible before dark, but the deepening snow made traveling difficult. She didn't want to be trapped attempting to get over the pass at Raton after dark. By now it would have been discovered that she was missing. Kidnapped. Deputy Hardcastle's body, unconscious on the floor of the sheriff's office, would assure everyone she hadn't escaped, but was the victim of vigilantes. Clare McIlhenney was dead.

The sun had just fallen behind Fisher's Peak to the north when Clare began descending the pass at Raton and into the New Mexico Territory. It was well after dark when she saw lights through the trees from a cabin ahead. She spurred her horse through the deepening snow toward it and was out of the saddle before her horse came to a complete stop. The door of the cabin opened and the silhouette of a woman holding a rifle appeared.

Clare made her way through knee-deep snow toward the door and took the rifle from Loretta's shaking hands. Loretta backed into the front room while Clare leaned the rifle against a small table inside the cabin door. She smiled and removed her hat coat, tossing them onto a nearby chair. Before she could say anything Loretta was in her arms, embracing her. Loretta's fingers lightly touched the red whelp encircling Clare's neck and tears filled her eyes.

"Are...are you all right?" Loretta asked.

"The marks will go away, but I never will again," Clare said softly.

No more words were necessary as Clare claimed Loretta's lips and devoured them. For the first time she felt free of the ghosts that haunted her past. As Loretta seductively pulled her toward the bedroom, the thought of touching Loretta's silken skin brought peace to Clare's soul.

Epilogue

JO WAS SETTLING her bill at the front desk of the Columbian Hotel when Ripley dropped his suitcase next to hers. Within a few hours they would be boarding the stage for Pueblo.

"Is that everything?" Jo asked.

"Yes, mother. I checked three times," he sighed. He leaned against the front desk counter. "We could have won," he said.

Jo shook her head. "Clare was right. We might have won the trial, but she would have lost eventually."

"Think they'll ever find her body?"

"Nope. There's a million places she could have been taken and killed or buried or whatever the hell they did to her. We'll never know."

"Damn shame. She was a pain in the ass as a client, but I liked her."

"Me, too."

"This was left here for you earlier, Miss Barclay," the young man at the counter said, holding out an envelope with Jo's name written neatly on the front.

"Who left it?" Jo asked.

"A little Mexican kid. I think it was one of Willis Manning's boys."

"Thank you," Jo said as she took the envelope and slipped it into the pocket of her coat.

Jo sat inside the stage office and took a deep breath. She reached into her pocket and withdrew the mysterious envelope, sliding her index finger under the flap to open it. She adjusted her glasses and began reading:

Jo,

Thank you for everything you did for us. I should have trusted Clare to work everything out her way without anyone getting hurt. She knew she couldn't win despite your best efforts. She killed Thaddeus Garner and believes Amelia shot Jack Coulter. But Amelia is still young and has a long life ahead of her. Cyrus and Hettie won't be forced to admit their past and leave town. Lastly, but not least, she killed Clare McIlhenney. I cannot tell you where we will be, but please know we are well and will live a peaceful life of our own choosing. Give our regards to Ripley. We wish you both well.

Loretta

Jo folded the letter and slid it back into her pocket. She removed her glasses and smiled to herself. She held the glasses loosely in her hands for a moment before slipping them back on.

"Bad news?" Ripley asked.

"No. Just a letter from a friend."

More Brenda Adcock titles:

The Sea Hawk

Dr. Julia Blanchard, a marine archaeologist, and her team of divers have spent almost eighteen months excavating the remains of a ship found a few miles off the coast of Georgia. Although they learn quite a bit about the nineteenth century sailing vessel, they have found nothing that would reveal the identity of the ship they have nicknamed "The Georgia Peach."

Consumed by the excavation of the mysterious ship, Julia's relationship with her partner, Amy, has deteriorated. When she forgets Amy's birthday and finds her celebrating in the arms of another woman, Julia returns alone to the Peach site. Caught in a violent storm, she finds herself separated from her boat and adrift on the vast Atlantic Ocean.

Her rescue at sea leads her on an unexpected journey into the true identity of the Peach and the captain and crew who called it their home. Her travels take her to the island of Martinique, the eastern Caribbean islands, the Louisiana German Coast and New Orleans at the close of the War of 1812.

How had the Peach come to rest in the waters off the Georgia coast? What had become of her alluring and enigmatic captain, Simone Moreau? Can love conquer everything, even time? On a voyage that lifts her spirits and eventually breaks her heart, Julia discovers the identity of the ship she had been excavating and the fate of its crew. Along the way she also discovers the true meaning of love which can be as boundless and unpredictable as the ocean itself.

ISBN 978-1-935053-10-1

Pipeline

What do you do when the mistakes you made in the past come back to slap you in the face with a vengeance? Joanna Carlisle, a fifty-seven year old photojournalist, has only begun to adjust to retirement on her small ranch outside Kerrville, Texas, when she finds herself unwillingly sucked into an investigation of illegal aliens being smuggled into the United States to fill the ranks of cheap labor needed to increase corporate profits.

Joanna is a woman who has always lived life her way and on her own terms, enjoying a career that had given her everything she thought she ever wanted or needed. An unexpected visit by her former lover, Cate Hammond, and the attempted murder of their son, forces Jo to finally face what she had given up. Although she hasn't seen Cate or their son for fifteen years, she finds that the feelings she had for Cate had only been dormant, but had never died. No matter how much she fights her attraction to Cate, Jo cannot help but wonder whether she had made the right decision when she chose career and independence over love.

Jo comes to understand the true meaning of friendship and love only when her investigation endangers not only her life, but also the lives of the people around her.

ISBN 978-1-932300-64-2

Reiko's Garden

Hatred...like love...knows no boundaries.

How much impact can one person have on a life?

When sixty-five-year old Callie Owen returns to her rural childhood home in Eastern Tennessee to attend the funeral of a woman she hasn't seen in twenty years, she's forced to face the fears, heartache, and turbulent events that scarred both her body and her mind. Drawing strength from Jean, her partner of thirty years, and from their two grown children, Callie stays in the valley longer than she had anticipated and relives the years that changed her life forever.

In 1949, Japanese war bride Reiko Sanders came to Frost Valley, Tennessee with her soldier husband and infant son. Callie Owen was an inquisitive ten-year-old whose curiosity about the stranger drove her to disobey her father for just one peek at the woman who had become the subject of so much speculation. Despite Callie's fears, she soon finds that the exotic-looking woman is kind and caring, and the two forge a tentative, but secret friendship.

When Callie and her five brothers and sisters were left orphaned, Reiko provided emotional support to Callie. The bond between them continued to grow stronger until Callie left Frost Valley as a teenager, emotionally and physically scarred, vowing never to return and never to forgive.

It's not until Callie goes "home" that she allows herself to remember how Reiko influenced her life. Once and for all, can she face the terrible events of her past? Or will they come back to destroy all that she loves?

ISBN 978-1-932300-77-2

Redress of Grievances

In the first of a series of psychological thrillers, Harriett Markham is a defense attorney in Austin, Texas, who lost everything eleven years earlier. She had been an associate with a Dallas firm and involved in an affair with a senior partner, Alexis Dunne. Harriett represented a rape/murder client named Jared Wilkes and got the charges dismissed on a technicality. When Wilkes committed a rape and murder after his release, Harriett was devastated. She resigned and moved to Austin, leaving everything behind, including her lover.

Despite lingering feelings for Alexis, Harriet becomes involved with a sex-offense investigator, Jessie Rains, a woman struggling with secrets of her own. Harriet thinks she might finally be happy, but then Alexis re-enters her life. She refers a case of multiple homicide allegedly committed by Sharon Taggart, a woman with no motive for the crimes. Harriett is creeped out by the brutal murders, but reluctantly agrees to handle the defense.

As Harriett's team prepares for trial, disturbing information comes to light. Sharon denies any involvement in the crimes, but the evidence against her seems overwhelming. Harriett is plunged into a case rife with twisty psychological motives, questionable sanity, and a client with a complex and disturbing life. Is she guilty or not? And will Harriet's legal defense bring about justice—or another Wilkes case?

Recipient of a 2008 award from the Golden Crown Literary Society, the premiere organization for the support and nourishment of quality lesbian literature. Redress of Grievances won in the category of Lesbian Mystery.

ISBN 978-1-932300-86-4

Tunnel Vision

Royce Brodie, a 50-year-old homicide detective in the quiet town of Cedar Springs, a bedroom community 30 miles from Austin, Texas, has spent the last seven years coming to grips with the incident that took the life of her partner and narrowly missed taking her own. The peace and quiet she had been enjoying is shattered by two seemingly unrelated murders in the same week: the first, a John Doe, and the second, a janitor at the local university.

As Brodie and her partner, Curtis Nicholls, begin their investigation, the assignment of a new trainee disrupts Brodie's life. Not only is Maggie Weston Brodie's former lover, but her father had been Brodie's commander at the Austin Police Department and nearly destroyed her career.

As the three detectives try to piece together the scattered evidence to solve the two murders, they become convinced the two murders are related. The discovery of a similar murder committed five years earlier at a small university in upstate New York creates a sense of urgency as they realize they are chasing a serial killer.

The already difficult case becomes even more so when a third victim is found. But the case becomes personal for Brodie when Maggie becomes the killer's next target. Unless Brodie finds a way to save Maggie, she could face losing everything a second time.

ISBN 978-1-935053-19-4-

.

Another Yellow Rose title you might enjoy:

A Table For Two
by Janet Albert

Ridley Kelsen is convinced she's not destined to find love. The singles scene is old and dating is terribly disappointing. Her closest friend tells her that love comes along when you least expect it and the very last thing Ridley expects when she accepts an invitation to join her friends for dinner, is that she will meet the most beautiful creature she's ever laid eyes on. Will this turn out to be yet another disappointment?

Dana De Marco moves to Philadelphia after her dreams for the future are unexpectedly shattered. Her new restaurant, Cafe De Marco is located on the city's famous South Street and has opened to rave reviews. It seems as if the pieces of her life are finally falling into place, except for one minor detail...she's unable to let go of the past.

The last thing Dana expects is that she's about to meet someone who will force her to face her demons head on. Does she have the courage to open her heart and love again?

ISBN 978-1-935053-27-9

OTHER YELLOW ROSE PUBLICATIONS

Vicki Stevenson	Family Ties	978-1-935053-03-3
Vicki Stevenson	Certain Personal Matters	978-1-935053-06-4
Cate Swannell	Heart's Passage	978-1-932300-09-3
Cate Swannell	No Ocean Deep	978-1-932300-36-9

About the Author

Originally from the Appalachian region of Eastern Tennessee, Brenda now lives in Central Texas, near Austin. She began writing in junior high school where she wrote an admittedly hokey western serial to entertain her friends. Completing her graduate studies in Eastern European history in 1971, she worked as a graphic artist, a public relations specialist for the military and a display advertising specialist until she finally had to admit that her mother might have been right and earned her teaching certification. For the last twenty-plus years she has taught world history and political science. Brenda and her partner of fourteen years, Cheryl, are the parents of four grown children, as well as three grandchildren. Rounding out their home are three temperamental cats and a poodle mix of suspicious parentage. She may be contacted at adcockb10@yahoo.com and welcomes all comments.